The Rose in the Clockwork Library

THE CLOCKWORK CHRONICLES: BOOK 3

LOU WILHAM

Midnight Tide
PUBLISHING

To Mom & Dad
who nurtured the story teller, the artist,
and the dream inside of me.

THE ROSE IN THE CLOCKWORK LIBRARY

A STEAMPUNK BEAUTY & THE BEAST RETELLING

LOU WILHAM

Daiwynn
Provence Four
Provence Two
Provence Three
Provence One
The Capital
Provence Seven
Provence Five
Provence Six
The Wilds
N
NW
NE
W
E
SW
SE
S

"I don't know why I agreed to this," Rose said, her fingers brushing down over the borrowed dress. It didn't fit quite right, too short where it had been adjusted to Persinette's smaller stature, but it would do in a pinch, she supposed. And in a pinch, they were, because Agnes had woken up two mornings ago with the inexplicable urge to get married, and Sully wasn't going to let that opportunity pass without seizing it. So, the crew of the *Duchess* had thrown together a wedding in haste. Rose wondered if it was more Tobias's funeral or the Wastes' steady approach on the horizon that had Agnes so anxious, but she wasn't going to ask him.

"Because you and Agnes are secretly best friends?" Persinette teased, a hopeful smile splitting her freckled face. The young co-captain had been trying to become Rose's friend since the moment Rose had stepped foot on the *Duchess*, and honestly, Rose was sick of it. She wanted to scream at the girl that not everyone had to like each other, but it felt too much like kicking a puppy, and Agnes did enough of that for all of them.

"That's not it." Rose pushed the short tight curls back from her forehead where they had begun to tickle. Persinette held out a headband, and Rose took it with a grunted, "Thank you."

"Because you're a closet softy?"

Rose's expression could have curdled milk, she didn't have to see it to know that, because Persinette's smile fell for a fraction of a second. Plus, her glasses were starting to cut into the wrinkle on the bridge of her nose. She'd had to adjust them, again, after they'd been knocked from her face in the engine room last week, and they weren't quite right.

"Okay, maybe that's not it either." Persinette lifted a hand to fiddle with her short lavender hair. It looked like she'd borrowed some pomade from Manu and was trying to wrangle it into something resembling neat, but there was a cowlick where a curl would normally have been that wasn't cooperating.

Rose sighed, taking the comb from the vanity, and murmured, "Let me."

. . . Maybe she *was* a closet softy after all.

They worked in silence for a few moments, Rose wrangling Persinette's hair into something more orderly, and Persinette fiddling with the long necklace around her neck.

"It's a shame Tobias isn't here," Rose said when the silence got to be too much for her. After years in the labor camp, she craved constant noise, to the point that Benard, the *Duchess's* first mate, had gifted her one of Manu's old gramophones from storage—not that she'd asked him to, mind you, she didn't ask for things from people. Why bother when she could get it herself? She didn't know what it was about the crew of the *Duchess*, but they did things like that for each other. They cared in a way that Rose had never experienced before. . . Well, not since losing her father, anyway. She didn't think she liked it. It was too much of an uncomfortable weight around her neck, a responsibility. That's why she said, "He'd have been the better choice."

Persinette reached back to still the comb, her fingers tight around Rose's wrist until Rose met her gaze in the mirror.

"It *is* a shame," she agreed softly. Persinette hadn't known Tobias long before he'd passed, but Rose had seen the way the two of them had connected. It was like they had each found a kindred spirit after all these years. Rose had been a little jealous of it, if she were being honest with herself. Which she made a habit of doing when she could be bothered. Tobias had been a second father to her, he'd raised her, but that didn't matter when she saw how happy he was chatting with the lavender-haired captain. Persinette squeezed her wrist again, pulling her back to the moment before saying, "but there isn't a better choice."

She wanted to argue. She opened her mouth to do just that, but Persinette shook her head, and Rose's jaw clicked shut. With a nod that was more for herself than for Persinette, Rose turned back to Persinette's hair.

"Are you two ready yet?" Sully asked, poking his head in through the door. He'd missed a button on his shirt, and the cravat Benard had picked for him was hanging askew around his throat, but for all the world he looked like the happiest man Rose had ever seen in her life. His dark eyes danced with joy, and the smile on his brown face could have lit the whole of Daiwynn with its brightness. If only she could bottle that joy, maybe then she'd be able to break it down into molecules and matter and understand it better.

"Almost." Persinette hummed, rising from the vanity, and brushing her hands down over her gown to check for wrinkles. "I feel like I'm missing something. Oh, my—"

Rose snatched the hat from the bed, and tucked it behind her back. "You're not wearing this feathered monstrosity to Sully and Hagnes's wedding, I don't care what Manu says."

"I wish you'd stop calling him that," Sully mumbled, though it sounded like he was laughing, at the same time

Persinette asked, "But then how will they know I'm a captain?"

"Trust me, they'll know." Rose scoffed, keeping herself bodily between Persinette's searching hands and the hat. It had a wide, floppy brim, and the plume dangling from it was so long that it brushed the floor, gathering dust, even when it was atop someone's head. It was unsightly. Agnes hadn't said he hated it, but Rose had seen the look on his face when Manu had given it to Persinette. If she wanted to get any peace at all for the foreseeable future, she had to keep Persinette from wearing it. "Now go on. Sully's waiting for you to walk with him. And for gods' sake, fix his shirt. Agnes will never forgive us if we let him go to his own wedding looking like that."

Persinette huffed, her hands on her hips, but when she turned to look at Sully she deflated. "Oh, all right. It is your day after all."

"It is," Sully agreed, that smile still in place though it strained at the edges now, not quite reaching his eyes. "And Agnes's. And if he sees that hat, he's told me he'll call the whole thing off."

"Manu will be disappointed." Persinette wilted further, her shoulders drooping.

"Manu will live, it's not his wedding." Rose tossed the hat into a corner. Hopefully it would be carted off by bilge rats, but if not, she could always light it on fire. She was sure if anyone would enjoy a bonfire at their wedding, it would be Agnes. "Now go on, before Agnes gets cold feet and takes the first dingy out of here."

Sully mouthed a quick 'thank you' as he ushered Persinette out into the hall, and Rose dipped her head. "Agnes is in our room, if you could. . ."

"I'll talk to him." *Yeah, I'm was definitely a closet softy*, she realized with a disdainful snort. That was the only way to explain how she'd been wrangled into being Agnes's best woman, walking him down the aisle, and now apparently dealing with his pre-wedding jitters. Tobias was probably laughing in his grave.

"Look at you, my little girl," she could practically hear him saying, a smile making his voice lilting and pleased. *"All grown up, with her own family. I'm so proud."*

"He's not my family," she muttered.

"Isn't he?" She imagined Tobias would ask.

He'd be right, of course. She didn't like Agnes, but she'd realized rather quickly, that you didn't have to like someone to love them. That didn't mean she was going to agree to such a thing out loud for the all world to hear. Nor that she was going to let Agnes or any of the others wiggle under her skin any deeper than they already had. No. Better to keep them at arm's length.

Shaking her head to dispel Tobias and his nonsense, she knocked on the door to Agnes and Sully's room. "Are you decent?"

"That's one word for it." Agnes grunted, and Rose assumed that meant she was allowed to enter. She found the unicorn sitting on the bed, facing the long mirror on the back of the closet door, his pale, nimble fingers fiddling with his cravat. It was blue, to match his eyes, and it looked hopelessly wrinkled like he'd retied it at least five times. The rest of him was immaculate, from the tips of his well-polished boots to his neatly trimmed pastel rainbow hair. "Did Sully send you to make sure I haven't gotten cold feet?"

"I think you know the answer to that." Rose moved to swat his hands away from his cravat, giving it a sharp tug.

"I suppose I do," he said his shoulders hunching forward a little, making him seem much smaller than Rose had ever seen him. Agnes was tall, annoyingly so. A head shorter than Sully, but that wasn't saying much when the kelpie towered over everyone else. "Tell me whose bright idea this was again?"

"Yours. Hubert, could we get a little steam?"

The robot tilted his head at her expectantly from where he stood near her hip, blinking his one working visual sensor at her. He'd gotten rather sassy since coming to the *Duchess*. Rose wondered if Felicity had mucked about with his programming, or if he was just learning it from Hiccup. There was only one way to tell. Rose sometimes wished people were as easy as robots. Able to be taken apart and put back together so that she could see how they ticked. Maybe then the crew of the *Duchess* would make more sense to her.

"Please," Rose amended, and Hubert's visual circuit brightened in approval before he let out a little puff of steam through the opening that some might call a mouth. Rose used it to smooth the wrinkles from the fabric. "There, that's better."

"He should be here." Agnes's voice was quiet, the words seeming mostly for himself, and Rose didn't have to guess at who he was talking about. It was strange how quickly Tobias had become important to all of them. Well, not strange, not really. Tobias was special that way, Rose had always known it. With the ability to burrow under people's skin and take root there, dandelion fluff on the wind just looking for a good place to go to ground.

"I like to think he's here in spirit."

Agnes huffed a laugh. "You believe in that kind of thing? I thought you were a woman of science."

"First rule of Thermodynamics," Rose said, retying the cravat into something less extravagant but definitely tidier, "no matter nor energy can be created or destroyed." She tilted her head to one side, then the other, looking at the knot from different angles until she was pleased with it. Then she gave a short *hm* before continuing. "Kind of hard not to believe in that sort of thing when you think about it that way."

Her words made Agnes unclench his jaw, his shoulders relaxing, and his chin lifting. It wasn't quite a smile, but Rose knew better than to expect one from him. "Thanks for that. I . . . I think I needed it."

"I think that's the first time you've ever said, 'thank you' to me." Rose teased, giving the cravat another sharp tug before she pulled away to admire her handiwork.

"You better burn it into your memory, it'll never happen again." Agnes grumbled, standing up, and heading over to the mirror to look at himself again.

"Felicity did a good job with the alterations." Rose tilted her head, surveying the way the lines of one of Owen's old suits had been pulled in to fit Agnes. It was amazing what one girl could do when motivated, and given free rein to pilfer through someone else's closet.

"Is that a compliment?" Agnes asked, a smile quirking up one side of his face.

"For Felicity."

"Of course." Agnes chuckled, shaking his head. "All right. This is as good as it's going to get, I think."

Pulling her watch from a pocket, Rose checked the time. "We've got about five more minutes for you to panic, if you're feeling like you need to breathe into a bag or something."

"You're the worst." Agnes huffed an annoyed laugh, but Rose would swear she heard some fondness in it—maybe they were *all* going soft. It was strange to have a friend like him in her life. It was strange to have friends at all. She'd spent the last twenty years avoiding everyone but Tobias, sure that at any moment they'd be ripped from her fingers, and she'd be alone again. Now she had all these. . . *people* who seemed to want her around whether she was grumpy or not, whether they legitimately seemed to like her or not.

"So I'm told." She took a breath, rubbing at the bridge of her nose under her glasses, feeling where the nose pads had left indentations behind in her skin. She moved behind Agnes to look at him over his shoulder in the mirror. She had to move onto her toes to accomplish it. "If you repeat this to anyone, it'll be the last thing you do," she warned, and Agnes lifted one dark, arrogant brow in question, tilting his head to look down his long aristocratic nose at her, even in the mirror. Bastard. "You look handsome. You know, if you're into pompous unicorns. Which Sully clearly is so. . ." She shrugged.

Agnes wrinkled his nose at her, but she could see the corners of his lips twitch upward into something that might have resembled a smile. "Well then, let's go get me married, shall we?"

"We shall." Rose stepped back, and held an arm out to him which he looped his own through casually, before they headed into the hall.

"I'm telling everyone you said that, by the way," Agnes said just as they reached the double doors into the galley.

"No one will believe you."

"Sure, they will. Hubert will back me up. Won't you Hubert?" Agnes nudged the little robot in front of them with his foot.

"I do not know what that means," Hubert said, voice grinding with gears. Rose wasn't sure if he was being sarcastic, or bluntly honest, but she had to choke back a chuckle either way when Agnes scoffed.

Agnes had just enough time to mutter the word 'brat' under his breath before the music started, the doors swung open, and it was time for Rose to escort her maybe-sort-of friend down the aisle.

Funny how the world can change in just a few months, she thought as she watched the beaming faces of the *Duchess* and *Sultana*'s crews pass by them.

TWO
KINDLE

The little robot's metal feet shuffled against the worn stone floors of the library. Its pincers were clasped tight around a well-loved picture book, holding it close to its chest as if the tome were something priceless, and delicate, and indeed, given the state it was in, it must have been precious. Read over and over until the corners were worn and scuffed, and the pages had grown soft.

"That one? Again?" Kindle asked, her hands reaching for the book to settle it into her lap where the reassuring weight of it would bring some small amount of peace to the turmoil that surrounded them. She'd read this particular book at least a thousand times over to the little robot. If she cared to, she could likely recite the story from memory alone, conjure up the carefully illustrated pictures in her mind, and watch the story unfold from beginning to end like humans once did with films. But that would negate the simple pleasure she and the robot both derived from reading a story every evening, and Kindle was not one to deny either of them such a thing. Not when so much else was going wrong in the world around them.

The robot chirped, and shifted on the cushions they'd built their little reading nest from like a child trying to find the perfect seat. Once it was settled, it looked up at her expectantly, glowing visual circuits unblinking.

"Yes, yes, here we go." Kindle snorted, and opened the cover, finding comfort in the way the spine crackled softly from age. The front cover was devoid of a title, as was the front page. All it showed was an illustration of a room full to the brim with books, and a rose made of gears, glowing faintly under a glass dome at the center.

She gave the little robot a moment to inspect the first illustration, it seemed to like to do that, even for all the times that it had done so before, finding new wonder in old things that Kindle envied. When it was through its inspection, it reached over to turn the page reverently, careful to not rip it from the spine, and then looked up at Kindle again.

Kindle took a deep breath, and waded in. "Once upon a time," she started, voice soft and low as it flowed over the words, "there was a great dragon king, and he wanted for nothing but hatchlings of his own to pass his kingdom to—"

The robot twittered, blowing steam out through its ears in a show of impatience.

"Look," Kindle grumbled, sitting up straighter, and lifting her chin, "either you want me to read you the story, or you don't. I'm not playing this game with you."

It huffed again, metal arms clinking and clanking as they crossed over its chest.

"I'll get to the good bits soon enough, you just have to wait."

With its chin tilted back defiantly, the robot made an aggravated noise that was part clicking gears, part hissing steam.

"No. I will not skip ahead. Now do you want me to read this or not?"

It released a soft whistle which might have been a groan, or a sigh, it was always hard to tell which. But Kindle took the noise to be reluctant acceptance, and returned to the book.

"As I was saying, once upon a time there was a great dragon king, and he wanted for nothing but hatchlings of his own to pass his kingdom to, and to share in his joy of the land." She could picture him, she'd always been able to. The tall, broad man, with dark hair, and a long beard that he would let his children braid when they were particularly bored. He had great red wings, and laugh lines around his eyes from smiling too often. In spite of how some might have feared him, Kindle always imagined that he had been a kind, benevolent ruler of the fae. A good man. The illustrations didn't do him justice. "And so, he married. . ."

And there was where the words faded into the background even for her, the reader, and Kindle saw the story behind her eyes as one might a memory. The great dragon king, and his wife, happy, and whole. They'd had three hatchlings, all fifty years apart, so that they would have time with their parents, but still be young enough to play together—for dragons aged much more slowly than any of the other fae.

"The first was born with blue wings, tipped in silver," Kindle said, the page turning as if by itself. "The second green tipped in bronze. But it was the youngest, the baby of the bunch, who was like their father, a great red dragon with her wings tipped in gold. It was known from the moment she hatched that it would be her who ruled.

"Even with that knowledge, the three siblings loved each other, and were happy. They spent their days running through the castle, laughing, and playing. . ."

"I'm gonna get you!" the eldest shouted, blue wings flapping and sending up dust motes, which left the youngest child who was running at full speed through the halls screeching in her joy. "You can't run from me!"

"Catch me if you can!" the youngest cried, her voice not

more than a squeak as she was young still, and the flapping of her wings left her short on breath. Her laughter flowed out behind her, so loud it echoed off the stone walls of the king's castle.

"Gotcha, brat," the middle child growled, arms wrapping tight around the youngest, lifting her up, and twirling her around as she squealed with more laughter before the three of them fell to the ground in a heap of wings, and scales, and giggles.

She should have known then. The littlest dragon should have known then what her siblings were capable of, but children always thought the best of the people they loved.

"It was not long after the youngest hatched that the dragon king fell ill," Kindle continued, tracing over the edge of the illustration of the dragon king in his bed, his children surrounding him. "He had meant to live much longer, but the magical world was in upheaval, destabilized by the war between the fae and the humans."

The next illustration sent screams through Kindle's mind. When the wards that separated the realms had fallen, there had been chaos, and so many had been lost as the realm of the fae supplanted the realm of the humans. . . or perhaps it had been the other way around. The history books weren't really sure how it had happened, and the science books had long since stopped trying to understand it. But the fact of the matter was . . .

"The moment the realms merged, the king was lost, and he knew it. So, he turned to his children, and imparted his last decree. . ."

He had begun to fade, his children could almost see the dark bedding through his body, or so the illustrations showed. And Kindle could imagine him reaching for them, pulling the three of them into a hug so tight that they felt it rearrange their bones.

"When I am gone, you will be left to rule," he said, his hand clasped onto the shoulder of the youngest. The heat of his big palm weighing her down, making her feel smaller than she ever had. "Trust your siblings, they will help you. But as the strongest, it is your magic that our people will need to keep them safe. To allow them full access to their power."

The littlest dragon had shifted under his tight hold, but had not denied what she knew, for she did know. The red of her wings and scales was a burden she had born since the moment she'd hatched, and her father had told her what it meant. Only red dragons could bear the weight of the world on their shoulders, their power immense, their fire unbeatable. Only red dragons could give the fae full access to their magic as opposed to the half-life many fae lived now. Maybe if the red dragon had been there when the world of the fae had fallen to the humans, she'd have been able to protect her people. She'd have stopped what came next. . .

"The king had faded by the following morning, his magic spent to ensure their people's safety as the two realms merged. The littlest dragon was lost in her grief. . ."

She'd been wailing, screaming, sobbing, crying, until she was sick with it. Until her own siblings had been sick of the sight of her, and their mother had given up trying to comfort her. It took days for the littlest dragon to come to terms with what it meant to lose the dragon king. But when she had, she emerged from her rooms ready to lead.

"Pity she never got the chance."

The little robot released another long gust of steam that might have been a mournful sigh, but it did not interrupt the story further, just leaned more heavily against Kindle, its metal shoulder digging into her own.

"For in her absence, her siblings plotted, and the night

before she was to be crowned, taking on the mantle of the dragon queen, they stole into her chambers. . ."

There was no moon that night, according to the book, just the dark of a winter sky threatening to snow. And the siblings had not even tried to hide their movements from the littlest dragon, for they knew she would not fight them. She loved them, after all. She had tried to scream—or maybe she hadn't, the book didn't show it, but Kindle imagined she had to have—in her terror, but the eldest had bargained with a witch for a sleeping powder, and once it was blown into the littlest dragon's face, she fell into a deep, dreamless sleep.

When she awoke it was to the silence of an empty place. "And they left her there, all alone."

The robot chirped, a low sound of sympathy, but it turned the page anyway to show the littlest dragon exploring her new home. A prison built from books and magic, room upon room full of stories that whispered long into the night, giving her nightmares. But there was one room, just one, free of books, or shelves, or any other trappings except a pedestal, a clear glass dome, and a clicking clockwork rose.

"They tied the littlest dragon's magic to the walls of her prison, stripping her of freedom, and autonomy, to power the great library that only they would ever be able to access for it moved at random, always one step out of reach of any other. And with her magic it updated, constantly, always growing, and filling itself."

The littlest dragon had always loved libraries as a child, she'd spent hours within the one in her father's castle.

"Maybe they thought they were doing her a kindness imprisoning her in such a place." Kindle doubted it.

The little robot reached over to turn the page again, and let out a disgruntled noise.

"How does it end?" Kindle repeated, frowning down at

the book. There was a space where pages had clearly been removed from it, ripped away, not just in the back but in the middle too. "What do you mean how does it end? You know as well as I do that the story stops there with the littlest dragon trapped in the library, and the rose ticking away towards twelve." The book never explained what the significance of the rose was, just that it was there, in a place of honor. Maybe it didn't mean anything. Maybe it was a taunt. One last cruel joke on the littlest dragon, to make her think that one day her time in that empty place might be up.

An irritated puff of steam left the robot.

"Yes, I know there are pages missing. There have always been pages missing. I can't exactly help that, can I?"

More puffs of steam made the air thick with humidity. The little robot ticked faster, and faster, winding itself up in its agitation.

"Well, there's no use in yelling at me about it. I don't have any control over—"

Crash. Bang.

The sounds reverberated through the floor and up into Kindle's bones, making her twitch. She narrowed her eyes on the gloom of the hallway adjacent to the main reading room.

"Do I even want to know what that was?" But she was already rising from the cushions, pushing her red hair back from her face, and making her way across the worn floors into the hall. She crept through the library, the robot huddled behind her, its pincers holding onto her anywhere that it could reach—a child hiding from a bogeyman.

They peeked into room, after room, each as perfectly maintained as the next, Kindle's frown grew, until they reached the fairytale wing. It was one that had been her favorite when she'd first come to the Great Library, offering her solace when there was no one to keep her company, that is until the robot had joined her. It was where they'd found the book about the dragon and the rose. Once, it had hummed with life, stories whispering excitedly from the walls, each book full of the tales mortals and fae alike would tell their children before bedtime. But over the years, it had grown quieter, and quieter. And when she pushed the door open now, she found the tomes buried under rock, and rubble where the roof had caved in.

She took a step back, to brace herself on the wall across the way, her lungs struggling to draw in air past the plummeting of her heart. "Can we salvage any of it, do you think?"

The robot didn't answer, and when she looked down at it, she found it frozen on its spot, one arm lifted, and completely silent.

"Blast. You need to be wound again, don't you?" Kindle sighed, scrubbing at her face as her shoulders sagged. She finally managed a shaking inhale. "All right. First thing's first. Let's get you moving again, you old bucket of bolts."

Lifting her gaze back to what was left of the room, Kindle shook her head, and spun on her heel to head back the way she'd come in search of the robot's turnkey. Her steps were measured, and sure, but they stuttered a moment later when a glowing red light caught her eye from one of the rooms that she was sure she'd closed off months ago.

There, in the center, sat a clockwork rose, the glass dome over it doing nothing to dim the faint glow of magic that surrounded the damned thing. Of all the rooms that fell to ruin in the Great Library, this would be the last, she knew that. The minute hand twitched one notch closer to twelve— the tick of it so loud it was a physical blow—Kindle jerked back, her red wings fluttering out behind her in agitation before she raced forward to pull the doors shut on the rose again, her ears still ringing with the tok.

Kindle drew in another trembling breath, her sweating palms slipping off the handles of the door. She could deal with barricading the door later, for now, she had other things to worry about.

T he party was in full swing. The crews of the *Duchess* and the *Sultana* laughing, and drinking, and dancing together along with the refugees they'd saved from labor camp 9C like they didn't have a care in the world. Like they hadn't just buried one of their own. Like there wasn't a war on the horizon.

Rose shifted, looking out across the wide expanse of nothingness that was more and more prevalent the closer they got to the wall. It was as if the people of Daiwynn were afraid to build anything too close to the Wastes, lest the creatures who roamed there get it into their heads to scale the wall and feast on them. Rose pushed away that errant thought with a jerk of her head. It wouldn't do anyone any good for her to worry about that now. They would be over the wall in a matter of days, and they would need their wits about them.

"Why aren't you dancing?" A familiar voice asked, and when Rose turned to look over her shoulder, she saw Benard coming up to join her at the rail. He had a drink in his hand, and his long, pointed, pale green ears were flushed pink. The goblin tipped his head a little to one side, waiting for an answer.

"Why aren't *you* dancing?" She countered, her eyes

flicking back to where Owen was spinning in a circle with some of the children from the camp, his head thrown back as he laughed. She didn't think she'd ever seen someone so jovial as Owen. His grins rivaled even Persinette's, who at times Rose had realized, was forcing them—for the people around her, or for herself, Rose had yet to deduce. "Your husband looks like he could use some company."

"I have two left feet." Benard winked, taking a long sip from his mostly empty glass. "And they only get worse after I've been drinking."

"Hmm." Rose hummed, turning back to look out over the darkness of a land uninhabited by people. That didn't mean there were no structures though, there were signs of life everywhere in Daiwynn, even in the places where life hadn't been for over a century. The humans that had inhabited the land before the realms merged, and the war grew in earnest, had crawled across the land like ants, leaving their marks everywhere. But no one inhabited these little square boxes which might have once been residences anymore.

"You should let yourself live a little," Benard said, his arms folding over the railing, the glass dangling dangerously from his fingers over the open air beneath them.

"Should I?" Rose wasn't even sure she'd know what that looked like, living a little.

"Yeah, you should." He lifted his glass to finish off the dregs of it, the extra joint in his fingers, indicative of goblins, tapping lightly against the bottom of the glass to get every last drop. "If there's anything this war has taught me, it's that we only get todays, no tomorrows." The wind picked up around them, and if Rose weren't looking for it, she might have lost Benard's voice for its softness. "And if we spend too much time worrying about the tomorrows, we miss out on the todays."

It sounded like something Tobias would have said to her,

had he been there. He had spent much of the last two decades trying to impart some wisdom to her. Trying to teach her that even in the gray world of the labor camp she could find color, and life, and happiness. She hadn't believed him, too stuck in the pain that cycled through her.

"And what would you suggest," Rose asked, pulling the sleeves of her borrowed dress down over her wrists to keep the chill at bay, "for not missing out on todays?"

Benard turned around, bracing himself on the railing so he could look out at the group of dancing people, and Rose followed to see what he was seeing. Once she was facing the right direction, he nodded to a figure who had her body turned surreptitiously towards Rose, but was making conversation with Persinette.

"That wouldn't be a bad start." Benard gave her a wink.

When Captain Stella looked their way again, Benard lifted his glass to her. She returned the gesture with a deep bow of her head, before going back to whatever she was saying to Persinette, long navy locks flowing out around her in an unruly tangle to hide her beautiful, bronzed face from view.

"That's not going to go anywhere," Rose scoffed, but still her eyes lingered on Stella. The captain of the *Sultana* hadn't put on a dress, like many of the other women had, and Rose could still see at least one pistol strapped to her hip as if she were expecting a fight at any moment.

"Who says it has to?" Benard tilted his head so he could look up at her again, his eyes twinkling in the lights from the ships. "I told you, stop worrying about the tomorrows. We only get todays. And today, that woman can't take her eyes off of you."

Without waiting for the disbelieving huff, or incredulous denial, Benard stepped away from the rail, heading back toward the crowd.

"Oy! Captain, you owe me a dance." He dipped into a low bow in front of Persinette who let out a loud laugh, and fell into a clumsy curtsy, then they were off, leaving Stella standing there with a bemused smile on her face.

Rose turned back to lean over the railing again, half-hoping that if she wasn't looking maybe Stella wouldn't have the courage to approach. But that was the thing about pirate captains, Rose had learned, they were recklessly fearless, and a moment later Rose heard the heavy tread of boots join her at the rail.

"Flirting with Persinette got me exactly nowhere." Stella huffed, leaning over the rail so far that one bit of turbulence would send her plummeting to her death. Recklessly fearless, just like Rose had said.

"So you decided to come and try your luck with me?" Rose pursed her lips to hide the twitch of an amused grin that threatened to take them over.

"You miss 100% of the shots you don't take." Pushing off from the rail, Stella turned so she could look at Rose, fixing her with those dark, dark, blue eyes—almost black—like the sky at midnight. "So. . . what do ya say?"

"What do I say to what, exactly?" Rose met her gaze with a quirked brow, and a tilted head. "Use your words."

Stella threw back her head, and laughed, her long neck elegant in the warm lights from the deck. She was beautiful, startlingly so. All sharp lines, and hard eyes, exactly Rose's type. Maybe Benard was right. . . maybe she ought to start living her todays a little more fully.

When Stella was done laughing, she lowered her head, and fixed Rose with a look that could only be described as sultry, the wind brushing her long navy hair into her face. "You wanna get outta here, Miss Rose?"

Rose sucked in a breath, swallowed down her doubts, and said, "Yeah. Yeah, I think I might."

Stella held out her hand, her head tilted just so, and Rose took it, letting the other woman lead her down the rail to the gangplank, and across to the *Sultana*.

ROSE HAD JUST DOZED OFF, her cheek smooshed against one of the fifty or so silk cushions Stella had in her bed. Who knew a woman who regularly had at least three weapons on her—at a wedding, no less—would be so infatuated with silk. She had silk sheets, silk cushions, a silk duvet, and even a curtain that hung from the bed, blocking it off from the rest of her quarters in a deep, midnight-blue silk, that Stella almost disappeared into once they'd fallen into the bed together.

It wouldn't have been so bad, but Rose found the fabric slippery, and uncomfortable after so many years dealing with the scratchy, coarse fibers of the labor camp. Another reminder that her life had changed yet again—that she had lost people yet again—that had her tossing and turning. But finally—*finally*—she'd managed to get comfortable, Stella's arm splayed over her waist, her long dark hair tickling Rose's bare shoulder.

And then there was a loud explosion from somewhere up on deck, followed by shouts.

"What is that?" Rose mumbled, but Stella was already up, rolling out of the bed and onto her feet as she grabbed for her pants. An alarm started not a second later, a deafening sound of warning that made Rose's eardrums ache. "What *is* that?!"

"We're under attack," Stella said, throwing her long coat on over top of her camisole, not bothering with the discarded shirt, and running for the door.

"Under attack?" Stumbling to her feet, Rose grabbed her wrinkled dress to tug it over her head, and slipped into her boots. She left the corset on the floor, it wouldn't do anything but slow her down, and raced out into the corridor after Stella as another explosion rocked the ship. "From whom?"

"Looks like an Uprising ship, Cap'n," a young man said, holding out a steaming tablet with a picture on it.

"Have Kelii and Persinette launched an offensive counterstrike?" Stella took one look at the tablet, and cursed, her feet hurrying up a set of steps with Rose close behind. When they made it to the helm, they found the crew in a state that could only be described as organized chaos. Each person dancing around the others, pressing buttons, and checking gauges at what looked to Rose to be random in their hurry.

"No. They sent word to only use defensive strikes. Their plan is to make it over the wall before the ship closes in." The young man shook is head, making deep purple hair fall into his eyes that he blew at to try to clear his vision.

"Of course, it is," Stella scoffed.

"What does that mean?" Rose asked, standing in the door to the helm, her hands wringing in front of her. She should be doing something to help. But there was nothing for her to do, and Stella's crew seemed to have it under control for the most part.

"It means, your captains don't want to start a fight with so many untrained passengers on board." Stella ground her teeth, her fingers working furiously over a control panel near the big bay window.

"It would be pointless to save all those lives only to lose them at the first sign of trouble, Cap'n." The young man had moved up beside Stella to help her along. Rose felt the ship take a sharp turn, and then there was an explosion that sounded like it had originated from them, followed by a more muted blast.

"I'm well aware of that, Nolan," Stella hissed, but Nolan didn't back down, and eventually she lowered her head to look at the screens. "That should dissuade them from tailing us too close. What do our munitions look like?"

"We're running a little lower than I'd like going into the Wastes, but we've done more with less." Nolan shrugged, his fingers flying over the tablet again.

"It looks like they're backing off, Cap'n," one of the other crew members shouted from their post.

"Good. Get Kelii and Persinette up on the screen, we need to make a push for the wall." Raking her hands through her tangled blue tresses, Stella stood, letting out a long, slow breath. For all the trembling of the ship below them, Stella looked like a general ready for war all perfect erect posture and tilted back chin. Her tanned skin pulled taught over a stiff jaw, navy brows narrowed. "Get me a damage report on both ships, Nolan. I need to know what kind of mess we're looking at."

"Aye, aye, cap'n." Nolan gave a little salute, and then pushed past Rose back out into the hall.

The view of the night sky out the window disappeared a second later, and was replaced with Persinette and Manu's faces in sepia tone, the co-captains looked ruffled, and sleep-worn, but alert.

"Anybody want to tell me why we were just attacked by an Uprising ship?" Stella asked, leaning over to brace herself on the control panel.

"Not particularly," Manu mumbled.

Persinette elbowed him—hard, if his wince was anything to go by—and said, "We told you our mission to save the people of 9c wasn't Uprising sanctioned."

"There is a difference between unsanctioned, and what just happened."

Rose frowned, watching the captains' faces on the screen. She'd heard what Agnes had said at Tobias' funeral, that enough was enough. That it was time that the Uprising and MOTHER both go down, but she hadn't really realized what it meant. Agnes, and the others. . .

"There was a direct order from Eddi not to do what we did." Persinette seemed to shrug, as if unbothered by the idea that she'd gone against one of the two most powerful people in all of Daiwynn, and wasn't that just Persinette to a T. "Our operation was pre-emptive. The Uprising planned to launch their own strike."

"And you interfered," Stella scrubbed at her face. She didn't seem surprised, but she didn't look happy about it either.

"To save lives," Rose said, when it looked like no one else would. Persinette and Stella's gazes fell on her, and Rose shifted a little under the weight of them. Grasping at what small amount of courage she had she pushed the words, "Right? To save lives?" from her tongue.

"Yes, to save lives." Persinette's lips twitched into an almost grin before she schooled her features. "Agnes felt that if the Uprising were in charge of the strike, they wouldn't care about the blood that would be shed. It would have been an attack, an act of war, not a rescue mission."

Rose's shoulders sagged under that knowledge. People had died in the escape from 9c, but not as many as could have, she knew that. She'd *seen* how the lives of those inhabiting the camp had been their rescuers' first priority. And from what she knew of the Uprising. . . Well, that wouldn't have been the case if Eddi had been in charge.

Stella's eyes narrowed for a moment, as if trying to gauge how much of what Persinette and Rose had said was true, then she took one quick breath and said, "All right then. We need to stay ahead of them."

"We do," Persinette agreed with a quick jerk of her head. "Our weapons cache is better stocked, we'll bring up the rear in case they get close again."

"We should be over the wall in two days," Manu added. "I don't think they'll bother us once we're there."

"No. But they might be waiting for us when we come back." Rose frowned. She'd never spoken to Eddi directly, all of the orders she'd received had come through Agnes first, but she'd heard enough stories of them. They weren't going to give up that easily. The thought sent a trickle of anxiety down her spine like sweat, dripping and pooling in the small of her back.

"We'll cross that bridge when we come to it." Stella rolled out her shoulders as if trying to shrug off an ill-fitting blouse. "They can't patrol the whole wall."

"That's the spirit!" Manu laughed, jovially, but Rose could see that his shoulders were tense. They all knew the implications of this, and they knew what it would cost them. But. . .

"Let's focus on getting these people to safety first," Persinette said, giving voice to exactly what Rose was thinking. They needed to focus on one thing at a time, and the first thing was getting their cargo to safety. Once there, they could decide what to do about the Uprising.

With the sun at her back, Kindle folded the long cuffs of her overalls, rolled up her sleeves, and tied her hair back in a tight tail at the base of her neck. She had never known hard work when living in her father's castle, but since her siblings abandoned her in the Great Library, Kindle had had to learn a great many things. The least of which being how to take care of herself, for there had been no one else to do so for many years, and by the time the robot had shown up she'd already figured it out.

Said robot let out a soft whirr, tilting its head back in disgust at the mess that lay before them. The fairytale wing wasn't the first of the rooms in the Great Library that had succumbed to age over the years, and Kindle was sure it wouldn't be the last, but every time the robot seemed to act as if it were above the manual labor required to scavenge through the wreckage.

"Oh, don't be such a priss," Kindle laughed, shaking her head. She propped the doors open with two chairs that had once belonged to a dining set in a wing on etiquette. Kindle had thrown a party when that room had gone—there had been paper decorations made from the books and everything —she could only wish it had been the first of them to fall.

The robot twittered its disapproval.

"I said what I said." Her hands on her hips, Kindle looked down at the little robot who was looking back at her, its visual sensors a little dimmer than usual as if it were glaring.

There was a chip—not a very large one mind you, and it was purely cosmetic—in one of the gears that made up the innards of its mouth, and it was flashing it at her as if it was baring its teeth.

"I'm not afraid of you."

She held out the little shovel they'd found in the tool shed, but the robot refused to take it, shaking its head, and grumbling a gush of steam from its mouth.

"Complain all you like, but just be glad it wasn't the seed library, this time," Kindle said, taking the robot by the elbow and forcing the shovel into its pincer before moving to grab her Kindle-sized shovel from where she'd leaned it against the wall. With a handkerchief tied over her mouth, she stepped into the room, and began the process of clearing away the rubble. They'd put it all in the etiquette room, if there was still space, and if not there then. . . well, they'd find someplace, they always did.

More twittering came from where the robot had finally started working, and Kindle lifted her head from her own work to glare at it.

"I know you don't eat, but I do. And things would have been a lot quieter around here if I'd have died from starvation or malnutrition in the first few years." Ducking back to work, she pretended to not hear the robot's continued mutterings that sounded vaguely like complaints about how maybe it would have liked things quieter. It didn't mean that, she knew it didn't, and sometimes it was just better to let it complain, and bluster, it made the work go faster.

IT TOOK them two days of constant digging to get enough of the roof moved out of the room that they could finally see books beneath the rubble. And that's when things really started slowing down, because the robot liked to take its time inspecting the books they unearthed, making sure all the pages were still intact, and cataloguing them as they went. Instead of cataloguing them once they were all removed from the ruined room, as Kindle had repeatedly told it to.

Which was where she found it on the afternoon of the third day after lunch, its nose stuck in a book as its visual sensors fluttered over the pages.

"There's at least another twelve feet of rubble to clear away, can't you wait to read them all later?" She frowned, taking another sip from the lemonade she'd made up the week before.

With a flap of its pincer, the robot brushed her off, not even bothering to lift its head from the book.

"Seriously, come on. We need to get this done before the first snow starts, or everything that's underneath will be ruined. You remember what happened to the early novels wing? I still don't know what happened with Elizabeth and Darcy." Leaning heavily on the shovel, she wrinkled her nose at the robot. It didn't seem to be paying her the least bit of attention. It had dragged one of the cushions out of the main room, and made itself quite comfortable just out in the hall where the lighting was the best to read by.

The turning of a page was the only movement from it, and brought a heavy sigh from Kindle.

"You're not going to help then?"

No answer.

"You're just going to sit and read that book?"

A disinterested shrug of metal shoulders, followed by the turn of another page, the robot's pincers gentle on the edges of the book.

"I really hate you sometimes, do you know that?" Kindle asked, but she'd already turned back to the work, for what else could she do? She hadn't been lying about the snow, and after reading everything the Great Library had to offer on weather patterns, she could see from the clouds that the first snow of the season could begin at any point. And water and books didn't mix. She'd learned that the hard way when she'd been reading out in the garden, and it had started raining. It had taken a full week for the library's sole copy of *A Picture of Dorian Gray* to dry out.

Sweat dripped down from Kindle's hair, into her eyes, before she could wipe it away with a spare handkerchief, and she was just about to shout another accusation at the robot when something tugged at her pant leg. It whistled at her, and she looked down to find the robot holding up the book it'd been inspecting for the last few hours.

"I don't have time to read that right now. Can't you wait for bedtime?" Her arms screamed at the strain of another shovel load of rubble, but she was getting close, so close, she could see a pile of brightly colored covers just in reach now.

The robot whistled louder, tugging on her pant leg so hard she worried the seams might give.

"All right. All right. Show me what it is you've found." Kindle growled, spinning around to give the blasted thing her full attention. She propped the shovel against her hip, and bent at the waist, giving herself a better view of whatever the robot had.

It twittered, pleased with itself, and held up the book for her to see the cover. There was a red rose under a glass dome in the middle of what looked like a derelict castle the illustration painfully reminiscent of her own book. The title read *Beauty and the Beast.*

"So?" she asked the robot, refusing to acknowledge the similarities between her own cursed rose, and the cover of this book.

The robot opened the book, and showed her a picture of a beautiful girl kissing the beast. It flipped the page, and there the beast was surrounded with light, before, on the page opposite, it turned into a handsome prince.

"I fail to see your point." Wouldn't it be nice if such a thing were even possible? It wasn't though, she knew that better than anyone. "This is a mortal fairytale; you know how those things are. There's no basis in reality. They took stories from us, and spun them all up with their own ideals, and happy endings to make themselves feel better."

Stomping its metal feet, the robot hissed at her.

"Go on and be mad about it all you like, there isn't a beautiful princess who's going to come and save us." Kindle thrust the book back toward the little robot, and bent to pick up her discarded shovel. "There's just you, and me, and our books. And if we don't dig out this wing, it'll just be you and me and a few *less* books."

Flapping the book at her, the robot pointed to the picture of the handsome prince again.

Kindle pinched the bridge of her nose, feeling a headache forming behind her eyes. How did one little creature manage to be so idealistic? It was all clockwork and bolts, and yet it always acted more like a child than anything else. Kindle didn't know what game someone had played with its programming, but sometimes she thought she'd have been better off if the thing didn't have a personality at all.

"Look, I see the similarities, trust me I do. But one." Kindle held up a single finger, then stepped back to spread her big red wings, taking up so much space they almost touched the edges of the room, for emphasis. "I'm not a beast. That creature is some kind of lion, man, wolf thing. I'm a dragon. See? Not a beast."

A soft grinding noise came from the robot, a begrudging agreement.

Kindle held up a second finger. "Two, this is not a castle, it's a library." Both of these were flimsy at best, and even Kindle knew it. But just because the beginnings were the same, didn't mean the endings would be, and there was no sense in the little robot getting its hopes up. "Three, he was cursed because he was horrible to someone who needed his help. I was left here because my siblings were jealous of my power, and wanted to rule in my stead. See? Not the same."

The robot let out a puff of steam. Flipping back to a previous page so quickly it almost ripped the paper from the binding, it pointed to the words about the beast being trapped as a beast by his curse.

"We don't know that it's a curse that's trapped me this way." She rolled her eyes, and lifted her shovel again to get back to work. The rubble wasn't going to move itself. "Maybe it's just that my magic is fading, so I can't hide my nature anymore. That happens, you know, to very old dragons." It didn't, or at least not that the history books on dragons she'd read said, but the robot didn't need to know that. She scratched at the scales on her cheek, hating the cold breeze that blew down from the opening in the ceiling, it always dried her skin out.

Lifting its shoulders, the robot puffed itself up, and let out a series of furious chirps and whistles.

"Calling people liars is a good way to get them not to read you bedtime stories anymore," Kindle growled, smoke puffing out of her nostrils threateningly, as her temper suddenly flared—an occurrence that seemed to be happening more and more as time passed. She tried not to think about what that meant, but she'd read enough magical medicine and psychology textbooks to know that it was either a byproduct of her losing control of her magic, or she was losing her sanity from being trapped for centuries with just a robot for company in the last few decades. Neither option was very appealing. "If you're not going to be useful, go sit over there and let me finish this."

It hissed out another long stream of steam.

"Go sit over there!" she snarled, baring pointed teeth at the robot in warning, and pointing toward the space next to the door that had been cleared already.

It eyed her for a moment longer, its visual sensors dimming again as if it were narrowing its eyes at her, and then it huffed, turned on its metal heel, and strode off down the corridor without another sound, taking the infernal book with it.

"Good! And don't come back until you're ready to work!" she shouted after it, before turning back to the pile of debris. A single snowflake fluttered down from the gray clouds above, landing on her nose where it melted into a droplet. "SNOW! Do you see this?! It's snowing now, on top of everything else!"

The robot didn't answer, and given that she no longer heard its clanking footsteps she could guess that it had disappeared into one of the far off wings. Well, good riddance! She didn't need it, or its company!

"Stupid robots, they'll believe anything." Kindle grumbled under her breath, her talons tightening so much around her shovel that the wood beneath threatened to give with a creak. When it started to splinter, she dropped the shovel, then took a pointed breath in through her nose, and out through her lips before returning to her work.

They were three days over the wall when the first jabberwock struck, and Rose idly wondered why it had taken so long. Well, perhaps not idly, as the moment the first hulking creature slammed against the *Duchess* all hell broke loose, and the thought didn't hit her until she was running across the deck in the twilight of pre-dusk, grabbing at one of the snapped lines that was attached to the balloon above. The coarse material burned her palms through her gloves as Rose tied it off again.

"Out of the frying pan and into the fire!" Rose heard Stella shout from the deck of the *Sultana*, her tone holding all the mad triumph of a woman who loved a good battle. She was running across the boards, a rifle pressed to her shoulder as she fired off little pops at the creature slowly lowering itself to be at eye level with them.

"She's loving this entirely too much," Sully grunted from where he'd come to help Rose tie down another line that had been pulled loose, and Rose had to agree. The wild adrenaline-fueled, hungry nature of Stella was baffling, and sort of off putting now that Rose was looking it right in the face. "We need people to help protect the balloon, do you have any spells—"

"I don't." Guilt sunk into her bones. Magic simmered through the air, summer heat rippling from the fingers of those who could wield it that way. Persinette was at the head of a small platoon of witches, her faintly purple magic flowing from her in waves that she directed up to the balloon to form a shield around it. "I wish I did."

"Then you'll need this." Agnes held out a pistol. "You know how to fire one, don't you?"

"Not really?" But she took the weapon, the metal cold even through her gloves, because what else was she going to do? Say that she couldn't help? Someone needed to protect the young and the elderly that lay beneath the deck from the monster snapping its jaws at their balloons.

"We'll worry about that later." Agnes held up his own pistol and fired a round of shots toward the head of the creature. They pinged off its thick scales, and made it roar louder. Rose heard an answering roar somewhere far off, and her stomach gave a lurch as the jabberwock's tail smacked against the *Duchess*, knocking it sideways for a moment before whoever was at the helm was able to wrangle control of the steering again.

"We need to chase it away!" Nolan shouted from the other deck, his hands cupped around his mouth.

"Brilliant! Why didn't I think of that?" Agnes snapped back, taking aim. The bullets pinged off of the creature again, only seeming to infuriate it further, and Rose wondered how many they had left before they were spent. "Just plant your feet, aim and fire, Rose."

"What about the cannons?" Rose asked.

"Don't wanna waste 'em!" Sully shouted, already running for another snapped line.

"My aim is terrible." The pistol weighed too heavily in her hand, making it hard for her to keep ahold of it. She was an inventor, damn it, not a fighter!

"It's a big enough target, I think you'll manage it." Agnes snorted. He took a step up to her, adjusted her hold on the pistol, kicked her feet shoulder width apart, and held her arm up to aim at the jabberwock. "Now pull the trigger."

Rose did as instructed, the recoil jarring the bones in her hand painfully, and the bullet bounced off the jabberwock's armored skin just as all the others had. Useless. Even when she managed to hit the target, she was useless. Her time would have been better spent below, seeing to the engines.

"Here comes another one!" Stella crowed in delight. Rose spun to watch as Stella's light steps took her across the shifting deck of the *Sultana*, almost like she was dancing, before setting up for another shot.

"There's something seriously wrong with that woman," Agnes muttered. He too was watching Stella drop her empty pistol to grab another from seemingly no where. "Just keep firing, Rose. The witches are working on cloaking us."

"Cloaking us? What'll that do?" Rose's voice went up an octave at the end as she watched one of the winged creatures crane its long neck to pick a crew member off the *Sultana*. The person had just enough time to scream before the jabberwock swallowed them down in a single gulp, the sound of its swallowing so loud it made Rose flinch back. Her stomach leaped up her throat, threatening to spill itself onto the tilting deck of the *Duchess*.

"Hopefully give us enough time to get the hell out of here!" Owen shouted as he ran past with something large, and ticking over his shoulder that looked remarkably like a cannon.

Another round of shots rent the air, and Rose watched as the jabberwock lunged for the people with firearms of some kind, no one else. Its neck stretched long to reach someone in the middle of the ship who was carrying a rifle, instead of picking off someone closer to the rail with a long sword in their grip.

"The heat," she muttered to herself.

"What?" Sully frowned at her upon his return.

"They're attracted to the heat, and the light!" Rose ran after Owen, not slowing down for Sully to catch up to her, or ask her to explain further. There wasn't time. She grabbed Owen by the back of his shirt, ducking down quickly when he spun around and almost smacked her in the face with the weapon on his shoulder. "Do we have any fireworks?"

Owen blinked at her for a minute, his eyes wide as he processed her request, then he jerked his chin toward the stairs. "If we do, they're down in the cargo hold near the other party supplies. Felicity should know where they are. Just—"

Rose didn't wait for him to finish, she grabbed Sully's wrist and said, "Come with me."

Sully was silent, letting her drag him down the steps into the cargo hold where Felicity was busy pulling crate after crate of munitions from their stores, a crowbar slung over her shoulder. "If you're here for bullets, I'm almost out."

"No." Rose dropped Sully's wrist and looked around the disorderly hold. There were open crates everywhere, their contents spilt all over the hold in the crew's haste to get to weapons and ammunition. "I need fireworks."

Felicity narrowed her eyes on Rose for a moment, and then shrugged. "They're just over there, under the crate of party linens. Why we've got party linens, I don't know. But then. . . I don't know why we have fireworks either."

"Thank you!" Rose called over her shoulder. It was the work of seconds for her and Sully to move the crate of linens, and get into the fireworks.

"Are you going to explain to me what you're thinking?" Sully asked pulling out a firecracker as large as his forearm.

"They came from above, likely from the mountains off to our west. Something attracted them, the ships are pretty quiet, and since we weren't exactly broadcasting our location. . ."

"It had to be the lights." Sully dug deeper into the box, pulling from the bottom the biggest fireworks he could find. "This one says it's a willow. Will that do what we want?"

"Should do. I'll grab a couple more just in case." Rose held them to her chest, and made her way across to the stairs again, with Sully behind her.

"I hope this works. If not, Manu is going to be very upset you used his fireworks."

"Me too. But if it doesn't, we'll probably be dead!" The words came out high and cheery, even as her stomach plummeted to her toes, and Rose smiled at him, all teeth and terror, drawing a chuckle from Sully.

"You're right. We probably will."

The deck was still in chaos by the time they ascended—a chorus of screams, shots firing in the dark, and there was something dark and slick painting the wood that might have been blood. Rose inhaled through her nose, realized it was a mistake as the heavy scent of metal and gunpowder clung to the inside of her nostrils, and decided to breathe through her mouth instead. A one quick look around found the perfect spot, forcing her focus on the problem instead of the carnage. "Over here, we need to aim them up and away from the ship. Hopefully, the jabberwocks will chase it."

Sully nodded once, and followed her orders, setting up the firework, and aiming it out so it wouldn't hit their balloon before pulling a lighter from his pocket. Lifting her hands to cover her ears in preparation for the blast, Rose hissed when the bright light burned her eyes. The shot fired off, far out over the trees, and then exploded into the dim twilight with a bang so loud she felt it in her chest.

The jabberwock roared, its head jerking to look at the fizzling firework off in the distance as its talons released the side of the *Duchess*.

"Another!" Rose shouted over the noise, and Sully lit the next.

By the time that firework had begun to fizzle, the jabberwock had moved around the *Duchess* and was headed toward the point where it still smoked among the trees, the second creature following behind it.

Rose motioned for Sully to light the next one, her breath still coming in hard pants that drew the sulfur and smoke smell into her lungs, making her cough. The jabberwocks were still moving, chasing the flittering smoke in the distance, and the gap between them and the ships was growing, the massive, winged beasts looking smaller and smaller.

"Brilliant!" an unfamiliar voice shouted, and Rose nearly jumped out of her skin in fright when a face popped up over the side of the rail to peer at Rose and Sully with eyes too big for its face. "That was bloody brilliant," the voice repeated, a smile splitting their face, too wide, almost manic. "But now you've got to dive."

"Dive?" Rose asked, her heart hammering in her chest. Her fingers twitched around the spent firework, an itch in her neck to turn and check that the jabberwocks were still flying in the opposite direction, but she refused to look away from this unfamiliar face.

"Yes, dive. The jabbers don't like the lower altitudes, you see, and so long as you're this high up, they're going to keep chasing you." Something flittered behind the face, and Rose's eyes flicked back to it to see translucent wings reflecting the lights of the ship.

"Why should we trust you?" Rose's jaw clenched around the words, but already over the person's shoulder she could see the jabberwocks turning back, their attention drawn to the ships again. *Blast.*

"Do you have any reason not to?"

They didn't. But they also didn't have any reason to trust them. Still, they had to do something, and the jabberwocks were already coming their way again. Rose made a split second calculation, and hoped that her math wasn't wrong. "Sully."

"Got it," Sully said, already scrambling to his feet to tell the others.

The pixie hummed, pleased, and let their wings flutter them up over the rail, to sit next to Rose before holding out one pale hand. "I'm Alys White."

"Rose Miller." Rose took the pixie's hand and shook it.

"Al. . . Al. . . *Alys!*" Someone was shouting from further up the deck behind them. When Rose turned to look, she found a dark-haired man with a set of griffon wings twitching behind him in annoyance, a pair of glasses askew on his nose.

Alys rolled her eyes. "I'm fine, Hatter. I just wanted to come meet the woman who thought to use fireworks to distract a jabber. Brilliant stuff, really. Did you see how they flapped right on after it?" Alys asked, pushing herself to her feet.

"Yes. I saw." Hatter's wings settled behind him, seeming to relax now that he had Alys in his sights again.

"We'll be landing soon." Alys turned back to Rose, offering her a hand up, and Rose took it, ignoring the dropping of her stomach as the ship started to dip. "Won't have to worry about a jabber on the ground." She winked at Rose, not letting go of her hand as they made their way to the railing to look down at the clearing where the *Duchess* and the *Sultana* were making to land. "Of course, there are other things to worry about on the ground, but at least it won't be jabbers." Alys laughed, the sound grating in its delight.

"Right." Rose shifted on her feet, clenching the rail tight with her free hand, the hand Alys held already growing too hot and uncomfortable in her grip. Below she could just see a settlement in the fading light. It was made up of refurbished train cars, separated into smaller units and given life by what looked like clockwork engines.

"That's home," Alys said, giving her hand one final squeeze before dropping it. "Doesn't look like much, but we like it."

"Al! They need to know where to land," Hatter called from up the deck again, and Alys let out an excited laugh before skipping away. Rose wiped the sweat from her hand onto her trousers.

"Just set her down anywhere." Rose heard Alys say. "There's plenty of space, and we can always move one of the cars." Rose's eyes followed her, a crease forming between her brows. Alys White.

"So, that's the woman who tamed the Wastes." Agnes came to lean against the rail beside Rose, watching the goings on of the ship as Alys, Hatter, and their people helped the crew of the Duchess check their lines, and pick a spot to land.

"She runs things here?" Rose turned to follow the movement herself. It didn't quite fit. The stories Rose had heard of the great Alys of the Wastes, and the fluttering woman who'd popped up over the side of the ship seemed incongruent with one another.

"Yeah. She was the first person able to survive over the wall, and make a life for people here." Agnes's eyebrows had lifted high on his face, his lip curled in a look of contempt. "She's a bit. . ." He flapped his wrist.

"Well, she'd have to be," Rose reasoned, not needing him to finish. Alys was an odd duck. That was for sure. "I mean. . . did you see that jabberwock?"

"Suppose so." Agnes frowned, tilting his head from side to side as if stretching out his neck. "I don't think I like her."

"You don't like anyone."

"True."

By the time Kindle had cleared all of the debris away, stacked the books in the hall, and blocked off the room, the little robot had forgiven her. Of course it waited until all the hard work was done to show its face again.

The robot tugged lightly on the leg of her overalls, twittering softly as if in apology.

"Oh *now* you're sorry?" Kindle asked, cutting the robot a glare that it had the nerve to tilt its head at in question as if it didn't remember exactly what it had done. She knew it did, the robot might be silly, idealistic, and immature in turns, but it wasn't stupid, and it seemed to remember everything. In fact, if it weren't in the wrong, they likely wouldn't be making up at all because the robot would have held a grudge for the foreseeable future. "I suppose you want to help catalogue what I managed to save?"

The little robot nodded its head so quickly that it almost toppled forward onto the worn wooden floors.

"Are you actually going to work? Or are you just going to sit and read all of the books while I catalogue and find new homes for them?" Kindle narrowed her eyes at it.

Its visual circuits dimmed and brightened like the robot was blinking innocently, as if that could fool her. She'd been living with the blasted thing for the last couple of decades, she knew it was far from innocent.

"That's not an answer."

A long stream of steam puffed out of the robot's mouth, metal shoulders sagging, as it leaned heavily against her, sullen. It looked up at her from where its head rested at about hip level, visual circuits dimming and brightening again.

"Oh fine. But I want these re-homed by the end of the week, do you hear me? We aren't having a repeat of the self-help wing where the books are *still* lining the hallway." She bent back down to the pile that she'd been preparing to go through to check for damage, then sort into piles.

Flapping its pincer at her as a brush off, the robot moved over to another stack and dropped down onto the floor, picked a book from the top of the pile, and started looking it over. It took all of five minutes—and three books from Kindle's pile—for her to realize that it was just reading them again.

Why am I still surprised? she wondered, letting out a long sigh, and getting back to her work. Her own pile was finished well before lunch, so she gathered up the stacks, and made to take them to their new homes. There was a new system to the place now, but it wouldn't make much sense to anyone else, especially after so many wings had been lost over the years.

Nudging the robot with her foot, she said, "are you going to come with me, so you can remember where these are going or are you too busy?"

It groaned with the creak of gears badly in need of oil, shoulders sagging as if it were put out by her request.

"You can finish reading that one after we shelf these, promise." Kindle couldn't help but smile at the annoyed grumbling from the robot as it climbed to its feet to follow behind her. "As a keeper of all of Daiwynn's knowledge, I would think you'd take this more seriously."

Grinding gears was the only response she got to the gentle teasing.

"Oh come on, we have an important job, don't we? We house every book ever written in Daiwynn. Do you know how many people today may have never even heard of some of these? After MOTHER's book burning. . ." She shuddered at the thought, and wiggled her shoulders to try to shake away the shiver crawling along her spine. That had been a bad time for the library. For years, it was like the books themselves were screaming in anguish. The first wing had crumbled days after the mournful wailing of books that had lost their kin started. It took her and the robot a long time to fully understand what had happened, but thankfully, some brave historian had kept a journal of it, and while journals very often did not get mass produced, or even reprinted, they did ultimately wind up in the Great Library. More proof that whether she had been abandoned by her family or not, Kindle had a purpose here. She was doing something important.

The robot chirped softly, patting her hand in sympathy.

"Yes. Well." Kindle cleared her throat. "Either way, we can't lose any more, can we?"

It whirred in agreement.

"I think we have some space in the main room for these, they're pretty thin, and if all else fails we can stack them in front of that reading chair I can't fit into anymore." She hated that reading chair anyway. It was a reminder of how things had started. Of how when she'd first been left in the library, she'd been mostly humanoid, able to shift between her full-fledged dragon form and a girl whenever she pleased. But over the years shifting had become more and more difficult until one time she shifted, and her wings didn't disappear.

These days her skin was a blotchy patchwork of scales, and leathery red bits. With the wings came the inability to sit in any of the beautiful wingback chairs.

The main room was the one she'd woken up in all those years ago. It was a large round space, with bookshelves curving around every wall except in the places where there was a door or a fireplace. And it had been empty, when she'd awoken, apart from a few logs in the fire to keep away the chill, leaving her plenty of space to fill the shelves with her personal favorites.

When they entered, Kindle set her stack down on the chair, and moved to the shelves with her hands on her hips to survey where they might be able to fit the new books in.

"How do we feel about these medical textbooks? Are they even still relevant? Or have we gotten everything we need from them do you think?" She was talking more to herself, she usually did, but it was nice to have the robot around to make it feel like she hadn't completely gone off the deep end just yet.

The robot shrugged, its shoulders making a horrible screeching sound that reminded her it was much in need of oiling. *Add it to the list.*

"Right then. We'll keep the most recent edition, but I doubt we need anything prior to that." Pulling books from the shelves, she sat them in the robot's arms, creating a small space where some of the more interesting fairytale books would fit. "And we certainly won't need anything on complex surgeries, no matter how interesting the pictures might be."

This seemed to annoy the robot, for it whistled at her in something close to a warning.

"I don't care if you like to look at the anatomy pictures when you're bored. You can go to the medical wing and look at them if you're so inclined." She dropped the next three books onto its stack with a decisive clap that made the robot stumble a little under the force. "Now go on, and return those to the medical wing."

Another annoyed sound, accompanied by a huff of steam.

"Do as I say, or I'll sing the entire time you're trying to read later." It didn't sound like much of a threat, but Kindle knew it for what it was, she couldn't carry a tune in a bucket, and her singing voice had only gotten worse since losing the battle to the scales on her throat.

Its visual censors dimmed, as if the robot were narrowing its eyes.

"Do you want to test that theory?" she asked, her lips curling up into a smile. "I haven't had the chance to try any of those shanties we found a couple of years back. How did that one about the barmaids go?"

She opened her mouth to start singing, but the robot didn't let her finish, it spun on its heel, hissing loudly with steam, and stomped off, the stack of medical texts still balanced on its pincers.

"That's what I thought," Kindle muttered to herself, and went back to pulling outdated textbooks from the shelves to make room for the stories she knew the robot would prefer to have on hand. Whatever it liked to pretend, she knew that this would make it happier than all the diagrams of a person's insides, or its own combined.

After wiping down the shelves, she put the new books in the space, then went back to the hall for the rest of them. That's where she found the robot, its nose buried in a thick tome. With a sigh, she returned to her work. There were at least another couple hundred books from the room to go through, and she'd prefer to have all of them done before it got too cold in the halls at dusk.

It took approximately an hour for the robot to flip to the back of the book, and let out a soft whirr of confusion as a sheaf of loose pages fell to floor. The soft shushing sound made Kindle stop what she was doing to look over at the robot.

"What is it?" She moved to crouch down beside the robot, watching as it carefully unfolded the paper to reveal illustrations that were strangely familiar, and yet so very new. "Wait. . . are these. . . do you think these are the missing pages from my book?"

The robot shoved the torn pages into her hands, then was on its metal feet, and shuffling down the hallway at breakneck speed. Kindle practically had to run to keep up, the paper flapping softly between her fingers. They made it to the main room in record time, and the robot pulled her book from the shelf, flipping it open to where someone had clearly ripped the pages from the back. It took the papers from Kindle, and set them in against the ragged page edges, examining them for a moment, before it nodded, pleased.

"So that's a yes," Kindle said more to herself than anyone else as she reached for the book, and flipped through the now recovered pages. There were five of them in total. One pictured an illustration that looked very much like the fallen storybook room, dust motes filtering in from the ruined ceiling. Carefully moving that page over to the other side, she was faced with a picture of a bright-eyed girl with tight curls, and spectacles perched high on her nose.

According to the page numbers, there were still some missing. Maybe truly gone, or maybe stuffed in some of the other books. But either way, she seemed to have the end, which showed the clockwork rose falling to pieces, the library crumbling around it, and Kindle's back turned to all of it, her hand wrapped tightly in the curly-haired girl's fingers.

"What does it mean, do you think?" She dropped down onto the cushions in the middle of the main room, a puff of dust fluttering up from under her. It couldn't be true. It just couldn't.

The robot chirped, and twittered, and whirred, all in such quick succession that she had a hard time deciphering the sounds.

"I wouldn't. . . I wouldn't just *leave* the library." Even if she could. Kindle's talons gripped the cover a little too hard, leaving behind indents where her claws had dug in. "I have a job to do here," she declared, but her shoulders hunched in, making her seem smaller, whether to avoid the robot's stare, or the heaviness of what was in front of her, she didn't know. "I can't just leave this place behind for some. . . for some *girl*. This is my home. And what about the books? Do you see what happens if I leave?" She pointed to the picture, jabbing her finger at the crumbling walls so hard her nail almost went through the paper as it shook. "It all goes away if I leave. We can't have that."

A whistle of disagreement followed the words, the robot's pincers flapping around as it let out clicking, ticking noises that sounded like it might be about to explode from everything it had to say.

"No. . . *No*. It's just a story." She pushed the book away so it was close to tipping off her knees. "Just another made up story by the humans. Put it back on the shelf, and let's get back to work."

Nudging her, the robot tapped on the part of the illustration where Kindle and the girl's hands were threaded together. It didn't look like the girl was forcing her, it looked like Kindle had gone willingly. Like maybe she was happy. But that didn't make sense. How could she be *happy* outside of the library? How could she be happy knowing that it would all turn to ash in her absence? Who would maintain the knowledge of Daiwynn if not for her? No one. Fury and fear sat like fire at the back of her tongue, making her skin hot, and the flames from her belly lick blisters into her throat.

"I said get back to work!" Kindle growled, snapping the book shut, and shoving it back onto the shelf where it had come from.

The robot shook its head at her, shoulders sagging, but dragged its feet back out into the hall to continue what they'd been doing.

The *Duchess* was in need of repairs, she was functional, but there had been no time to stop and fix things over the last couple of months. Then they had been attacked by the Uprising, and a pair of jabber-wocks, on top of the damage from the rescue mission at 9c, so there was plenty that needed doing. And honestly, Rose preferred being elbow deep in grease to dealing with people. Engines, she understood. Machines, made sense to her. But the inner workings of finding all of their refugees lodgings amongst Alys's people, grouping them up in a way that would work, was a puzzle that Rose just didn't *want* to apply her considerable gray matter to. So she'd volunteered to help repair the ships.

"There you are!" Alys dropped down beside her, heedless of the oil that Rose hadn't had time to clean up yet as it soaked into her brown breeches. "I've been looking all over for you."

"I've been here the whole time." Rose buried herself deeper into the stabilizer that she was trying to repair, ignoring the way Alys pressed in close—to see what she was doing, or maybe to try to get her attention. Whatever it was, it wasn't working. Rose had more important things to do than to entertain Alys. She also wondered if Alys was one of those people who would go away if she ignored them long enough. It hadn't worked with Tobias, but there was enough evidence that it worked with most people for Rose to be willing to try it at least one more time.

"What're you doing?"

"Repairs." Rose swore she heard Felicity muttering something on the other side of the engine room, but she couldn't make out what it was. It had been so peaceful with just the two of them occasionally asking for opinions or tools. Why couldn't it have stayed that way?

"Persi said she invited you to the meeting."

Rose should have known being down here wouldn't allow her to stay out of the political talks. Persinette seemed intent on including her in their organization's leadership. Why? Rose, didn't know. She just wished that hiding out in the engine room of the ship would have been enough to deter them.

Alys leaned back, her feet kicking out in front of her, scuffed boots a little too close to the internals of the stabilizers for Rose's comfort.

"Could you not?" Knocking her feet away, Rose moved onto her knees to press herself deeper. She just needed to reach a little further, and tighten that bolt, and . . .

"The meeting was supposed to start ten minutes ago," Alys pressed again.

"Well, I'm obviously busy." She wasn't really. This was something she could have done later, or even left to Felicity. It wasn't like this repair was particularly complex, but Rose didn't *want* to go to the meeting. She'd thought she'd made that clear to all of them. Agnes seemed to understand it, at least. Why couldn't everyone else?

"Obviously," Alys said, tone doubtful.

Rose didn't for a second think that that was the end of the conversation. She hadn't spent much time with Alys over the last couple of days, but she'd learned enough about the other woman to know that she was tenacious to a fault. She'd have to be to survive in the Wastes like she had. Still, when the silence stretched on for too long, becoming a weight around Rose's shoulders, Rose foolishly pulled her head from the innards of the stabilizer so she could fix Alys with a frown. "Don't you have someplace to be?"

"We've postponed the meeting until you have a free minute to talk." Alys leaned back onto her palms, a smile stretched wide across her face.

"Why?" Rose narrowed her gaze, her fingers tightening around the wrench, the cold metal edges leaving indents on her palm.

"We all want you there." Crossing one ankle over the other, Alys tilted her head back to stare up at the ceiling of the engine room.

It was a lie. Rose would bet that at least one of them didn't want her there—Agnes. At least two didn't care one way or the other—Hatter and Manu. The people who wanted her there were Sully, Alys, and Persinette—mostly Alys and Persinette. Unfortunately, it was those three who seemed to be the most vocal about these things.

Setting the wrench into the toolbox on her other side, Rose grabbed a screwdriver, and reached over to reattach the panel she'd removed to work on the stabilizers. Alys moved onto her knees to help hold it in place as Rose replaced the screws, and Rose tricked herself into believing maybe that was the end of the conversation.

"I think you have something to add to the conversation."

It sounded reasonable when Alys said it that way. Like they just wanted Rose's opinion on a few things and then she'd be left alone to her machines. But she knew better. She knew that the moment she stepped into that meeting, that would be it. She would be considered part of leadership.

There would be no escaping the responsibility that would rest on her shoulders, the lives she would have to make decisions for. She didn't want that, she never had. Even when she'd helped Agnes with the Uprising while she was under MOTHER's roof, she hadn't wanted that. She'd wanted to do something good. To help. To get vengeance for her father, and herself. But she didn't want to lead. She wouldn't be *good* at it. Not everyone had to be.

And besides. . . what had fighting the power ever done for her other than get her locked up in a labor camp when Agnes had needed a pawn to sacrifice? No. Forget that.

"I have no desire to be a part of your revolution." Rose dropped the screwdriver back into the toolbox, and stood, rubbing her greasy hands on her coveralls. She also didn't desire a confrontation about it, but it would seem she wasn't being given a choice in that either.

Alys stood, leaning heavily on the stabilizer so she could look up at Rose thoughtfully—she was almost two heads shorter than Rose, but it didn't feel like it when Alys was fixing her with that gray stare. She tilted her head to the opposite side, white hair escaping from the bandana she'd used to keep it back, and falling into her face as her wings fluttered behind her. Rose wanted to escape from the careful scrutiny, hide away from those all-knowing eyes. Alys had seemed too curious, and wild on the day they'd first met, and strange beyond belief, but Rose had watched her since then. Alys was smarter than she let on. A woman who always knew what was going on around her, and how to play it to her advantage.

"Come now," Alys said, her lips spreading into a sharp smile that made Rose's stomach turn. Whatever she was about to say would be something Rose couldn't ignore. Something that would drag her to that meeting whether she liked it or not. Rose dug her heels into the metal beneath her, as if in doing so she could keep Alys from dragging her along for the ride. "We both know you're too smart to really believe you have a choice."

"Am I?" Rose's hands tightened where they held onto the legs of her coveralls. Felicity was strangely quiet on her side of the engine room, and Rose wondered if she was even still there at all, or if she'd ducked out when it looked like Alys and Rose were going to have an argument. Probably had. The young woman was observant, no fool.

"You are." Alys tilted her head, still smiling, it was unsettling. "MOTHER and the Uprising have made sure that you can't opt out, as it were, none of us can."

"I could stay here in the Wastes, leave the fighting to the others." Rose didn't know how much she liked that idea. Not because she wanted to fight, or because she really cared about what happened to the *Duchess* and her crew, but she did owe them her life and her freedom. And there would be no living with Tobias if she sat out on the final battle. "It'd probably be better for everyone if I did. I'm not a fighter."

"Don't lie to yourself," she heard Tobias hiss in her ear, his words scolding. She lifted her shoulder to rub her ear against it, pushing his voice away if just for the moment.

"See, that's the thing about a war against MOTHER and the Uprising, we don't need fighters." Shaking her head, Alys clicked her tongue softly. "We need thinkers. And you, Rosevelt Miller, are one of the quickest thinkers I've seen in a long time. I wish you'd been here to help me start my settlement. Things would have gone so much more smoothly."

"Flattery won't change my mind." Rose turned on her heel, intent on putting space between herself and Alys, but the pixie just flitted around her, moving to stand in the doorway.

"I know what they took from you," Alys said, her tone sympathetic, and soft. "They took my family too. And do you know what the Uprising did about it? Nothing. Eddi left me alone to sort my own way out. The Uprising likes to pretend it's here for us, to help the Enchanted fight the power of MOTHER, but it's not. The Uprising just wants to rule."

"I told you, I don't want to be a part of your revolution." Rose pushed past Alys into the hall, frowning when she heard her following behind, boots squeaking.

"And I told you, this isn't a choice any of us get to *make!*" Alys sped up her pace, the toes of her boots nipping at Rose's heels. Her fingers brushed Rose's wrist, trying to grab hold and force Rose to face her, but Rose wasn't having it. "Maybe when things first went south, it was. But maybe that's why we're in the predicament we're in. Too many people decided the revolution wasn't for them, or it wasn't that bad. They stayed in the pot too long, not realizing the water was heating up, and now it's *boiling.*"

"What are you even talking about?" Rose snapped, turning around, and grunting when Alys ran right into her.

"I'm talking about the fact that we *need* you."

Heaving a sigh, Rose scrubbed at her face, heedless of the grease she was no doubt smearing over her cheeks. "All right. I'll go to the meeting, if it'll get you to leave me alone. But I'm not making any promises that I'm signing on."

Alys's smile widened, eating up her whole face, before she grabbed Rose, and dragged her down the hall toward the galley. The others were waiting for them there, sat in chairs, or on the tables, almost pointedly relaxed, with Persinette standing at the center of it all. Funny how one small, mousey girl could wind up being the head of everything.

"Oh, thank you Alys." Persinette clapped, bouncing a little on her toes. "So glad you were able to convince her. Please, have a seat."

"I'll stand." Rose moved to lean against the table next to where Agnes and Sully were sitting on a bench, Agnes looking as annoyed at this impromptu meeting as she was. At least she wasn't alone in that.

"You said you had information for us?" Agnes asked, his gaze cutting to Alys. He still hadn't warmed up to her, it would seem, and Rose was starting to understand why.

"I know how to find the Great Library." Alys brushed a loose white hair back behind her ear, and tilted her chin as if proud of this accomplishment.

Rose fought back a snort. "What? The Great Library is a myth."

"It's not." Alys puffed out her cheeks, clearly annoyed.

"It is. Everyone knows it is. It's just a children's story." Roy shook his head, rubbing at the bridge of his nose. He looked tired. Worn around the edges from the last three days of being in charge of getting the refugees settled. Rose didn't envy him the task, she was just glad he'd taken it up since he seemed so genuinely good at it. Even still, humans tended to age more quickly under stress, with no magic to fuel them like the Enchanted. How much longer before he collapsed?

"It's not. It's how I got here. How I survived here." Alys pulled something from her pocket, and unfolded it carefully, then she held it out for them to see. Rose wrinkled her nose at it. It looked like a journal page.

"What are we looking at?" Agnes asked, reaching for the page, but Alys's grip held too firmly for him to snatch it away. Which didn't make her story any more believable in Rose's mind.

"Always so suspicious," Tobias said, and Rose rubbed at her ear with her wrist to try to silence him.

"This is a page from the queen's personal diary. I got it from the Great Library when I was there some years ago. The keepers of the library are how I wound up in the Wastes, they helped me escape when I didn't have a ship to get over the wall. They gave me seeds for crops so I wouldn't starve, and books on trains so I could rebuild the one I found in the woods. If I hadn't had them, I would have died."

Alys passed the page to Rose reluctantly, letting her examine it. She had no way of knowing if it was authentic or not. It could be forged—she'd never seen the queen's signature before, who was to say this was it?

"They told me the Great Library is constantly updating. It's a wealth of information. If we can get back there, we can use that information to bring both MOTHER and the Uprising down with minimal loss of life."

"Say that we believe you," Rose said, her fingers brushing over the letters on the page, feeling the indentations where 'Queen Eloise' had pressed a little too hard in places. "How would we even find this place?"

"That's where Manu and I come in." Persinette raised her hand, her freckled nose wrinkling. "We have a hair from one of the keepers. Manu got it before the extraction at Headquarters. Sully has found a witch amongst the refugees who knows locator magic. We just need to get everything together. We can begin as early as next week."

Rose blew out a long breath, letting it rustle the short curls that clung to her forehead. "I don't think this is a good idea. Even if this place does exist, how do we know the keepers will just let us access what we need?"

"You let me figure that out," Persinette said, which didn't make Rose feel any more confident in this plan, but she supposed this, like everything else in her life to date, wasn't really up to her.

"If you don't stop following me with those bloody book pages, I'm going to dismantle you for parts!" Kindle snapped, baring her pointed teeth at the robot. She'd heard enough about the blasted pages to last her a lifetime. There wasn't anything new in them, nor was there anything that could really help her. The robot obviously thought otherwise though. It seemed to think that if she went out of her way to find the woman in the pictures, then that would solve everything. It was missing the part where the library collapsed, and Kindle lost everything, after finding said woman.

The robot twittered on, ignoring the threat, as it generally did. It got stuck on things sometimes, and became a broken record, unable to stop skipping and repeating the same soundbite over and over. Kindle often wondered if there was a way to reboot it entirely. Just turn it off, wipe its data stores, and turn it back on. If she knew how, she'd have done it days ago just after it had found the damn book pages.

"There are still pages missing, you have no idea what happens after that. Maybe the library just ceases to exist! What happens then, huh?" Her throat clenched around the words, *what was it all for?* Because that would be the worst of it, wouldn't it? If she'd spent the last few centuries keeping the library functioning, growing, and relatively organized, for it to just fall apart in the end. What good was that? What good was *she*?

A huff left the robot, steam fluttering up from its mouth, its shoulders jerking with it as if it thought she was being particularly obtuse, on purpose. She wasn't. She just didn't see how the library falling apart could ever be a good thing. It was the only home she'd ever known for centuries. And it needed her. It needed its keeper, to look after the books, and take care of the rooms that collapsed, and tidy up. That was her job. She couldn't leave it behind to chase some selfish ideal that she didn't fully understand, or even want.

The robot released another series of chirps.

"No. I will not look for the other pages. We have more important things to focus on." Like the fact that the first snow had started in earnest, and they hadn't had time to move the last of the plants from the garden into the greenhouse because they were too busy dealing with the fable room. Or that they needed to check on their oil and wood stores to make sure they had enough to sustain them through the cold winter. Then there was always the dusting to do. There simply was no time to worry about—

A sharp tick-tock came from the little robot, derisive, and annoyed.

"I am not making up tasks just to avoid the truth." Kindle spun around so quickly the robot nearly walked right into her, and when it stopped to keep that from happening it wobbled dangerously on its little feet. Her muscles twitched to reach out and stop it from falling over, but she forced herself not to move. If the robot was going to be a pest, it could fall onto its back in the middle of the hall and sit there like a turtle, legs and arms flailing, for hours until she decided to come and help it up.

It jabbed her with one of its pincers, whistling in a tone so high pitched it made Kindle's ears ring. Her hands flew up to cover them, wings curling around her as if to protect her from the assault. They couldn't. The damn robot was good at making noises so shrill and piercing that Kindle swore sometimes they might burst her eardrums. And it seemed to have no compunction about weaponizing those sounds against the person who regularly oiled and wound it.

"Yell all you like. I'm not going to waste any more time on this. If you want to go digging through all the other books, have at it. It'll take you years, decades even! But I've got to make sure I survive through the winter so there's someone to keep my annoying robot buddy in working order." With that she spun on her heel and continued on her way. She ignored the calling clicks of the robot's continued chatter. If it had something to say, it could damn well come and say it out in the greenhouse, and make itself useful in the process.

KINDLE HAD FOOLISHLY THOUGHT the robot would drop it. Why she'd thought that, she didn't know. It never had before. It had a long memory, and the ability to be more tenacious than a hound on a scent. Still, she hadn't seen it for a couple of days, which she'd never admit out loud made her feel lonelier than she'd expected, but wasn't wholly unusual. Sometimes it did that, buried itself in a new crop of books, or went to reread something it hadn't read in a few years. She'd find it later, hidden behind what looked like a leather-bound fortress, locked up and in need of winding.

So she'd thought that after a few days, she'd find it that way, or it would just show back up like nothing had happened, chirping happily about some new journal it had found. Instead, the robot came barreling up to her where she was working in the greenhouse, paper flapping from its pincer, a shrill whistle leaving its metal mouth.

"What is it? What have you found now?" Kindle turned, her arms crossed over her chest, pulling the sleeves of her sweater down over her knuckles to keep the chill at bay.

The robot held out two new pages from the book, its pincers practically shaking in its excitement as it looked up at her expectantly.

Kindle rolled her eyes, and took the pages to survey them. She'd said she was done with this whole thing, but it would be better to placate the robot than to have it throw another fit. Maybe if they could get this whole obsession over with, then they could finally move on. But as the paper rustled in Kindle's fingers, she realized that there were still more pages missing. At least one, if she had to guess. Maybe they'd never find it, the library was so large, there were so many places it could be stashed. And if whoever had destroyed the storybook had wanted the answers to the library to truly stay hidden, then they could have simply destroyed the most important pages.

With a sigh, Kindle moved to the wrought-iron bench along one wall, and sat down, careful to sit on the edge so she wouldn't squish her wings, the metal creaking under her weight. The robot climbed up beside her, its little legs dangling over the seat where it kicked them back and forth. It tapped on the pages in Kindle's hand impatiently, and she let out another long exhale before she smoothed them out on her thighs.

"What am I looking at here?" she asked, talons moving carefully to keep from ripping through the paper. But she didn't need the robot to explain what she was seeing. It was an illustration of a letter left behind by her siblings. One that she was fairly sure she'd never seen, but had apparently been attached to the very book she'd read hundreds of times to the little robot.

Dearest sister,

We hope you will be comfortable here.

With your love of books, you will be happy to know that every time a new book is written, the library will receive a copy, all you need do to maintain this collection is stay here. It is your magic that powers this place, the moment you leave it will cease to update, and collapse, robbing the world of this vast resource.

Here you will be out of the way, but consider the alternative.

Be happy, dear sister.

Kindle's fingers tightened a little around the pages, making them crinkle. Something in her had cracked open and grown raw at the words. She hardly remembered her siblings apart from vague blurs, and voices, but to know that they had thought her imprisonment a *mercy* hurt more than she knew how to handle. So instead, she lashed out. "There? You see? If I leave, the Great Library ceases to exist. Is that what you want?"

The robot was looking up at her, its visual circuits wide. To answer her question, it released a soft, curious whirr.

"I don't know what it means that the rooms are collapsing." Kindle set the pages down on her lap to rub her face with her hands, careful of her sharp talons. "I assume it's just because the building is getting old. These things happen, you know. Stonework doesn't last forever."

The robot let out a long puff of air, shoulders sagging as if what she had said hadn't made sense to it at all. She supposed it didn't, or maybe it just wasn't what the robot had wanted to hear. It wanted her to go off on some high-flying adventure. To leave this place like people left home in all the books they'd read. But books weren't life. Adventures didn't happen to creatures like Kindle. Happy endings were a ploy to sell more copies.

"And even if I didn't care about what happened to the library," she said, her fingers fiddling with the edges of the paper, "there's still my appearance to contend with. I'm not exactly normal looking anymore, am I? Can't pass for human, can I? And you know what MOTHER is doing to people like me, don't you? They're rounding us up, and locking us away. What do you think they'd do to a dragon?"

Reaching over to take the page that Kindle had been examining, the robot tapped on the one beneath it. It was a drawing of a steamship. Although they were small, Kindle could see people on the deck, leaning against the railing, they were waving. One of them had red wings spread out behind them.

"Okay?" Kindle asked, not really sure what the robot was getting at.

It tapped the page again, almost hard enough to poke a hole through it, insistent.

"Just because an illustration says that there'd be people who accept me, doesn't mean it's true. This is a story. You know that, as well as I do. And people like happy endings. No one wants to read a sad story."

The robot let out an annoyed twitter, its arms crossing over its chest with a metallic clank.

"Look, you've found most of the pages, can we stop this silliness now? If the stonework really is giving way, then we need to start thinking about ways to reinforce it."

The robot slid to its feet, with muted ticking noises.

"No. I don't think the fact that the rooms are falling apart has anything to do with my own magic." Except, she did think that. She'd been thinking that for days now, and this page from the storybook had all but confirmed it. The question was, why had the page been torn out? Had her siblings removed it? Or had someone else? She shook herself, folding up the pages, and tucking them into the pocket of her pants.

Clanking footsteps followed her as she made her way back to where she'd been pruning back one of the trees in the greenhouse. The robot seemed to be waiting for something, its gears moving silently, but Kindle could hear a soft tapping noise, like it was clanging its pincer on its own hip, impatient.

"What?"

It released a lowered twittering sound that might have been a grumble, as if she had missed something patently obvious.

"I don't know what all this has to do with the clock on the rose. You got me there. Maybe the last page has something about that on it. Either way, why bother with something that'll never happen? Why don't you go and search the books on magical construction? We must have something that could—"

Another crash rent the air, so loud it shook the ground under Kindle's feet. She was running before she thought about it, following the rumbles of settling stone down corridor after corridor until she was pulled to a stop by a collapsed hallway. The rubble piled so high that she couldn't even see the top of it. It might have reached the ceiling, it was hard to tell from where she was standing.

Panting hard, Kindle braced herself on her knees, waiting for the robot to catch up to her. When it finally did she asked, "what are the odds it was just the hall and not everything in the west wing?"

The robot shook its head.

"Yeah. I didn't think so." Running her talons through her hair she let out a long breath, trying to steady the pounding of her heart in her chest. Her home was falling apart. It was collapsing in on itself, one room at a time. The dust burned her eyes, and she coughed around where some of it had gotten in her throat making it feel tighter than before. How much longer did she have before she had no home *left*?

A pincer patted her lightly, and the robot let out a soft whirr of sympathy.

"We should try to find the last page." She felt stupid saying it, but that book was the only clue they had about what kind of magic her siblings had used to create the library. "I just. . . I don't know what else to *do*." She choked on the last word, but hid it behind a cough. "This doesn't mean I'm looking for that girl in the pictures though."

Another whirr was followed by a nod from the robot. A pledge to do its best to help—and a brush off of their arguments over the girl—that Kindle appreciated far more than she'd ever be able to say. She reached down to take the cold pincer in her own hand and gave it a gentle squeeze.

"Let's get to work."

ose had made up her mind. She had decided even before the meeting, but the meeting sealed it for her. The Great library? A fictional place that Enchanted children learned about in bedtime stories? It wasn't anything more than a fever dream in Rose's opinion, whatever Alys might say. And she wasn't willing to stake her whole future on it. Or to put her neck on the line to find it. No thank you. She'd stay in the Wastes and take her chances with the jabberwocks. She knew what MOTHER and the Uprising were capable of, and in her opinion, they were worse than anything that could live in the Wastes. Let Eddi and the queen duke it out on the other side of the wall, they'd kill each other eventually.

"So that's it then?" Tobias' voice asked in her head, a tickle at the back of her mind, urging her to make a different choice. Blast, he was stubborn even when he was dead. *"You're just going to look out for yourself? Forget everyone else? What would your father think?"*

"My father's dead. Just like you, in case you forgot," she growled back, tightening the bolt on the capacitor harder than she likely should have. The wrench skidded dangerously, like maybe she'd stripped the screw threads underneath. *Damn it.* She hissed when she looked at it, clenched her jaw with an annoyed grunt, and loosened it a little. "The queen made sure of that."

"You joined the Uprising before, to make him proud, didn't you?" Tobias pressed, because he never did know when to give up. And even the version of him that her mind had conjured up was a persistent old bastard. That's probably why she had taken to him like she had. He reminded her so much of her father sometimes, it ached.

"Yes," she grunted in response, "and look where that got me. Look where it got any of us. Agnes. Sully. Persinette. Manu! Our want to do the right thing, what did it get us?"

"It brought you together." Tobias pointed out in that obnoxiously reasonable way of his. Gods, she hated him sometimes. Why couldn't the voice in her head just shut up for once? One would have thought that when her father figure died, he'd have ceased to be her conscience, but it wasn't so. Instead he now lived, rent free, in her head to tell her all of the ways she needed to do better. To continue to push her.

Rose rolled her eyes. *Brought them together*, as if that mattered. As if it gave her something she was missing. It didn't. She didn't need the makeshift family Persinette and the others were building. "And look at what helping them did to you. You're *dead*."

"Yes, but I got to breathe free air before I went," he said as if that were some kind of accomplishment. It wasn't, not in her opinion. What was free air when it came at the price of life? Everything came at a cost, yes, but no price should be that steep.

"It wasn't free though, was it?" she countered, banging her wrench against a piece of pipe that refused to budge, and baring her teeth at it as if she could snarl it into submission. Sometimes that worked with machines, most of the time it didn't, but she was always willing to try it on the off chance. Especially since beating on a machine helped to relieve some of her own stress. Normally. Now was not one of those times. She was wound up, a coil tightened one too many times, and this conversation with Tobias wasn't helping. "It came at the price of your life."

"You know what I mean."

She was glad she was alone in the engine room of the *Sultana* having this conversation with Tobias. There had been a couple of times over the last few days where he'd gotten her going when she wasn't alone, and the others had looked at her as if she were one traumatic incident from losing her grip on reality entirely. She had a grip on reality, she knew Tobias wasn't real, but he'd always helped her talk things out before, and she wasn't about to stop using him as a sounding board now. Plus, he gave the best advice.

"Do I?" Rose countered, swiping sweat from her brow with the back of her hand.

"You damn well do, and we both know it." He sounded irritated, which would have been funny if he were alive so she could see the way his wrinkled face would pucker like a child eating a lemon, his pointed ears twitching. But he wasn't alive. And the thought that she'd never see that again caused something to slice through her chest, a stabbing pain at the center of her that would never go away.

"And what would you have me do, Tobias? Sacrifice what little I have left for a cause I don't believe in anymore? Go up against MOTHER again, just so I can fail, and die with the rest of them? No, thanks. I'll stick it out here." She grunted around the tightening of a valve, and sat back to eye the replacement pip with a speculative look. It would hold. It might even work better now than it had when it was new. But there was no sense of accomplishment to it, no gentle warmth that made the corners of her lips twitch upward. Just a hollowness at the realization that everyone around her, everyone who knew her name, and gave a damn about her, would probably die in the coming months. That's why it was better they weren't friends.

"*You know, Rosevelt Miller,*" Tobias said, his tone soft and sad, "*I never took you for a coward.*"

Rose jerked as if she'd been slapped, her head banging against the piping behind her. She hissed, lifting a hand to rub at the back of her head, which was already starting to pound, grateful when it didn't come away bloody. "Excuse you?"

Tobias didn't answer. In fact, her mind had gone strangely quiet, only echoing her own thoughts, no one else's. She pressed her fingers into the sore spot on her skull, and scowled. It seemed like forever since she'd been alone in her own head. Months since Tobias had taken up being the angel on her shoulder. And now there she was. . . alone again. Maybe she was a coward after all. She swallowed around a tightness in her throat, rubbing away the blurriness of her vision. It was just the pounding headache that was slowly forming. That's all it was. She didn't *miss* him. His words hadn't stung. She didn't secretly think he was right.

"Rose?" Stella asked, poking her head in between the pipes to look for her.

"Yeah?" Rose pulled herself free of where she'd been working to meet Stella's gaze. Grabbing the handkerchief that Felicity had given her from her pocket, she wiped down her hands. "What's going on?"

"You need to get back to the *Duchess*, Agnes says there's something you need to see." Stella wrinkled her nose, stuffing her hands into her pockets, miffed at being forced to play errand boy for Agnes. Rose could relate. She resisted the urge to scoff, grabbing her toolbox instead, and heading for the door.

"Did he say what it was about?"

"Something to do with somebody named Gaston?" Stella

scrubbed at her nose. "I don't know. He just said to come down and get you."

"Gaston?" The name echoed off the sudden emptiness inside Rose's skull. Warping, and growing louder instead of softer as an echo ought to, until it was a blaring alarm instead of a name.

"I think so." With a shrug, Stella led her back to the steps that would take them to the deck.

"You're sure that's the name he said?" Her hand tightened painfully around the handle of her toolbox, knuckles paling as Rose fought to keep a grip on her control, and the box which was starting to slip through her sweaty fingers. It couldn't be. It wasn't possible. Or. . . well, it was *possible*. The last she'd seen of Gaston, he'd been alive, so she supposed he could come back to haunt her. But he wasn't smart enough to have risen through the ranks at MOTHER, even if he'd used her as a bargaining chip. And she'd spent the last several years in 9c, surely he was too old to be leading any kind of charge? Still, she knew that name. And the fact that Agnes was the one calling her in, meant that it had to be *that* Gaston, as if there could be any other.

Stella tilted back on her heels, her chin tipping up to stare at the ceiling as if in thought, and then she dipped her head to meet Rose's gaze again. "Definitely. He said you'd know who that was. So. . ." She stuffed her hands into her pockets. "Who is it?"

Rose didn't answer. She wasn't going to drag her dirty laundry out in front of a one-night-stand. Besides, if Gaston were really after them, Stella would know soon enough the kind of man he was. He never had had enough sense to keep his mouth shut. The gangplank was still up from when she'd crossed earlier. She could have gone down through the cargo hold and across the ground, it would have been safer and had less chances of her falling to her death in between the two ships, but she didn't have the patience for that. Never would, very likely. And honestly, what would it matter now if she fell to her death? If Gaston was truly back, she likely didn't have much longer to live anyhow. He wouldn't stop until he'd hunted them all like a bloodhound. Except unlike a bloodhound, Gaston liked to play with his food.

Stella stayed behind her, dogging her steps even once they'd reached the deck and she could have broken away from Rose. Maybe that should have bothered Rose, left her with a feeling that Stella was sticking her nose where it didn't belong, but that seemed to be the way of things with this group of people, and she was too distracted to be bothered with it. Too busy swallowing breath after breath to keep that baby-bird-caught-in-the-mouth-of-a-dog feeling at bay.

It wasn't working. The world was narrowing down to a tiny point of light.

Agnes was at the helm, his long form flopped into the captain's chair like he belonged there, one leg kicked up over the arm. The room was otherwise empty, and Rose felt a small swell of gratitude for the unicorn at allowing her this little privacy. He above all others would know how traumatic this would be.

"Thank you for finding her, Stella. You can go," Agnes said with a dismissive flick of his wrist that made Stella's shoulders go rigid. Her jaw ticked as it tightened, the teeth grinding together so hard that Rose could hear it. Stella was a captain, and no one gave her orders, but Agnes didn't seem to give one whit about her status, which was very on brand for him.

"It's all right Stella. I can handle this from here." Rose gave her a little nudge with her shoulder, hoping to keep them both from fighting as sweat trickled down her back. She didn't need that, not right now.

Stella's navy eyes flicked down to Rose, a dark brow

lifting in question, as if asking if this too were an order. If it were, Rose was sure she'd lash out against it, even if it was coming from someone she liked.

"Why don't you go and see how the *Sultana* is running since the repairs? Let me know if there is anything else that needs looking into?" A diversion that Rose was sure would work, because Stella loved her ship, and the temptation to start her up, and see how well she was flying after so long landlocked, would be something that no captain could resist. Especially one like Stella.

Stella took one last look at both Rose and Agnes, then dipped her head once, and practically ran out of the room and down the hall, her boots slapping hard on the floors outside.

"Remind me to never let you see my weakness." Agnes scoffed, turning the chair back to the big screen that had lowered from the ceiling.

"Oh Haggy, I already know all of your weaknesses." Rose forced a laugh, hoping to sound more relaxed and hide the tell-tale tremble in her voice. She dropped her toolbox and made her way over to lean against the arm of the chair, arms crossed over her chest, hands tight on her upper arms—she could feel the heat of her palms through her sleeves—as if she could hold herself together that way. She couldn't. It had never worked before, and it wasn't about to start now. She asked, "Gaston has surfaced?"

"He has." Agnes pressed a button on the control panel to the other side of the chair, and a picture appeared on the screen of a square jawed, blond man, with straight teeth, and pale colored eyes. No one would be able to tell from the black and white pictures, but Rose knew those eyes were ice blue, and beautiful if you were into that kind of thing, because she'd felt them slip over her like an unwanted caress more times than she could count. Had met them, stared into them, as he'd read her crimes out loud. "We got this from one of my Uprising contacts."

"You still have contacts?" She didn't know why she was surprised by that. She shouldn't be. For all she hated Agnes, his people had always been strangely loyal. She'd blame it on the unicorn magic if she didn't know that that's not how unicorns worked.

Agnes lifted one shoulder in a shrug, and pressed another button on the panel to make the video play.

"That's right, ma'am, MOTHER has issued a kill on sight order for the escapees of 9c," Gaston's voice said out of time with the movement of his mouth on the video, giving Rose a strange sense of vertigo that only added to her already turning stomach. "We have been told by an anonymous source that they escaped over the wall into the Wastes on two former Uprising ships, the *Saccharine Sultana*, and the *Defiant Duchess*. Of the escapees, our intel lists a unicorn named Agnes, and a half-elf named Rosevelt Miller as the leaders of the break. We have been told to bring them in, dead or alive."

Agnes pushed another button, and the image paused, Gaston's smile fixed on his face in a sinister rictus.

"How do they know what ships were used?" Rose asked, rubbing her sweating hands over the sleeves of her coveralls even as a chill made her skin pimple with gooseflesh. They'd listed her as a leader of the break. Not Sully. Not Tobias. Not Roy. *Her*. She didn't know what that meant, or why they'd picked her out of the group that had escaped, but she knew it wasn't good.

"Eddi told them." Agnes drummed his fingers on the arm of the chair. "I haven't told the others yet, but this kill order changes everything. It means Eddi is utilizing MOTHER to do their dirty work."

"It means they have more weapons at their disposal."

Something tight and sharp had settled in Rose's throat, making it hard to swallow without feeling like she was going to cut herself open. "So what are our choices?" She asked before she even thought about the words. *Our* choices. But once they were out, she knew they were true. She was one of them now, Gaston had made sure of that by showing his face, and calling her name as a target. He'd made sure that she couldn't avoid a fight, and she was going to finish him once and for all.

"The library, I think, is our best option. The others have pinned down a location. If Alys is correct in how it works, we could enter from here, and exit from somewhere over the wall, far away from MOTHER or the Uprising's notice."

"And then what?"

"And then, I guess we hope we have enough of a surprise advantage to take them both down quickly before they notice where we are and come after us." Agnes continued to drum on the arm rests, the rhythm picking up a little in his agitation, each tap of his fingertips landing too hard, pounding against the steadily growing ache in Rose's temples.

"That's pinning a lot on hopes, and chance." Rose didn't like it. She'd never been the type to do such a thing, and she didn't think an all-out war against two much better equipped forces was the time to start.

"Yeah, well, that's all we've ever done, really." Agnes smiled a little, the curl of his lips looking more sinister than it had any right to under the slowly growing scruff on his face. His hair had begun to come back in, but it wasn't as vibrant as it had once been, Rose noticed. Likely a reaction to the trauma he'd suffered. Sully had made it clear that if anyone mentioned it, he'd personally gut them, and after seeing him rip out a man's heart to protect Agnes, she wouldn't put it past him. So she'd kept that particular revelation to herself. Still, it made her wonder sometimes what the trauma of camp 9c had done to her. How it had affected her magic.

"I don't like it."

"You don't have to." Agnes murmured scratching at the scruff along his jaw. "Besides if Alys is right, and this place has any and everything that's ever been written down as a source. . ."

"We won't need luck." Rose realized, a little bit of something warm like hope curling up in her stomach, and chasing away the cold sweats of fear. A trilling trailed up her spine that was mainly adrenaline, excitement following in it's wake. She was still afraid, terrified really, but the idea of having that much of a leg up on Gaston? On Eddie? It was exhilarating. "We'd have blueprints, formal plans, lists of weapons, and—"

"Exactly." Agnes tilted his head back to give her an even wider grin, it made his eyes narrow into a squint that almost had him looking boyish. Almost had Rose seeing the man Sully had fallen in love with. Almost. He was still a bastard underneath, after all. "We should inform the others. It'll be time to start the ritual to find the library soon, and they should know about this before we set foot there."

Rose ran her fingers over her clothes. "We'll need a list of everything we should search for."

"You'll be in charge of that." Agnes waved his hand like a king assigning a task to one of his underlings. "That was always your specialty."

"All right." Rose straightened her spine, happy to have a task ahead of her that she might actually enjoy, and turned to get cleaned up so she could get to work.

Just as she reached the door, Agnes stopped her with a soft, "Rose."

"Yeah?"

"Glad to have you on the team."

Rose didn't say anything to that, there was nothing to say. He knew exactly why she was joining up, even after she'd been so adamant that she didn't want to. He'd probably known as soon as the message had come through and it had been Gaston in the video. Agnes was a manipulative little shit, and he'd played her exactly right. Rose would have chafed under that realization if it didn't mean she was finally going to get vengeance on Gaston for everything he'd done to her.

"You just let me be the one to bring that bastard to his knees, and we'll be even. All right, Agnes?"

"I think I can have that arranged," Agnes said and it sounded like he might be laughing, but Rose didn't stop to find out as she strode out into the hall to set to work.

Finding a missing book page in a library was like looking for a needle in a stack of needles, near impossible. It had been some days since they had been cut off from the west wing, and even with Kindle and the robot working night and day to search for it, still there was nothing. It was becoming increasingly likely that the page had been destroyed altogether, or that it was hidden in the west wing, where they couldn't reach.

Twice, Kindle had stood on the edge of the debris, and thought about how long it would take her to dig her way through to the other side. Twice, she had discarded the idea. Because the reality was, she didn't want to know what was on the other side. If the entire wing had collapsed, that was centuries worth of texts gone in a flash, a whole portion of her home destroyed that she would never get back. Even if they could rebuild it, and salvage a good portion of the works that had been stored there, it would never be the same, and it would never be enough. There would still be things that were lost, that had slipped through the cracks. Then there was the seed library to think of, which was either on the other side of that pile of rubble or gone entirely. And that is what finally broke Kindle, had her curling in on herself most nights, her wings wrapped around her like a blanket, insides twisting and turning. That bloody pile of rubble, blocking her off from the remainder of her home. Yeah, the not knowing was safer.

"All right," she said one day, as they had just finished going through the vast collection of books on botany that she didn't think she'd ever really looked through. She probably should have, it may have made her a better gardener, but everything in the seed library had come with instructions, and there were just so many other things to read at the time to bother with books on boring plants.

The robot chirped in question.

"All right, let's find that girl," Kindle answered, her shoulders hunching forward in defeat. It had been so many years since someone else had stepped foot in the library, and she didn't like the idea of someone seeing it like this, but they needed help. Gods did they need help. And Kindle was not so proud as to not ask for it, especially if that meant she had the chance to save her home. "There must be some way to conjure a person, surely."

A tilt of its head and a soft whirr, followed by a curious blink was the only answer she got from the robot.

"What does it matter what changed my mind? This is what you wanted, isn't it? For us to find the girl, and have her come and help us?" She grumbled, defensive, talons too tight on an outdated book on pollination. Really, they should have gone through at some point and gotten rid of everything that would never be of use again. Outdated medical texts, books with incorrect information on biology, technology that the world had moved past, but Kindle found it hard to part with any of her beloved collection. Especially after she'd read the history of what MOTHER was doing out in the world. Burning books. Despicable behavior, but not the worst of their sins.

The robot whistled.

"No, I haven't changed my mind about staying." She never would. The library was her home, and if she left, all their carefully stored knowledge would be lost. She had to hope that maybe one day the world would be ready to acknowledge all of these texts, to understand the people who had come before them, maybe not today, but someday. It would be selfish of her to leave it behind to chase after an adventure that wasn't really her own, and let this all turn to ash in her wake. "But I do think she and those people on the ship could help us. We definitely need more hands to clear the mess in between us and the west wing."

The robot's visual censors dimmed, as if it were narrowing its eyes at her, and Kindle frowned. She hated it when it did that. She knew the robot wasn't equipped with any kind of x-ray capabilities, but it always felt like the little thing was seeing too far down into her when it did. She didn't want it to see all the squirmy dark bits of her that sometimes wished her siblings had just killed her and been done with it, nor the bits that were actively afraid of the world beyond the walls of her library. She was imprisoned there, in a way—and she knew that's what her siblings had meant to do—but she also didn't want to leave. She'd long since stopped dreaming of the world outside. Content to watch it all through the safety of books.

"Don't look at me like that." She squirmed under its knowing gaze.

The censors dimmed further, and the robot leaned in closer, its hinges squeaking a little at the motion it didn't normally perform.

"Are you going to help me or not?" Kindle huffed, leaning her weight back on her heels to escape the robot's searching gaze. She wasn't sure what it thought it would find, but she was sure that she didn't want it to find it.

A soft trill left the robot, and it pulled back before shrugging.

"Good. Then let's start in the magical theory section. I know there aren't any actual spells there, but it might be able to point us in the right direction where it comes to spell books. That stuffy lot was always very good at citing their sources." She stuffed the book she'd been looking at back where it belonged on the shelf, and spun on her heel to head toward the southern wing of the library without waiting for the robot to follow, but follow it did, if the soft clanking from behind her was any indication.

IT WAS DAYS LATER, and although they had a pile of possibilities sitting at the center of the round room, they hadn't stumbled upon anything definitive yet, which Kindle supposed she should have been prepared for. This was the theory section, of course, not the practical section. Maybe it would have been better to start with the spell books after all. But she hadn't wanted to slog through all of them, especially with the way some of the magic had bled into the pages, making them buzz, and hum, and prickle at her skin when she touched them. They also sometimes made the robot short out, which would be unproductive as then she'd have to get it going again, and that always took so much longer than it ought to with how her talons got in the way while she worked on its innards.

"Bunch of blowhards," Kindle grumbled, tossing another book onto the stack of their discards. "All these experts, and not a single one can make up their mind how to conjure a single person."

The robot twittered a response that sounded optimistic, and Kindle clicked her tongue.

"Yes, there's plenty on how to summon demons, but I don't think the woman we saw in the pictures is a demon, do you?"

It seemed to give the suggestion some thought, and then disregarded it with a huff, and a shake of its head.

"I didn't think so," Kindle agreed, grabbing for the next text. Her neck was starting to get sore from where she'd kept it bent over reading far too long, and the light from the windows up near the ceiling was fading. She massaged the skin under her hair, careful of the scales that lingered there. Soon they'd be left with nothing but the oil lamps, and she always hated reading by those when she could help it, they made her eyes feel tired and fuzzy.

One glance at the table of contents told her this book wouldn't be useful either, but just as she was about to add it to their discards, the pages flipped of their own volition, and a bit of paper fluttered from between them down onto the floor. She frowned, bending down to pick up the folded piece of paper, and set the book on the top of her stack.

The robot whirred in question.

"I don't know what it is yet, I just picked it up. Have I opened it yet?" Kindle snapped, moving over to the table to click on one of the lamps, and unfold the bit of paper carefully. Smoothing out the folds, her brows raised, almost disappearing into the mane of red hair on top of her head at the sight of what might be the final page from her storybook. But where they'd thought it might provide answers about what the rose meant, or an ending beyond the page of her waving from the deck of a ship, it appeared to be an illustration of her and the robot drawing a summoning circle onto the floor of one of the bigger rooms of the library in chalk.

An excited exclamation left the robot, high pitched, and piercing.

"Instructions? I don't think it's instructions." She frowned, shaking her head. She couldn't even properly make out all of the symbols on the floor, and she doubted the circle was the whole of it. There were no words to recite, no ingredients to include, just her winged back to the illustrator as she and the robot sketched out the circle.

The robot chattered, almost too quickly for her to fully understand what it was trying to say.

"Wait, you're telling me you've seen this exact circle before?" Kindle turned to frown down at the robot. How could it even tell? Some of the characters were so far from the perspective of the illustrator that whoever had drawn the pictures had blurred them intentionally. There was no way it could—

It took off, clanking loudly in its rush to leave the room and jet down the hallway.

"Hey! Wait a minute! Explain this to me!" Kindle dropped the page onto the desk, and ran off after it, her clawed feet tapping loudly on the stone floors. "Don't just say something like that and run off. You have to tell me what's going on."

It didn't dignify her words with an answer, feet continuing to clank until it made its way to the room full of journals, which was surprising, she'd been sure it'd head for the spell books. Because why wouldn't something like that be amongst the other spell books? It only made sense! Kindle panted, clutching her knees, as she glared at the robot, which had already moved to the shelves to find what it was looking for.

"Are you going to explain this, or are you just going to run around being all mysterious?"

A twittering laugh followed the question, and if the robot

weren't her only friend, Kindle really would have disassembled it for parts, little brat that it was.

"You're not cute. You know that right?"

It shrugged, grabbed the journal it was looking for, and moved to the desk to drop the book onto it with a thud. It didn't even bother turning on the desk lamp, already flipping through pages at a speed that would have been impossible for anyone not made of clockwork bits. Kindle moved up behind it and peered over its shoulder, her hands stuffed deep in her pockets to keep herself from reaching out and snatching the journal away to find the answers herself. The robot seemed to know what it was looking for, she'd just have to let it do its thing.

Finally, it stopped on a page, and pointed to a large circle that spanned the gutter between the opposite pages. Above someone had written "to summon a person" in a hand so hurried, that she almost couldn't make it out.

"Are there any other instructions?" Kindle asked, reaching down to flip the page, but the pages after that one were blank, as if the person hadn't been able to continue. Wrinkling her nose, she went back to the page before, and found something about burning the person's name inside of the circle. "Well that's not helpful at all, we don't know her name. What do we do then? Do they say?"

The robot shook its head, but let out a soft chittering noise that made Kindle's head ache. Gods, she was going to really regret this decision, wasn't she?

"All right, we can try burning the storybook pages. Maybe her likeness will call her." Kindle scrubbed at the back of her neck, letting the coarse scales ground her. "Go on and get the chalk, and I'll find us a clear space to do this."

A little cheer left the robot, its arms lifting above its head with a loud squeak before it dashed off to do as she'd told it to.

Half an hour later, they had the circle sketched out in the middle of the historical room. It was the biggest one they had left, and while Kindle didn't see why they needed that much space, it showed them using it in the illustration, and she wasn't going to chance this not working simply because they hadn't provided adequate room for the spell.

The robot had found her a little brass bowl from somewhere, probably the dining room where neither of them had stepped in some decades, and sat it on one of the spots in the circle that was clear of characters. Kindle scratched her jaw where a fresh crop of scales had begun to break the surface, leaving behind the gritty feeling of chalk on her leathery skin.

"That should do it," she said, standing up to survey her work. It wasn't even perfectly circular, but she figured it was the thought that counted. And she was already putting a lot of faith into what could very well just be a storybook, why not put a little more into her ability to draw a magic circle?

A soft whir left the robot as it held up the book page.

"Yeah, good luck," Kindle muttered, looking down at the image of the girl again. None of the illustrations really showed her face, not full on. Her profile in one, the back of her head in another, her from a distance on the ship. Kindle couldn't help but think it was a shame, but she shook the thought aside. Then she sucked in a breath, pursed her lips as if to whistle, and blew out a small flame that caught at the corner of the page. Dropping it into the bowl, she and the robot stepped back.

A blinding light burst forth from the center of the circle, followed by a loud bang that shook the very ground Kindle stood on. She ducked behind her wings to protect herself from the searing light, and hissed as it burned at the delicate skin pulled taught across her hollow bones. The book really should have warned them about that! Why hadn't—

The robot let out an unfamiliar noise that Kindle unfortunately recognized the exact meaning of.

"Whoops? What do you mean *whoops*?" She lowered her wing, her eyes narrowing and frowned at what she saw. The room, and circle, had expanded to several times what it had been, large enough to house an entire ship, in fact. And at the center of it sat the pirate ship they'd seen in the drawings. Kindle's head swam a little just looking at it. "Whoops."

It was too easy. Rose didn't trust things that were too easy. Sure, they had spent a couple of days gathering ingredients for the spell, but everything they'd needed had been readily available in Alys' greenhouse at the back of her train caravan, or in the surrounding forest. They hadn't had to travel to the top of a mountain and battle a jabberwock for some rare herb or anything. They also hadn't had to translate anything—the spell book the witch had was written in Daiwynn standard, with instructions so simple that a child could have performed the spell.

The only thing that had added an air of difficulty was the fact that they had needed five witches to power the locating array because they had made it large enough to encompass the whole of the *Duchess*. And even with that, they hadn't had to be particularly powerful witches. They just needed five because they had to have a magical presence at every cardinal point, and one inside. If they were sending a single person, this could have been completed with three witches, as a witch's hand would count as a magical presence.

Either way, it had been too easy. Persinette's pale purple magic had just begun to bleed into the symbols on the deck of the ship when the air shifted like heat overflow coming from a grate, warping, and going all misshapen, and the outside was suddenly the inside, and much, much darker. Rose blinked, taking a moment for her eyes to adjust, as she rubbed at the right one.

Where the forest had been before, now there were shelves lined with books, each stuffed to bursting, curved all the way around the ship. Rose tilted her head back and looked up to find that they were at least twenty shelves high, probably more, it was hard to count that many at a glance, and some of them disappeared into the high ceiling. She wondered how anyone could read that many books, least of all reach the ones at the very top up near the skylights. Whoever wanted to read those books would have to be able to fly, there was simply no other option, even if there were a ladder that went all that way up.

Rose's breath caught in her throat at the thought of having time to look through all of those books. Of being able to sit and read without being bothered or interrupted. Such a place truly would be a haven. And then the realization of what she was looking at caught up to her, and she lost her breath anew, her heart tripping in her chest.

The Great Library. They had made it to the *Great Library*.

Every book ever penned or published was here somewhere among these shelves. The room spun around her at the realization, her fingers twitching with the need to reach out and learn everything she possibly could from all those years ago. MOTHER had gotten rid of so many books before she'd even been born, and now, here they all were, hers for the reading. All Rose had to do was reach out and touch them.

She leaned over the rail of the ship, intent on doing just that, but her hand met resistance, palm pressed flat against something hard, and cold, like glass. Frowning, she pulled her hand back, and tried again. Still, it would not go any further past the edge of the rail. Curling her fingers into a fist, she rapped her knuckles on the barrier, frowning when they made a sound like knocking on a door.

Rose turned to tell the others, but found everyone else on the ship had collapsed onto the deck. Persinette was nearest, and Rose bent quickly to make sure her pulse was still thumping lazily along, her chest still rising and falling in a relaxed rhythm.

"They're fine," a voice said from over her shoulder, "just sleeping."

"What did you do to them?" Rose's shoulders stiffened as she rose to her full height. She may not have particularly cared for any of the people who she had been forced to team up with, but they *were* her team, and without them she would be left to face MOTHER and the Uprising alone. Which was not something she wanted, nor thought she could handle.

"Just a little sleeping spell. I wanted to be left alone with you, to work out a deal." They sounded casual, unbothered by the fact that they had just put a whole ship of people to sleep for no other reason than to have some privacy.

Rose bit down on the end of her tongue to keep from saying something that might cause them to lash out at her as well, her hands tightening into fists at her sides. She wanted to scream at them, to tell them that it wasn't right to use magic that way, but if they could do such a thing without even being a little bit winded, what could they do to her for being rude? Better not to find out. She shifted on her feet, readying to spin around and face this new threat.

"Don't," they said, something strange and almost frightened in their voice, a quiver threatening to break the word. Which made no sense at all, because didn't they have *her* hostage here, not the other way around? "Don't turn around, please."

"Who are you?" Rose's spine straightened further, her chin lifting, as she resisted the urge to turn. She had to know what her captor looked like. Not just because she was curious but also because she needed to make sure they weren't a true danger to her or her people. Maybe they were from MOTHER, and had lured them here to finish them off. Or maybe they were one of the Uprising's people. Not that laying eyes on them would be enough for her to tell, but it would make her feel better. Still, she wasn't willing to risk her own neck for that information. Not yet anyway. She'd see what she could get out of them without it first.

"A keeper of the library." They let out a breath, and Rose could imagine some faceless person's shoulders slumping forward a little as if in defeat. "I brought you here to help."

Well, that certainly answered one of her questions. Of course it hadn't been that the spell had worked, it was that someone had been working their own magic on the other end. Someone had been calling for them. Maybe the wires had crossed, and enhanced the magic on both ends. Or maybe someone had just interfered and changed their destination.

"I didn't mean to bring the entire ship though," they muttered, but it was too loud in the quiet that surrounded them for Rose to miss it. They sighed, shifting their weight around enough that Rose could hear their clothes move with them.

"So you meant to bring just me here. Why?" Rose turned her head, hoping to catch a glimpse of the person from the corner of her eye, but all she saw was a vague red shape, that gave her no indication about who or what they were.

They made a soft, surprised sound, and Rose heard them take a step back, making the floorboards on the deck creak loudly. "Oh. Umm. . ." They laughed nervously and moved around some more, their movements too loud in the silence of the sleeping crew. "This is really embarrassing."

Rose swallowed down a scoff. If they thought this was

embarrassing, they should see how the crew was going to feel when they all awoke. Especially Agnes, he was going to be livid. Oh, she was definitely going to rub this in his face once he woke up. The great and powerful Agnes the ornery unicorn, laid flat by a sleeping spell. He was going to be unbearable to live with. It would be delightful

"Well it's no picnic for me, either," Rose snarked.

"Of course. Apologies." They huffed a little, and Rose would swear that they were pouting, but she didn't turn her head to see. They cleared their throat, likely straightened up a little as if to be more in control of the situation. Not that they needed that help, they had put her entire crew to sleep, and Rose wasn't about to test the limits on what else they could do. "We found your picture in a book, and it seemed like you might be able to help us with saving the library."

"Saving it from what, exactly?" Rose pressed her weight onto the balls of her feet, the shining surface of a dagger catching her eye. If she changed her posture just a little, maybe bent down to check on Persinette again then she'd be able to see the person behind her in the reflection. She squatted, her fingers reaching out as if to check Persinette's pulse, making her lean over a little more, bracing her weight on her free hand.

"It's. . . It's. . ." They struggled with the words, and Rose heard them swallow around whatever they were trying to force from their tongue. They opened and closed their mouth a few more times, the sound like a fish struggling for breath, and then with a loud sigh they let it all out. "The Great Library is crumbling, I'm afraid. And I need someone—"

"It's what?!" Rose jerked her head around to look at them, and her stomach lurched at the sight before her. The person —no, woman, she was a woman—had giant red wings spread out behind her, a long draconic tail wrapped around her ankles as if to comfort herself, and what skin Rose could see poking out from her sweater and overalls was covered in angry red patches. Rose couldn't tell if they were scales, or some kind of illness. She yelped, stumbling back onto her bottom beside Persinette, almost sitting on the other girl's prone body. The impact sent a jolt up her spine that had her hissing. But she didn't squeeze them shut. No. she couldn't. Not when there was . . . there was . . .

"I told you not to turn around!" The woman shouted, smoke pluming out from her nostrils as her eyes blazed blood red, her wings lifting behind her to make her look far more threatening.

"You're a. . . A. . . A. . ." Why couldn't she get the word out past her tongue? Why was Rose choking on it, finding it hard to swallow as her jaw opened and closed uselessly? Rose had never been at a loss for words, not in her whole life. But at that moment the word 'dragon' was stuck somewhere between her lungs and her voice box, and she didn't think any amount of coughing would get it back.

"A dragon," the woman finished for her through clenched teeth. She looked furious, as if she'd really thought she could hide what she looked like from Rose. "I am aware."

At some point Rose's hand had lifted to cover her mouth, but she didn't remember lifting it herself. Her eyes were so wide in her face that they were on the verge of watering. "Are you going to eat us?"

"What?" The woman growled, her gaze narrowed on Rose, jaw clenched so tight Rose would swear she could hear her sharpened teeth grinding. "Of course not! I brought you here to help."

Help. Was the dragon even really asking? Or would she just force them to do what she wanted under threat of death? And why had she wanted Rose in particular? She'd said something about a picture. None of it made sense, Rose felt her heart pounding against her chest in fear, threatening to leap free of her ribcage and splatter against the floor. It was too loud in the quiet of the sleeping crew. The dragon was going to hear it. And then what? Rose pressed her hand to her chest trying to quiet it, for fear the sound of it might further trigger the dragon's rage.

"So you will help," she said, leaving no room for argument. "You and your crew will help me rebuild what we've lost, and then help me reinforce our walls with magic if need be."

"Or what?" Rose asked, not even really sure she wanted to know the answer. Her fist was so tight where it gripped her shirt that she could feel her nails leaving crescent shaped wounds in her palms, threatening to rip holes in the fabric.

"Or I'll send you back to Daiwynn and let MOTHER do with you what they will." She lifted her head, imperious, the kind of woman who was used to getting what she wanted, and not having to answer to anyone.

"What if I want to make a trade?" The words sprouted out of nowhere, Rose didn't even remember thinking them, but there they were floating around in the air between them. They needed answers, and if she had to make an exchange with a dragon to get them. . . Well, Rose wasn't above that. There was an untold amount of things she'd do for information, she'd learned over the years.

"A trade?" she asked, tilting her head to one side so her long crimson hair fell over her right shoulder. "What sort of trade?"

"We'll help you rebuild, and clean up, if that's what you need. But in exchange you'll give us access to anything you have on the Uprising or MOTHER." Rose's throat had gone dry, and it was impossible to swallow past the feel of cotton and grit that had filled it to near choking. Her voice was rough with it, but that wasn't going to stop her. They had come to the library for one thing, and one thing only, and she was going to get it.

"And why should I?" Talons scratched at her jaw, as if she were giving it some serious thought.

"Because a happy worker is a good worker?" It sounded silly, and it was. Who was she to bargain with a dragon? Especially a dragon who had put her entire crew to sleep without seeming to break a sweat. It was foolhardy to think that she had any power at all in this situation. And the dragon proved that quite soundly.

"No!" the dragon snarled, baring sharp fangs in a fury that seemed to come from nowhere. "You will do as I say, or I'll leave your entire crew asleep, and they can waste away to their deaths for all I care!"

Anger lit in Rose, sharp, and hot. She pushed to her feet, and was across the deck, poking at the dragon's chest in seconds. She didn't even know where it had come from, but she couldn't seem to stop it either. "You have no right to do that to us! You. . . You. . ."

"Beast?" the dragon asked, a sharp, jagged smile curling up one corner of her lips to show off every pointed tooth in her mouth—and there were a great many. Rose swallowed down a throat full of bile. The dragon advanced, and Rose took a step back, nearly tripping over someone's arm. "I will not bargain with children."

Then with a flap of her wings, that sent Rose reeling onto her backside again, the dragon lifted into the air, and left Rose alone with her sleeping crew, and no way out of the array that was keeping the *Duchess* contained. Rose rubbed at her bottom with a scowl. "Well, she certainly treats people like she's a beast."

"Did you hear what she called me?!" Kindle growled, her talons raking through her hair as she paced just outside of the history room that now housed *an entire pirate vessel* by some strange twist of fate. Which wasn't her fault, and she'd say as much until the day she died. Because the journal should have noted that the summoning circle could be powerful enough to bring an *entire ship* through, if it had, maybe Kindle wouldn't have used the picture of the girl standing on the ship. In hindsight, she really should have thought about that a little more. But she was still going to blame the mysterious writer of the journal.

Thankfully, she'd had enough sense upon seeing the ship to put the crew to sleep while they were still dazed. It had drawn on her magical reserves, leaving her vision fuzzy, and her head pounding, but a least it meant the crew couldn't attack her.

The robot hadn't answered, and it wasn't until Kindle had made a third circuit out in front of the door that she realized this. When she looked at it, she found it standing in front of the door, its little metal arms crossed over its barrel chest, and its visual sensors dimmed to a glare.

"Well? Did you hear her?" she prompted again.

A single chirp of confirmation was its only reply.

Kindle stopped where she'd been rubbing circles into her temples, and frowned at the robot. "What's gotten into you? The spell worked, I thought you'd be excited."

It stared at her, visual censors dimming further as Kindle shifted on her feet, a bead of sweat trailing down her neck. She hated when it did the stare down thing. It made her feel like a scolded child when she was anything but. Lifting her chin, Kindle met its eyes and didn't look away.

"Do you have something to say?" Kindle crossed her own arms over her chest, mirroring the little robot's posture. If it wanted to act disapproving, two could play that game, and Kindle wasn't about to be shamed by a creature that had to be wound at least once every couple of weeks to keep ticking. "Because if you do, then say it."

Letting out a long, loud whistle, the robot tilted its head back as if praying for patience, and then descended into a long diatribe that consisted of twitters, chirps, the grinding of gears, and a couple of ticks and tocks. By the time it was through, the twinge that had settled into the base of her skull when first faced with that insufferable girl on the ship had grown into a full-blown migraine.

Pinching the bridge of her nose, Kindle exhaled, hoping the outward breath would relax her bunched muscles, and untense her shoulders. It didn't. Everything felt just as wound up as it had a moment ago, only now her lungs were empty, and screaming for air.

"Look," Kindle said, holding her hand out to stop the continued tirade of the little robot. "You can be mad at me all you like, you bucket of bolts. It's not going to change anything."

An angry whistle left the robot, so loud it felt like it was drilling into Kindle's skull with a screwdriver. She gasped against the pain, covering her ears, and curling her wings around her head to protect herself from the onslaught. The robot didn't let up, instead it advanced on her, poking at the soft membrane of her wings with a pincer.

"Enough!" she shouted, her wings flaring out, and knocking the robot back into the door where it banged loudly, no doubt denting the wood. "I don't care what you say! They're not leaving that circle until I've gotten her agreement that they'll help with rebuilding the library! Or have you forgotten that we may have lost the entire west wing?" Kindle hissed, leaning forward to press her face close to the robot's. When the robot didn't answer, she scoffed. "Didn't think so."

She straightened, ignoring the way the robot stood up as well, running its pincers down over its front, as if straightening clothes that it wasn't wearing. Such a strange little creature, always acting more person than clockwork.

"Now, if you're quite finished berating me—"

The robot whirred, annoyed.

"I'm going to get some sleep. Maybe our guest will be more willing to help after she's spent a night alone with the books, and none of her friends for company." Kindle spun on her heel, striding away from the room which she had barred shut, just in case.

Another grinding sound came from the robot. She didn't hear its footfalls behind her, and she wondered if it would try to enter the room without her, she didn't think it could. At least not right away, it would have to find a way to reach the bolt that was relatively high up on the door first. So for one evening, her prisoners would probably stay prisoners.

"Yes, well, I can deal with your disdain for the moment." She huffed, but just as she was about to turn the corner into another corridor, she heard it grind out something else, the sound like nails on a chalk board. "Call me a beast ever again, and I really will dismantle you for parts."

It was still glaring at her when she stopped to look at it, but in spite of the threat, it didn't seem worried. Foolish little bot.

SHE SPENT all evening tossing and turning over what had happened with the girl on the ship. And when she had managed to sleep, Kindle was plagued with dreams of her siblings, their wing beats so loud in her ears that they drowned out everything else, growing ever closer, and closer. What would they do this time should they catch her? Would they finish what they started all those years ago? Had she outlived her usefulness?

When the murky light of a winter's morning finally broke the barrier of Kindle's bedroom curtains, she felt groggier than when she'd gone to sleep. Scrubbing at her face, Kindle forced herself from the bed, and got dressed before heading down to the kitchen to make breakfast.

She'd decided sometime during the night that maybe she hadn't approached their guest in the best way. Maybe if she'd come bearing something other than demands, the woman would be more sympathetic to her plight. Honestly, she wasn't sure what about the proposed arrangement had set her off when the woman had offered it. Maybe it was the headache, and fatigue licking at her spine that had made her grumpy, irritable. Or maybe it was that she hadn't thought the girl would try to barter with her, and after decades with nothing but the robot for company she had been wrong-footed, put off by the very notion. Whatever it was, she'd do better this time.

With a tray full of pancakes topped in blueberries fresh from the greenhouse, Kindle made her way back to the history room. The robot was still perched outside, looking grumpy. Although it had dragged a chair from somewhere, and based on the scrapes against the door she could tell that it had tried to get in while she slept.

"I wouldn't do that, if I were you," Kindle warned, patting it on the head, and resting the tray on her hip before she reached up to unlock the door and let herself in. The room was silent, but for the whispers of the books, and when Kindle stepped over the line into the containment circle, she didn't even see anyone stirring up on the ship's deck. Flapping her wings, she made her way up again, only to find that someone had moved all of the people from the deck, leaving behind clear marks that they'd been dragged somewhere.

"It's not right to leave them sleeping on the deck like that. It could cause lingering health issues. I got them all into bed," a voice said, and Kindle turned to watch the woman climbing the steps from the lower decks.

Kindle wrinkled her nose a little at the words. She hadn't thought of that, of how uncomfortable it must be for them to sleep on the wooden floor. Or how it might cause lasting issues later. She shook herself and held out the tray, hoping to hold the guilt at bay with it. "I come bearing a peace offering."

"I already had breakfast," the woman said, making her way to the railing and looking out over the floor to where the books were again. She was worse for wear than when Kindle had first seen her. Bags under her hazel eyes, her glasses askew, and her clothes were wrinkled as if she'd slept in them. This too, Kindle was certain she was supposed to feel guilty about. She didn't. Or at least she told herself that's not what the pit in her stomach was.

"More for me then." Kindle shrugged, biting down on the inside of her cheek to keep from saying something nasty, Kindle set the tray down on the rail next to the other woman and leaned against it.

The woman grunted, not seeming to care one way or the other for the utter waste of it. She didn't know how Kindle had to ration her food, especially during the winter months. She didn't know that those were the last blueberries she was likely to see until spring. Kindle couldn't yell at her for that, because this woman didn't know the situation. Which was what she'd come here to rectify. She'd come to tell her all about the library, and why she needed to help. To convince this woman to save Kindle and her dusty old books.

"I'm Kindle," Kindle offered, holding out one taloned hand. The woman looked down at it, her brows raised when she saw the long, pointed fingers, the sharp nails, and Kindle instantly retracted the appendage, hiding it behind herself where the other woman couldn't look at it, and judge her.

"Rose."

"What?" Kindle's brows pinched together.

"That's my name, Rose." Rose blew out a breath, brushing her fingers through her curly hair to push it away from her forehead. "Rosevelt, really, but I go by Rose." She turned back to look out at the books. "How many books are there?"

"A lot more than this." Kindle leaned over the rail to look at where the walls had expanded, and still there was no space between the books. It had to be a trick of the light, otherwise how had the shelves filled up so fast when they should have already held every history book in existence before? She shook herself, forcing her attention back to her guest. "This is just the history room."

"There are more rooms like this one?" Rose's head jerked

around, her eyes wide behind her glasses when she looked at Kindle. Maybe they were getting somewhere, if they could keep this tenuous truce then things might just turn out all right.

Excitement twitched at the corners of Kindle's lips. It had been so long, too long, since she'd talked to someone who loved her books as much as she and the robot did. "So many more. We have whole rooms on botany, and mechanics, and magical theory and—"

"And yet you won't let me access anything on the Uprising and MOTHER," Rose accused, her eyes narrowing on Kindle, lips pursing in irritation.

A tightness settled between her shoulders, and Kindle bristled at the insinuation, and the continued insistence that she submit all in one. "No. I won't. Anything else you'd like to research, feel free. But not those things."

"Are you working with them?"

"Of course not!" Kindle hated what MOTHER and the Uprising had done to their world, to their people, she couldn't possibly be working for them, but then why *wouldn't* she let Rose access those parts of the library? Why wouldn't she lend a hand to help bring them down? They had burned books! They were burning the world around them! And it wasn't like Rose was asking for Kindle to run head long into battle right alongside the others. It wasn't like she was even asking for Kindle to participate in the planning of MOTHER and the Uprising's downfall. Just provide some information. Just let Rose look at some texts. But Kindle felt a strange resistance at the mere thought of anything happening to either organization.

"Of course not," Rose said, a doubtful tone, and turned back to the books. "Then why won't you let me research the queen and Eddi?"

"Because. . . Because. . . " *Think Kindle think!* "Because the library is a neutral party in all of this. We cannot be taking sides."

"Is it really taking sides if you're helping to bring down *both* corrupt organizations?" Rose seemed to muse out loud, but it was a pointed barb, and Kindle had had enough already. Her sharp teeth gnashed at the inside of her cheeks, making her taste blood.

"And who are you to decide if they're corrupt or not?! You're what, fifty years old at the most? What do you know of corruption? You're a child!" Kindle snarled, wings flaring out behind her, and knocking the tray from the rail down to the floor far, far below, where it clanked and the ceramic that'd been on it shattered to pieces that she was sure even the little robot wouldn't be able to glue back together. "Look what you made me do!"

"I made you?" Rose laughed, throwing her head back to show off the elegant line of her throat, and Kindle wasn't sure if the itch in her palms was to strangle it or stroke it. So she just growled again, and stomped her foot, showing off teeth tinted in blood that she hoped would scare Rose.

"Yes you. And your demands. And your insistence that you have a say in this at all. You're in *my* home, *my* library, you will do as *I* say!" Her wings spread out further, flapping a little, the displaced air ruffling Rose's curls in a way that would have been beautiful if Kindle weren't so furious with her.

"Or what?" Rose asked, leaning back against the rail looking completely unruffled by Kindle's ire in a way that Kindle wasn't sure she'd ever seen before. Not that she'd had many guests, mind, but that wasn't the point! She was a ferocious dragon. The dragon princess. The heir to the throne of the dragon king. This little fae person should cower before her. Still, it was admirable, and if the heat of anger weren't licking at her very bones, Kindle might have taken a moment to admire the proud tilt to Rose's nose, and the subtle twitch of sarcastic amusement on the edge of her mouth.

"Or I'll leave you and your friends here to *rot!*" Kindle shouted and then left the way she'd come, flying up into the air, and straight through the door before slamming it behind her again.

An empty threat, that's what Rose assumed Kindle's little tantrum was. She'd spent most of her life dealing with people trying to intimidate her. She'd seen enough of it to know that most people didn't have the gall to back up what they said they would do. So when Kindle said that she'd leave Rose's friends to rot, Rose had shrugged her off.

It was just an intimidation tactic to get Rose to bow to what Kindle wanted, and Rose wasn't about to do that. Not just because Rose was as stubborn as they came, and she thought Kindle was blowing hot air, but also because Rose didn't like the idea of signing the crew onto something without discussing it with them first. A task which Kindle had made impossible. Then there was the matter of why they had come at all, and the fact that Kindle seemed unwilling to offer them the information they needed. So no, Rose wasn't going to be the one to cave first.

But it had been three days. Rose sat beside the bed she'd managed to wrangle Sully and Agnes into. They'd been the hardest of the lot to move, especially Sully with his substantial height, and the muscle mass hidden beneath his dark brown skin. But she'd gotten them into their bed somehow, and now they just looked like they were asleep, faces relaxed.

She didn't think she'd ever seen Agnes so peaceful in all the time she'd known him. Sully almost looked like he was smiling, a dimple threatening to appear on his left cheek that she was sure was half the reason Agnes had fallen for him in the first place.

"I know what you'd say if you were to wake up right now." Rose laughed a little to herself. She shifted in her seat again, lifting one thigh and then the other, peeling the skin away from the hard chair, before reaching out to feel at the pulse on Agnes's pale wrist. It was still as calm and steady as it had been the day she'd put them both in their bed, but she could see the way the days without food or water were already starting to take their toll. She didn't know how much more of this they'd be able to endure without an IV, and as clever as Rose was, she knew absolutely nothing about medicine. "You'd call me creepy."

She'd checked to see if Hubert was awake, hoping whatever spell Kindle had done hadn't touched the androids on board, but it had. Hubert and Hiccup had both stopped right where they'd been in the middle of their respective tasks, locking up to the point where she couldn't even wheel them out of the way, their innards humming faintly like they were in power-save mode.

Sighing, Rose scrubbed her face, and stood from her vigil to check on the others. She'd never heard the halls of the *Duchess* so quiet, not even on the day they had buried Tobias when it had seemed like the world had fallen still. The *Duchess*'s crew just weren't the type to grieve in silence. They were the type to sob loudly, and make vows to change things. The type to go through life swinging if they had to. They were fighters, and she'd grown to admire that about them, even if she didn't actually *like* anyone on the ship.

"*Now, that's not true,*" Tobias said in the back of her mind so clearly it had her spinning around to check if he was standing behind her. He wasn't. But she hadn't heard his voice in days, not since he'd called her a coward. Maybe he was right. Maybe she was a coward. If she weren't, she might have fought harder against Kindle. Maybe taken the tray of food and smacked her over the head with it, knocking her unconscious so she could escape the ship, and get what they needed. But violence had never been Rose's way. Maybe that did make her a coward.

"What's not true?" Her boots padded softly down the corridor to the room where she'd lain Persinette and Manu. She knew they didn't sleep together yet, and that Persinette had her own room, but keeping people together in pairs made checking on everyone regularly quicker, and she doubted anyone would hold this against her. Especially as sometime during the night Persinette's hand had sought out Manu's, seeking comfort even in her dreams that only he seemed able to provide. It was nauseatingly romantic, and she wasn't going to mention it to either of them for fear it would make her seem like she cared.

That you don't like them. If he were there, Rose imagined he would have his hands on his hips, and be looking at her thoroughly unimpressed with anything and everything she could possibly say in response. Which, she supposed, was entirely fair. It was hard to bite back at such a comment without sounding at least a little bit petty. But she'd never really cared about sounding petty.

"And what makes you think that I do?" Her fingers brushed Manu's pulse, counting the beats in her head, and letting out a little relieved noise when they matched her metrics from the morning. They remained steady, frozen in place by whatever spell Kindle had cast, but she didn't think that could last much longer. Eventually the lack of food and water would wear on them, and their hearts would slow, their bodies would give up. What would she do then?

"Oh, I don't know. . ." She had the very distinct feeling that Tobias was watching her keenly, even if he wasn't there. Which was more annoying than anything.

"I can't have them dying on me," Rose said definitively, dropping Manu's wrist perhaps a little harder than was strictly necessary.

"Mhm." Tobias hummed in a disbelieving tone that grated on Rose's nerves more than any other sound ever had in her long life. She remembered him doing that to her when they were at the camp, and she'd said that the only reason she'd agreed to help with the escape was because she didn't have anything better to do. That had been a lie, and she supposed to some extent this was too. She couldn't have the crew dying on her, that was true, but the why of it she was still unsure about. She did want to see whatever crazy, hair-brained thing they decided to try next. But also, she had begun to genuinely like them to some extent, small as it was. And there were so few people in Rose's life who she could claim she'd actually liked even a little bit, it seemed a shame to lose these.

"Mhm yourself." Rose brushed him off, and headed for the stairs up to the deck. She needed fresh air, not that the air out on the deck was any different anymore. It was all musty, and tinged with whispered voices that she couldn't figure out the origins of. There were no other people in the room aside from the *Duchess*'s crew, and all of them were under the dragon's spell. For about half a minute she'd thought that maybe the voices were in her head just as Tobias's was. But Tobias was so clear, and distinct, and his was a voice she recognized, these were none of those things. And when she'd been able to pick them apart she'd realized that some of them were in languages she didn't know. The only thing she could conclude was that they were possibly coming from the books.

Leaning against the railing, she reached out for the barrier again. She'd been testing it regularly every hour or so to see if it faltered, or weakened, so far it hadn't. And just like all of those times before her hand *thunke*d softly against a cool, hard surface that was utterly invisible.

"I wonder how high up it goes," she murmured to herself, hoping Tobias wouldn't answer. He'd probably decide this was a bad idea, but Rose was the kind of person who had to know the answer to these questions once they struck her. So she climbed up onto the railing, and walked along it, her arms outstretched to keep her balance, until she reached one of the ropes. She'd never been particularly good at climbing, but Rose wasn't about to let that stop her. Giving her gloves a firm tug, she wrapped her hands around the rope, and started to pull herself up little by little.

Her arms burned, her lungs squeezed, and her legs had begun to turn to jelly. She was sure she'd made it up at least halfway, but when she looked down, she found that she was only a couple of feet from the rail. Letting out a loud huff, Rose reached over to check on the barrier. Still there. Taking a deep inhale, she started the climb again.

She didn't get very far before she heard the doors to the room bang open, and looked down to find a little robot teetering on a stack of books sitting on a pyramid of chairs. Rose had just enough time to wonder how it had gotten up there before she lost her hold on the rope, and skidded back down to the rail, hitting her tail bone on the hard surface with a jolt of pain.

Groaning, she slipped to the deck, leaning heavily against the rail so she could lift her hips and rub at the base of her spine.

The little robot let out what sounded like a squeak of concern, and then it somehow got through the barrier, and onto the deck. Rose didn't think it could fly, so either it had jumped, or it had climbed the side of the ship, both seemed equally unlikely. It was twittering beside her, its pincers flapping through the air like a mother hen trying to find where its chick was hurt. Rose waved it off.

"I'm fine. Just a little sore. Nothing is broken, I don't think." Rose's eyes flicked over the robot's shoulder to see the still open door. It wouldn't help her friends to escape, but maybe she could get someone to lift the spell and get them out. Maybe there were other keepers around, someone more reasonable than Kindle. Or a way to contact Alys and the others. She had to try. "But my friends. . ." She said, forcing her voice to quiver a little, to play on the robot's sympathies. "It's been three days, I don't know how much longer they can stay like they are. Is there. . . is there nothing we can do to help them?"

The robot looked around, seemingly checking that the coast was clear, then it relaxed a little. It held a pincer up to its mouth as if to shush her, and took her wrist in its hand to guide her to the rail. When she looked down she found a rope ladder hanging over the side. *Well, that answers one question.* Whistling softly, the robot motioned for her to make her way over the railing, and Rose wrinkled her nose, but followed its instructions over the side of the ship and down the rope ladder.

Clanking down beside her, the little robot took a hold of her wrist again, and looked up at her with a wide grin, showing off a chipped gear on the inside of its mouth.

"I could fix that for you, you know?" Rose tilted her head, her eyes narrowing in on the chip. It almost made the little robot look sort of cute. Like a child who had lost their front teeth, but didn't let that stop them from smiling.

It shook its head at her, and chirped a reply, lifting one pincer to cover its mouth as if protective of the little chipped gear.

"No? You like it?" Rose smiled a little, her nose wrinkling. "All right then. I think I'll call you Chirp, what do you think about that?"

Twittering happily, the robot nodded so fast it almost knocked itself over, but was able to maintain its balance by holding on more tightly to Rose, tugging her into an awkward side bend. It hurt, a little, the metal pincers rubbing at her skin, but she didn't complain. Not if Chirp was going to help her find a way to help her friends.

"All right, lead the way." Maybe she shouldn't trust Chirp, it in all likelihood worked for Kindle, but it was the first friendly face she'd seen in days, and Rose wasn't above hoping that it would give her something to help the crew.

When they reached the door—they hadn't been stopped at all by the forcefield that seemed to block everything from the railing up on the *Duchess*—Chirp poked its head out of the room and looked both ways before determining the hall clear, and tugging her along. It did this at every corner, or doorway, seeming to be looking for someone who might stop them, but Rose hadn't seen another soul since leaving the history room.

Every room they passed whispered just like the one they'd come from, but Rose didn't see any people, Enchanted, mechanical, or otherwise. She was beginning to wonder if Kindle and Chirp were the only inhabitants of the library when Chirp stopped in front of a room that was much louder than all the others. It pushed the doors open, and the whispers reached a crescendo that broke over Rose like a tidal wave. She stumbled back a little, only managing to stay in place by the force of Chirp's pincer around her wrist.

"What is this place?" she asked, taking a careful step inside, wincing when the whispers grated against eardrums too accustomed to the silence of a sleeping crew. They made their way across the round room—which was much smaller than the one where the ship was currently housed, Rose noted, but no less tall—and Chirp dropped her wrist so it could point at a particular book on the shelf. "That one?"

It rocked eagerly on its heels, letting out a soft whistle of approval.

"Why couldn't you bring that to me then?" Rose reached out for the book. Her fingers brushed the spine and a little static shock jumped from the leather to her skin, causing her to jerk back.

"Oh, that's why." She laughed a little, shaking her head, and then reached out to grab the book again, now prepared for the jolt of electricity that licked at her fingers, and crawled up her arms, raising every hair in its wake. "Which page?"

Chirp followed her over to a table near the center of the room, and tried to say something via soft ticking sounds that she couldn't make hide nor hair of. Clearly, it was used to those around it understanding its meaning without any trouble, but Rose just wrinkled her nose. With a loud sigh of steam, the humidity of which made Rose's hair curl more tightly, Chirp reached out to grab a pen from the desk, and write a number on paper.

"I apologize," Rose laughed a little, flipping to the page it had indicated. "I'll endeavor to understand your unique dialect better."

A soft twitter was all she got for her troubles, but Rose didn't care, because right there in front of her was the incantation that would wake the crew. Her fingers tightened around the edges of the book, and she let out a relieved breath.

"Thank you for this," Rose murmured softly, bending down to kiss Chirp's head which made it let out an embarrassed whirr, steam coming out of its ears.

Being scolded by a robot wasn't unlike being scolded by a cuckoo clock except, if possible, more annoying. Because when a cuckoo clock was finished announcing the hour or half hour, it was quiet for a little while before it made its ticking clock everyone else's problem again. The little robot did not give Kindle such respite, and she'd started to wish she hadn't wound it just the day before because at least then she'd know that it was going to freeze up sometime soon. But no. She liked to get ahead on the winding to make sure they didn't run into moments where she needed it and it wasn't there, so she'd taken to winding it on a schedule that overlapped. Which meant it was very rare these days that it just stopped. Unless it was mad at her and disappeared, of course, which was entirely its own fault.

Rubbing at the base of her skull, Kindle tilted her head one way and then the other to stretch out her neck where an unfamiliar tension had taken up residence. Who knew holding a ship hostage could be so stressful? Not only had the pirates worked the robot into a tizzy, but they were taking up the entirety of her historical room. She knew she could go in there at any time to get what she needed, but she didn't want to deal with the feel of Rose's icy stare from the deck of the ship, so Kindle had largely been avoiding the room altogether, which had not gone unnoticed. That's how they had gotten into this conversation—or lecture rather—in the first place.

"What do you mean I need for her to *like* me?" Kindle asked, and the knot that was building in between her shoulder blades twisted just a little bit tighter. "I don't need *anyone* to like me!"

She really didn't. It didn't matter what the robot thought was going to come of all of this, the fact of the matter was that nothing could. Rose hadn't looked at her the way the girl in the picture had. She didn't seem to want to help the way the girl in the picture was shown helping. Kindle was beginning to wonder if she wasn't the girl in the picture at all, but that didn't seem likely. Either way it had all been for naught, in Kindle's opinion, and the west wing was still blocked! That meant they couldn't reach the seed library. Which wasn't a big deal right at that moment, but it would be come spring when it was time to plant the crops. Kindle knew the robot wasn't worried about all that, because it wouldn't be the robot that starved, but she for damn sure was.

The robot kept muttering to itself, its chatter almost background noise as Kindle worked on pulling rubble from the pile that blocked the west wing. She'd been at it for an hour already, and thus far the robot had not lifted a single pincer to help. All it had done was stand there, and go on and on about Rose. As if it and Rose were suddenly friends. Honestly, dismantling it and starting from scratch was sounding better and better every day. Maybe she could build a bot that would actually do as she told it to instead of making idle gossip while she did all the work.

Some of its comments caught in her ears, the chastising click clacking of a very irritated alarm clock, and she jerked to a stop, a big stone from one of the walls held so tightly in her fingers she could feel it scraping against her roughened skin.

"She's not going to *save* me," Kindle growled, lowering her head so she could snarl into the robot's face, baring pointed teeth at it in an obvious threat. She had to tighten her fingers to keep from dropping the stone on her bare feet, but it was worth it. "I don't need to be *saved* by some. . . some. . . entitled, loud-mouthed, self-important half-elf!"

The robot stopped its twittering and stared at her with an expression that Kindle might have considered aghast, if robots could even look that way. Its metal mouth had dropped open to reveal the chipped gear, and its eyes seemed to glow even brighter.

"What?" Kindle dropped the stone into the wheelbarrow she was using to cart them away. They'd run out of space in the dining room, and she wasn't sure where else to put them, so she'd started a little pile out in the garden. It would do until they started to rebuild, when she assumed they'd need the raw materials again, because it wasn't as if she had access to a quarry in the library. So they'd just have to settle for what was available to them. She could only hope that enough of the stones were still in a condition to be useful.

Another scolding note left the robot, and Kindle scoffed, wrinkling her nose.

"I didn't say there was anything *wrong* with being a halfling. Just that this one wasn't going to save me, or you, or the library for that matter. She doesn't want anything to do with us. She's just too—"

With a smug note, the robot chittered something that made Kindle stop dead where she'd been pushing the wheelbarrow to the back door. She turned slowly to eye the foolish bucket of bolts and found its arms crossed imperiously over its chest as if it had done something leagues beyond Kindle.

"You did *what*?" she hissed, eyes narrowing. Translating

what the robot said was never exact, but she thought it'd just told her that it had let Rose out of the containment circle. Which couldn't be right because the robot wasn't that—

Shrugging its shoulders with a faint grinding noise that likely meant it needed to be oiled, again—she wouldn't be doing that any time soon, let it grind its gears down to nothing, see if she cared!—it repeated itself.

Stupid.

"You foolish little nuisance!" Kindle snarled, her wings lifting her off the ground, before she flew away from the broken-down walls and toward the historical room, leaving behind a robot who seemed intent on lecturing her further if its noises were anything to go by. She'd hear no more of its idiocy, not where Rose was concerned, not where the storybook was concerned, none of it. She was through. She'd heard *enough*.

"Oh there you are," Rose's voice called when Kindle opened the door to the history room. In spite of the robot having helped her escape just the previous day to get a spell book, Rose was still up on the deck of the ship, sitting on the rail with her leg dangling over the edge like she hadn't a care in the world. Kindle didn't know if she should be thankful or annoyed by the fact that Rose apparently hadn't learned the secret to escaping the forcefield on her own in her little adventure outside of the history room. She was leaning towards annoyed. "I was wondering when you'd come and make sure we were still alive."

Definitely annoyed.

"I heard the robot let you out for a stroll yesterday." Kindle took her time pacing around the edge of the circle, making sure all the characters were still carefully drawn on the floor. She couldn't have Rose and her crew escaping one way or the other. If they got out into the library, they could just take what they wanted. But if they left the library entirely, they could lead others back. Kindle couldn't have that.

"So what if it did? At least someone in this place knows how to treat a guest." Rose's posture had grown more rigid, her chin tilting back as if in challenge, daring Kindle to rise to the bait. It wouldn't be long before she did, Kindle was sure of that. But for the moment, she had better control over herself.

"You aren't a guest, you're a prisoner," she said with a shrug, continuing on her rotation around the edge of the circle. Everything looked to be in order. "I see no reason to show hospitality to a trespasser."

"Am I a trespasser, a savior, or a prisoner? You're going to have to make up your mind." Rose's voice carried through the space between them even if she wasn't shouting, and Kindle heard no other voices. So either her crew hadn't risen yet, or they were incapacitated from the days in bed. Not that Kindle cared one way or the other.

"It won't happen again. That stupid bot won't be able to get through the door the next time I lock it!" Kindle rose up on her wings so she could meet Rose's eyes from outside the circle, and glare at her directly. It didn't seem to faze Rose half as much as it had some of Kindle's other "guests".

Rose just raised one brow, her brown face set into an expression of impassivity that made Kindle's blood boil. "Its name is Chirp, and you ought to be nicer to it."

"Excuse you?" What kind of person named someone else's robot without consulting them first? What impertinent, arrogant, brazen behavior! Rude. She was so rude! Kindle had never met someone so rude in all her years.

"It told me it likes the name," Rose said with a careless shrug, and *that*, that was too much.

Roaring, Kindle flew out the door, slamming it shut behind herself and retreated to the gardens. The snow had started in earnest, covering the ground, and biting cold into her bare arms, but she ignored it. Instead, she flew up, up, up until she reached the magical barrier that let the snow, rain, and sunshine in, but had never let her out.

She'd tried it once, when she was much younger and angrier at her siblings for trapping her there. When she'd cared less for the work they were doing. But upon reaching the very top, where the round walls of the courtyard ended and there was only gray sky above, she'd found she could go no further. It was like reaching the end of her tether, something had yanked her back by her ankle.

Kindle didn't fly that high today. Just high enough that the clouds seemed to be within reach. The itch to extend her arm and try to touch their damp fluffiness sat like a buzz under her skin, but she wouldn't give into it, because she had had enough disappointment for one day, thank you. She didn't need to add to it with the crushing realization that not all things that were in reach were actually attainable. Freedom, for one. Rose's help, for another.

How long she stayed up there, she wasn't sure, but by the time her wings were too tired, and the cold had begun to sink into her leathery skin, the gray skies had faded to a starless night, and the snow had slowed.

Setting foot on the ground again did nothing to quiet the agitation under her skin, so she did the next best thing, she went to work again. She blinked back every sign of fatigue, and pushed through any physical indication that maybe she should take a break. Because there was no time for that. If the robot wasn't going to help. If Rose wasn't going to help. That just left Kindle to do it.

She'd stop when she couldn't keep her eyes open anymore, Kindle told herself. She'd let herself rest when she had cleared this little section. Just one more stone. Just one more brick. Just one more shovel full of rubble. Just one more...

The pile made a noise like the earth rumbling during an air strike, a sound Kindle was unfortunately all too familiar with from when she'd been a child, and the war between the humans and Enchanted had only just begun. She had just enough time to look up and realize her mistake before the top came down like an avalanche, burying her under the weight of half of the wall.

Something snapped. *A bone, probably*, she realized in that strange distant way people think bad things happen to other people. There was a searing pain coming from one of her wings but she couldn't tell if it was from another break, or a tear in the thin membrane between the bones.

And oh gods. . . oh *gods*. . . she was buried under half of the corridor, and no one was coming to help her!

S ully was, thankfully, the first of the crew able to get up and move about once Rose had broken the sleeping spell by way of the burning of some incense she'd found buried under the good linens. They were probably Owen's, but he wouldn't mind that she'd used them to save everyone, she was sure.

The others were awake of course, but Rose could escape their searching gazes, and questions by extricating herself from their rooms, because they were still fairly weak. She'd left Hubert to tend to them. That was better for all of them. She had never been a nursemaid, and Hubert was a med-droid after all, that's what he was designed for.

"So are we going to talk about what happened while we were all out?" Sully asked, munching on a piece of dry toast as he leaned against the rail to look at the books just out of reach, the thick ropes of his arms shifting under his dark brown skin. He hadn't asked any questions in front of Agnes, and Rose supposed she should be grateful for that, because if anyone was going to blame her for what happened, it was going to be Agnes.

"Does it really matter?" Rose ran her fingers over her tight curls, pushing them down to lay flat against her scalp for a moment. They sprung right back up when she released them, and the motion really did nothing to ease the tension she felt at the impending conversation. Sully was going to keep pushing. That was his nature. He'd have been a good friend, if she were looking for friends. It almost seemed a shame that his kindness, and generosity were wasted on her. But then, he was wasting them on Agnes too, so maybe he was just a horrible judge of character. "It's not going to change the predicament we're in."

"No, but it'll help us understand it better." Sully stuffed the last of his toast into his mouth, and rubbed the crumbs off of his fingers onto his trousers, then stood up to his full height, towering over her. If it weren't for the gentle wrinkle between his brows, softening his dark gaze, he may have been pretty intimidating—especially as Rose was intimately acquainted with exactly what the kelpie was capable of. "And maybe help us get out of here quicker."

He didn't sound like he was going to press, but Rose knew he would if he really thought it would help, and she refused to answer. Her best bet was to tell him what she knew without diving into the feud it seemed she'd started with the dragon who was keeping them there. She didn't need the crew of the *Duchess* mad at her on top of everything else.

"There's not much to tell." Rose scratched at her ear, tugging on one of the short curls that hung around it. "One of the keepers of the library is a dragon, and she seems intent on keeping us here until we help her rebuild the library."

"But you said that it seemed like there was something wrong with her."

"Other than her abhorrent crankiness, you mean?"

Sully's lips twitched in amusement, but he hummed his agreement.

Rose sighed, scrubbing over her face, knocking her glasses askew and then taking them off to slide them back into place where they belonged. "I've never met a dragon before, so I don't know how normal it is for them to be in the middle of a transformation like that. She had the wings, and the tail, and several patches of her skin that might have been scales or dragon skin, but she was about Agnes's height, and had a humanoid face. I suppose it could just be a form she takes to scare people."

Sully hummed thoughtfully, tapping his fingers against the rail. He didn't seem to have any more answers than she had, and suddenly Rose wished Tobias were with them. The missing him sat always like a dull ache in her chest that she only really noticed when she thought about him, but it was ever present, and right then it throbbed anew, a fresh wound. Tobias would have known what to do about Kindle. He'd have been able to talk to the dragon and bring her over to their side, Rose just knew it. But he wasn't there, it was just her, and the skeleton crew they'd brought along from the Wastes. The next best option might be Persinette, but she was still too weak to even get out of bed, and Rose had the sinking feeling that Kindle might eat her alive. They needed someone with a spine made of steel, and a voice of velvet. They needed Tobias.

Pulling the sleeves of her coveralls down over her grease-stained hands, Rose curled in on herself. She hated the feeling of the air on her skin all of a sudden, it was too cool. Winter had well and truly set in, and whatever heat the library might have had, it wasn't being used to warm the room where the *Duchess* was housed. Maybe Kindle thought she'd freeze them out, and then take their ship. Rose wouldn't put it past her, and it might work, Rose had always hated the cold.

"We should get you back to bed. I'm sure Agnes is looking for you." Rose pushed off from the rail, and moved to Sully's side to help him across the deck. It was a distraction tactic, mentioning Agnes that way. One she was sure Sully would call her on, but he didn't. Instead he smiled, eyes crinkling under the weight of his love for a man Rose found foul at best.

"Oh, so you *do* know his real name." Sully teased, a chuckle rumbling through his chest where it was pressed into her side as they both stumbled along.

Biting down on her own laugh, Rose shook her head. "If you tell him, I'm just going to deny it."

"You two are terrible."

The door to the history room opened behind them with a clatter of wood against the wall beside it, and Rose looked over her shoulder to see Chirp rushing in, its pincers waving frantically as it screeched as loudly as it was capable. Stomping through the circle, it made its way up the ladder at a speed that Rose wouldn't have previously thought it capable of, and over the rail.

"Chirp?" Rose leaned Sully against the wall, and moved to the little bot so she could bend before it, and give it a once over. It was a little dusty, but it didn't look like Kindle had done anything to damage it. There were no open panels, or dents in its plating, just the wide-eyed look of its visual sensors turned up so bright it hurt to look right at them. "What's wrong?"

Chirp whistled, the sound like a tea kettle about to boil over, as its arms continued to flail around, nearly smacking Rose in the face.

"What's it saying?" Sully bent down beside them, his balance was a little unsteady, but Rose wasn't about to argue with him about how he should be in bed, resting, instead of dealing with an upset robot. He was a grown man.

"I have absolutely no idea. Do you think Hubert is done looking after everyone?"

"I'll go check. You try to get Chirp calmed down."

Rose watched him over her shoulder as he took his time

on the stairs, clutching the banister a little tighter than he might normally. She'd be glad when they were all out of this awful place and back in the Wastes with the jabberwocks—add that to things she never thought she'd miss. Meanwhile she shushed Chirp softly, patting its shoulders to try to calm it. This at least made the ear-splitting whistling stop. Hubert and Sully joined them a moment later.

"What seems to be the problem?" Hubert turned his good visual circuit to Chirp. Rose had offered to replace the other one with some spare parts she'd found in Felicity's stash, it wouldn't match exactly but it would be close. He hadn't wanted it, apparently, he'd grown quite attached to the eye patch. It did look rather pirate-y, which she supposed was fitting given their circumstances. And it wasn't like lacking a second visual sensor upset his depth perception as it might a person.

Chirp started twittering so quickly that Rose was worried it was in very real danger of grinding its gears to the point of them being unusable, or overheating, but that didn't seem to stop it. The robot's arms were flinging out wildly, trying to get its point across as efficiently as possible it seemed, or perhaps it was just upset and didn't know how else to deal with those feelings. It was hard to tell, the robot seemed so much more alive than robots tended to.

Hubert didn't even let it finish, before he was making his way to the rail, expecting the others to follow. "They say someone named Kindle is stuck under a pile of rubble near the west wing. Chirp doesn't know how long they've been there, but they can't get Kindle to respond. Sullivan, I suggest you help me down to the ground."

"I'll go grab the medical kit," Rose called over her shoulder, already running down the steps and to the med bay. She grabbed the kit and threw it over her shoulder, ignoring the questions hurled her way from the patients in the beds.

Sully had strapped Hubert to his back, and was making his way slowly down the ladder on unsteady legs when she returned to the deck, an expression of discomfort twisting up his already sweating face. Chirp was on the ground, their little arms raised high overhead as if they could catch Sully and Hubert should they fall.

Shaking her head, Rose started her own descent. Once they were all on the ground, she turned to Sully. "Sully are you going to be okay?"

Sully was out of breath from the rope ladder, sweat clinging to his temples, as his hands clutched the rungs for support. "I'll be fine. Just go on ahead. Send Chirp back if you need me." He waved her off, leaning more against the side of the ship.

With a nod, Rose turned to follow Chirp and Hubert out into the hall. She looked back once, to make sure Sully was at least still upright, and sighed a little in relief when she found him still leaning against the ship. Then she turned back to the task at hand, racing after Chirp down the darkened corridors of the library till they reached a part of the hallway that had collapsed in on itself.

Rose didn't see any signs of Kindle at first, but when she drew closer Chirp shined their visual sensors on a bit of bright red hair peeking out from under the rubble.

"Okay," Rose said letting out a calming breath that really didn't do much to calm her. "We need to move the rubble carefully, we don't want it to fall on the rest of us, or shift too much and make her injures worse. Do you think you two can do that?"

Chirp gave a quick nod, and Hubert murmured his agreement.

"I'm going to get as close as I can without stepping on any of it. I'll start picking pieces from the top, I'll hand them back to you and you two put them out of the way. I don't want anyone stepping on the actual rubble in case she's under there." The work would be easier if they had more people, especially Sully, but with the condition the rest of the crew was in, Rose wasn't willing to risk their weakened state making the situation worse. So she'd just have to go at it alone, and hope that none of it was heavier than she could handle.

Nodding to herself, she set down the medical kit, rolled up her sleeves and got to work.

It took them too long, far too long, to dig Kindle out. Rose's muscles were screaming, her stomach turning, and every breath felt like she was fighting against a vacuum to inhale it, but finally a red wing peeked out amongst the rubble. There was a tear in the soft membrane of the wing, but the bones looked intact. Sucking in another ragged breath, Rose worked faster, the little robots keeping up with her by sheer force of will.

"We're going to need a stretcher," Rose told Hubert when they uncovered Kindle's arm and found it lying at a strange angle. Hubert would be able to x-ray it, and set it, but they needed to move Kindle without further injuring her. "And if Sully is up to it, bring him too."

Hubert jerked a nod, and sped off, leaving Rose and Chirp to finish up. Bending down, Rose checked Kindle's pulse, and was relieved to find it steady, if a little faster than she'd like, probably from the shock, and her chest moving with shallow breaths.

"Can we roll her over do you think?" Sully asked. He had the stretcher slung over his shoulder, and was looking at the scene with wide dark eyes. "I told Agnes we might need more help, and I'd send Hubert back if we did."

"I think you and I can manage. But I want Hubert to do an x-ray before we try moving her. Just to make sure her back and neck are all right. Hubert?" Rubbing her sweaty palms on her pants, Rose stepped back to let Hubert do his thing, sending up a thank you to whoever was listening for the little med droid. *And Agnes said we should've left him behind in the camp*, Rose thought with an internal scoff.

"She is fine to be moved. Just be careful of her wing and arm," Hubert said, rolling away from Kindle's prone form so that Rose and Sully could shift her carefully onto the stretcher.

"I don't think it's safe to try to lug her up the rope ladder of the *Duchess*. Where's her room, Chirp?"

The little robot looked conflicted, their face turning from Rose to Sully and then down to Kindle's unconscious form, after a couple more glances between the three they released a hiss of steam that sounded like a groan, and started off at a slower pace back down the hall. Chirp led them past several closed doors, but there was one that was open, and Rose had just enough time to catch a glimpse of a glowing red sculpture in the middle on a pedestal before Chirp hurried them past.

They reached Kindle's room a moment later, Chirp pushing the double doors open wide to allow them in. Rose stopped, nearly dropping her end of the stretcher as Sully kept walking, when she got a look at the room. It was covered, floor to ceiling in colorful nick knacks, stacks of books, and tapestries, she couldn't even tell what color the walls were. Sully, with his considerable height, wound up sending a kite and a beaded mobile into each other with a clatter when he was unable to duck under them. The floor, too, was a maze of piles of books and artifacts. Rose thought she saw a nesting doll, and a tiki carving stacked on top of a pile of books that looked like it would fall over if it was breathed on too hard. But Chirp navigated through the mess like they were used to it, leading them through a winding path to the bed where they were able to deposit Kindle carefully.

"Do you need any more help?" Sully asked. He was out of breath again, sweat leaving a sheen on his neck now too.

"No. I think I've got it. You go and rest, Hubert and I can handle things from here." Rose sat the med kit on the edge of the bed next to Kindle, and pulled up a little stool from under what could have been a vanity or a side table, she wasn't sure, to sit on. Sully took one last look at Kindle, and Rose, rubbed at the tip of his nose, then left her to it.

SIXTEEN
KINDLE

Kindle roused bit by bit to a wet something brushing over her face—*a cloth*, she thought, *it must surely be a cloth*. It was nice against her over-warm skin, cooling it, and leaving behind a trail of moisture that raised the fine hairs along her hair line, drawing a shiver up her spine.

Opening her eyes enough to see who it was tending to her, she groaned at the sight of soft, brown skin, and the glint of a pair of metal spectacles on the person's long, elegant nose. Rose.

"Oh good, you're awake." Rose pulled the cloth away, sitting back in her chair with a soft creak. "How are you feeling?"

"Why do you care?" Kindle groused, closing her eyes again to keep the infernal light above from burning at her still sensitive retinas. How long had she been asleep? When she tried to lift her arm to rub at her face, something heavy kept it rooted to the spot, and there was a catching like a thorn dragging against her skin but from the inside. Wincing, she turned her head to look at where a hard cast had been wrapped around her arm. Lovely. A broken arm. That was going to slow things down significantly.

"It's fractured. I don't know exactly where, Hubert would

be able to tell you better, since he did the scans. I just helped out." Rose reached over to take a glass of water from the bedside table. "You should drink something."

"I'm not thirsty," Kindle said, ignoring the way her tongue threatened to stick to the roof of her mouth for how dry it was, rubbing like sandpaper against slightly fuzzy-feeling teeth. Rose had helped her enough, and she wasn't weak, she didn't need *her* help.

"I didn't ask." Rose leaned closer, forcing the glass to her lips and holding it there until Kindle took a begrudging sip. It felt wonderful running over the roughness of her throat and tongue, but she wasn't going to give Rose the satisfaction of seeing that relief. She tilted her head away from the glass after only a sip, even if she'd have happily drunk the entire thing. "Hubert said I can give you more pain medicine in a couple of hours, but not before."

"I don't need pain medication." Kindle lifted her chin, challenging Rose to argue with her. She probably did need it. There was a dull ache, lingering in her bones, waiting to flare into shooting pain when whatever they'd already given her wore off. By then maybe Rose would be gone. Back to the ship and out of Kindle's hair.

Rose raised a single brow, her lips quirking up at the edges, and then she scoffed. "Of course not. Because you're a big *scary* dragon."

It was a struggle not to jerk back from the comment, and how it stung far more than it should have. That's what she'd wanted, isn't it? She'd wanted to instill fear, to make sure that Rose wouldn't rise against her and try to take from her the only home she'd ever known. But those words slung so casually. . . they made something sharp jab against her ribs that she was sure had nothing to do with her injuries from the hall collapse.

"How did you get out?" Kindle shifted in the bed, ignoring

how that same catching sensation happened in her wing too. She must have a break back there as well. Rose reached over to help her sit up, rearranging the pillows behind her like a dutiful nurse without even having to be prompted. A growl started in Kindle's throat that she swallowed, and then turned into a cough before she could completely get rid of it. She choked down the words to tell Rose that she didn't want her pity.

"Do you need more water?" Rose's hands twitched for the glass on the table.

"Why do you care?!" Baring her teeth, Kindle leaned forward to let Rose see their sharp points, a threat, ignoring the way it throbbed to lean on her injured arm. *Note to self: do not put pressure on a broken appendage even if it is in a cast.*

"Because you're hurt." Pale hazel eyes met Kindle's without a trace of fear or revulsion, just disappointment. "Only sociopaths don't care when other people get hurt."

Those words *did* make Kindle jerk, jarring her injuries enough to elicit a soft wince, her face contorting in pain. She could feel Rose's eyes on her, watching every subtle shift in her movements, even with her eyes squeezed closed. Blast. What was she *looking* for? A hint of weakness, no doubt. But why bother? Kindle was already trapped in her bed. She couldn't do anything to stop Rose from burning the blasted place to the ground if she wanted to. But maybe Rose just liked having the upper hand. She didn't seem smug about it, but she could be hiding it, Kindle didn't have enough experience with other people—nor this one in particular—to know when someone was lying.

"I'm going to have Hubert prepare you some more pain medication when he comes back," Rose said, tone brokering no argument.

"Who's Hubert?" Exhaustion tugged at Kindle's words, making them soft as she slurred out the name. Rose leaned in to help her lay back down, careful of her injuries as she adjusted the pillows again, then pulled the blanket up to Kindle's chin, tucking her in like a child. Gods, it had been so long since someone had tucked her in. How long? Centuries, upon centuries, probably. Not since her father, had anyone ever bothered to tuck her in. Not even that blasted robot. Although, she'd never really asked it to either.

"He's a med droid I saved from the labor camp when we escaped." Rose's voice had gone hushed, and lulling, and Kindle wondered if she was weaving sleeping magic into it, but Kindle didn't think she had the energy to combat it even if Rose were.

"Labor camp?" Blinking heavily, Kindle yawned into the blankets, frowning a little at the smell of her breath, all sulfur and brimstone from the fire that lay in her belly and however many days of not brushing her teeth.

"Hmm," Rose hummed her answer. "I think that'll be a story for the next time you wake up."

There was something else Kindle wanted to say to that, but as the words filtered across her mind they were lost to the groggy haze, and soon she was asleep again, pulled under by her body trying to knit itself back together.

THE NEXT TIME SHE WOKE, she could hear voices in the hall. They were hushed, like whoever it was was trying to keep from waking her, or maybe they just didn't want to be overheard. But Kindle recognized Rose's voice, and the voice of a man.

"This is foolish, Rosevelt. We can't continue to waste our time here if they won't help us find what we need." His voice was hard, tone aggravated, like they'd been having this discussion for a while now and he was annoyed with the fact that Rose was being stubborn. It was nice to know that Kindle wasn't the only one who brought that side out in Rose. It'd be annoying if she were. Although, something roiled in her stomach, something sour, that might have been jealousy at the thought that Rose could turn that temper on anyone else. Whatever medicines they were giving her must have been affecting Kindle's mind, because she definitely wasn't jealous. She didn't care if Rose fixed her blazing hazel eyes on someone else. Not at all.

"We can't leave her like this. Once she's well, we'll deal with getting out of here." Rose sounded unbothered by the man's irritated tone, and although Kindle didn't know her well, had only had a handful of conversations with her, she could almost imagine Rose looking at him as if he were nothing more than a fly trying to ruffle her.

"What if we just started loo—"

"No," Rose said, voice abruptly much harder than Kindle thought she'd ever heard it, and she'd had the other woman yelling at her, so that was saying something. "We will not *steal* information, Agnes. If we do then we're no better than the people we're fighting against, and I will not lower myself to the level of Eddi or Eloise."

Eddi. Eloise. Why did those names sound so familiar? Where had Kindle heard them before? She tried to think—to remember—but it was like coming up against a wall. The harder she pushed the more painful it became, her body seizing up with an ache she almost recognized.

The man said something else, but his words were nothing more than a soft rumble, and then Rose was at her side again, gentle hands pressing Kindle back down into the bed where she hadn't realized she'd been arching off of it in pain.

"Shhh. . . Shhh. . ." Rose hushed, and Kindle felt the

pillows move underneath her. "Lay back down, it's all right. Lay back down."

Kindle had little choice. She lowered herself into the pillows with Rose's help, and the moment her body relaxed, she was asleep once more.

GROGGINESS PERMEATED EVERYTHING. Every single fiber of Kindle's being felt crusted with sleep, and it was a struggle to pull all of them into wakefulness when all some of them wanted to do was drift back into the bed, and never wake up. Things would be easier that way, she knew. But there were other parts, like the skin on her fingertips that were brushing over the soft blanket that someone had laid over top of her, which wouldn't go quietly into that good night. Which was a crying shame, if you asked her.

"You need some more water," Rose said, already shifting Kindle up to sit without her even being fully awake yet. But it felt good to sit up, it cleared her head a little, and lightened up the load on her eyelids so she could crack them open to eye Rose incredulously. "Trust me, it'll help with the grogginess."

"How long have I been asleep?" Kindle frowned at the brush of Rose's calloused palm over her wrist as she lifted it to press the glass of water into her fingers. The water wasn't cold, if the temperature of the glass was anything to go by, but Rose was probably right, it would sweep away some of the lingering fog. The question was, why bother?

"A couple of days. Hubert says your bones have all but mended though, likely because of your dragon blood. We'll remove the casts in a few more days, I think." With the glass firmly in Kindle's grip, Rose leaned back in her chair to watch her with an expression that Kindle could only describe as guarded. Like she was waiting for Kindle to lash out again, or have another attack like she'd had when she'd woken up before.

"So I can hold my own water glass now?" Kindle asked, and tried not to let herself acknowledge how the words almost sounded teasing. She was not teasing Rose. They were not to that point, and likely never would be, because they didn't like each other. Because Rose had come to the library for information. She'd come to *steal*.

Rose's brows lifted into the short, curled fringe that almost hid her forehead. "I can take it back, and continue to treat you like you can't take care of yourself if you'd prefer. But I think we both know neither of us particularly cared for me playing nurse, did we?"

"No." Kindle tightened her hold on the glass and lifted it to her lips where she quickly drained it dry before leaning over to put it back on the bedside table. Rose didn't say anything or move the entire time, instead Kindle could see her jaw working out of the corner of her eye, seeming to be chewing on her words, unsure what to do or say, as she watched Kindle drink. Kindle saw Rose's head move in a little jerk, brushing her ear against her shoulder.

Rose exhaled a loud breath through her nostrils, and then straightened up when Kindle looked at her again. Nodding to herself, Rose met her gaze. "The crew and I are willing to help rebuild the wing of the library that has collapsed. We are also willing to help you find ways to reinforce the walls so that this will not happen again."

"But you want something in return." Kindle wished she still had the glass in her hand, if just to have something to do with her fingers other than to pick at the blanket resting over her lap. It was already threadbare and faded from years of use, it didn't need her sharp talons picking at the loose threads, but those thoughts couldn't stop the creeping crawling anxiety under her skin. The itch to move. To do. If she weren't sequestered to a bed, she very well might have been pacing.

Pursing her lips, Rose drew her brows together and puffed out her cheeks for a moment, determined, before releasing the words, "We will need access to anything and everything the library has. That includes information on the queen, MOTHER, and the Uprising leader. If you cannot provide us with that, then we will leave." all in one breath.

"Leave?"

"Yes. Leave. With Chirp's help we have found a spell that might help us escape whether you want us to or not."

Kindle's talons had picked a hole in the blanket, she stopped, smoothing it out over her legs. "Why not just take the information while I slept?" She knew the reason, but she needed to hear Rose say it. To hear the ring of the truth or a lie in it. Not that she'd likely be able to tell the difference, but people were less likely to do something wrong when they had to look someone in the eyes before they did it. "You could have grabbed every book in the library and taken them back to wherever you all are hiding from MOTHER, and left me with nothing."

"Because that would be stealing." Rose wrinkled her nose, making her glasses rise up a little the way some's eyebrows might, shaking her head. "We're not in the practice of stealing."

"What *are* you in the practice of?" Kindle tilted her head, curiosity tugging at her chest like a fishing line. Maybe she'd been wrong about Rose from the beginning. Maybe the book had been too. She wasn't a savior, no. But she wasn't a thief either. She wasn't here to rip everything Kindle loved out from under her, like Kindle and the book had thought. Kindle still didn't have the desire to hold her hand—well maybe a little—like she had seen illustrated doing in the pictures, but this was a start toward understanding one another that Kindle appreciated.

"Let me stick around, and maybe you'll find out." A little smile quirked the corners of Rose's mouth, the gesture a taunt, but not an unkind one, that sent Kindle's stomach swooping toward her toes with some unfamiliar emotion so quickly it left her dazed, and dizzy.

Kindle's brows raised at the suggestion, and though there was still a part of her that railed against the idea of these people in her library, hunting for information to start a bloody war that would no doubt end in many more deaths, she found herself nodding and saying, "All right. But only *you* are allowed to interact with the texts that Chirp, and I show you, no one else."

The smile on Rose's face spread wider, still teasing, but almost delighted. "Chirp, huh?"

"Do we have a deal or not?" Kindle grumbled.

Rose hummed, lifting her hand to scratch at her cheek as if she needed to consider Kindle's offer for a minute longer, but there was a light in her eyes, the way they were a little wider than usual, that told Kindle she was poking fun at her.

"Well?"

"Deal," Rose said, holding out a hand for Kindle to shake, and to her credit, not pulling back when Kindle extended her own to clasp it, sharp talons poking at Rose's wrist.

Rose watched as Kindle looked over the *Duchess*'s crew, her nose curled just slightly. They were a little worse for wear, but that was to be expected after everything they'd been through. Even Persinette—who Rose didn't think she'd ever seen without a kind look, or a smile in the last few months—was too tired to try to fake it in the face of someone who clearly held only disdain for her.

"Is this all there is?" Kindle asked, her nose curled up further in something that might have been disgust, or might have been curiosity. Rose didn't know her well enough to be able to tell yet, but she was going with disgust. Which really wasn't helping Kindle's case with Agnes, Rose could see that already. It was only by sheer force of will on Sully's part that the unicorn hadn't started shouting at Kindle yet. But it wouldn't be long before even Sully's presence couldn't keep Agnes in check. Her gaze jerked down to where Chirp was hiding behind Kindle's outstretched wings, their visual sensors bright, and laser focused on the people in front of them. She couldn't tell exactly who they were looking at, but whoever it was, was making Chirp *tick-tick-tick* nervously. She thought it might be Manu given the direction they were turned but she could have been wrong. Either way Rose needed to speed this along before Chirp exploded from the strain, Agnes said something that got them all killed, or Kindle lost what little control she had over her temper. *Damn it all.*

"Before we did the spell, Alys told us that we wouldn't be flying in open air. And there was still so much to do back at the Wastes to get the refugees settled in." Rose shifted her weight to one side, waiting for Kindle to argue with her about this, because Kindle seemed to like to argue about everything in Rose's limited experience. "So, to answer your question, yes, right now the crew of the *Duchess* is just the nine of us."

Kindle made a noise in the back of her throat that sounded distinctly dismissive. The sound made Benard's ears twitch, Penny take a step forward even with Roy holding her back, Agnes's eyes flair dangerously, and Manu smirk as if he'd heard it all before. He probably had, Manu seemed like the type who was used to being scoffed at, often because people didn't think he was worth anything. Rose had learned differently during their time together since leaving the camp. None of these people were to be trifled with, that's why she'd been comfortable leaving the rest of the crew behind in the Wastes. If they had to fly the *Duchess* with just the nine of them, they'd be able to without a problem, she knew that, but she could see how someone like Kindle who hadn't seen them all in action, wouldn't guess what they were capable of on sight.

"Let her underestimate them," Tobias said, a cheeky smile in his voice. He was enjoying this far too much. Had been enjoying *all* of this far too much. Including the bit where Rose played nursemaid to the worst patient to have ever lived.

Rose chewed on the inside of her cheek to keep from answering him out loud. They had all grieved differently, but she didn't think knowing that he had become an imaginary friend, or her conscience, or whatever Tobias was, would make the others feel very confident in her ability to get the information they needed from the library. He was right though, it was better if Kindle underestimated them. If she realized the true danger the crew of the *Duchess* could pose to her, she'd lock them back on the ship, put them all back to sleep, and let them fade into nothing. Better she didn't think much of the ragtag group.

"And I can trust these . . . *pirates* not to steal from me?" Kindle's red brows raised high, her dark gaze sweeping back to Rose. That was fair, Rose supposed, plundering, lying, cheating, and stealing did seem to be in the pirate job description once upon a time. Before they'd become rebels of a different sort.

"Persinette will keep them honest." Rose resisted the urge to wink at Kindle. All that would do was make it look like she wasn't taking this seriously. Which she was, mostly. She saw Persinette straighten up a little taller under the praise out of her periphery. Was that the first time Rose had ever paid her a compliment? She couldn't remember. She hadn't exactly been looking to ingratiate herself to these people since leaving the camp.

"Of course, it is," Tobias said, his tone a reprimand that had words crawling up Rose's throat. Excuses. An explanation. They'd have to have that discussion later where there weren't so many ears to overhear it. She rubbed at the hinge of her jaw, pulling at her ear a little to try to silence Tobias, or at least keep the crackle of his voice out of her ears.

"Hey," Sully spoke up, a frown marring his handsome features.

"And Sully, of course." Rose swallowed around a laugh, her voice trembling with it. "The rest are loose cannons and can't be trusted."

Agnes's gaze bore into the side of her face, leaving behind

no visible mark, but she could feel it there, heated and annoyed. She didn't have to see Persinette, Owen, and Roy to know that they were laughing too even as Sully coughed into his hand to try to hold back his own chuckles.

Rose met Kindle's searching expression with a serious purse of her lips. She just hoped Kindle wouldn't see the laughter dancing in her eyes. The way she was making fun of the crew, and Kindle as a whole. Because really, how ridiculous could Kindle get? Did she need help or not? Her reluctance in accepting help she clearly needed was getting more annoying by the second.

"You've instilled me with a supreme amount of confidence in your crew," Kindle drawled, her head turning to look at them as if she could perhaps see something that she'd been missing before, or maybe she was looking for a tell that they were planning to just take what they wanted and leave, regardless of what Rose had promised her. Her lack of trust chafed.

"Oh, they're not *my* crew," Rose said, a forced lightness to her voice that she knew sounded strange based on the way Sully's gaze narrowed on her. Out of all of them, he knew her the best. They were almost friends, if Rose had had friends on the crew, which she didn't. "They're Manu and Persinette's, but you're welcome."

"We're a team," Persinette amended for Rose, and Rose had to clench her teeth not to argue with her. "And we're here to help."

The wings on Kindle's back shifted, her weight rocking back on her heels. If Rose didn't know any better, she'd say that Kindle was uncomfortable with the direct address. Maybe she was, from what Rose had gathered, Kindle and Chirp were the only inhabitants of the library. Alys said she had been here before, but she'd never specified how long ago, if it had been decades or centuries even, that meant Kindle had maybe been that long without any other companionship. Or maybe, Kindle just didn't like large groups like this one. That would make sense too, considering that she lived a solitary life. Whatever it was, Kindle didn't give Rose time to ask before she turned back to her, a tightness around her eyes that hadn't been there before.

"You'll come with me to start researching. Chirp will be in charge of the others. Gather whatever you need to get started." Then Kindle turned on her heel, and walked out into the hall without a backward glance.

"Well. She's a delight," Agnes snorted the moment Kindle was out of sight.

Sully swatted him lightly. "Shush, she can probably still hear you."

"Oh? Can I be rude once she can't anymore?"

"No." Persinette frowned, giving Manu's hand a pointed tug as they all clustered together. "We're not going to be rude to our host."

"She put us under a sleeping curse for days while terrorizing Rose," Benard pointed out, his tone entirely reasonable. He hadn't taken his gaze away from the door through which Kindle had disappeared, the sharp, glowing, green eyes narrowed in distrust. Rose couldn't blame him. For as little confidence as Kindle had in them, she hadn't exactly engendered trust in herself either. "I don't think it's rude to comment on her lack of decorum."

"Regardless." Persinette lifted her chin, trying to appear taller while surrounded by men like Owen and Sully who towered over her. It didn't really work, but they all looked to her with a deference, begrudging or otherwise, that Rose found absolutely fascinating. Persinette was tiny, soft spoken, and far too kind for her own good. But she'd earned their respect, even Agnes's. What Rose wouldn't do to pick her apart, dissect her, try to figure out how she worked. She couldn't. Things like that weren't exactly socially acceptable. So she settled for watching the way the group reacted to her instead. "We are going to give Kindle the same respect we'd give anyone else. Am I clear?"

There was a chorus of mumbled agreements before the door creaked open again and Kindle called through, "Are you coming or not, Rose?"

With a loud exhale, Rose rubbed at the space between her brows as all the others turned to look at her expectantly. They were counting on her, they didn't have to say as much, to get the information they needed. That's why Agnes had convinced her to come, after all, she couldn't back out now. "Yes, in a moment."

Kindle clicked her tongue, and the door shut again.

"Will you be all right with her?" Owen asked, his forehead wrinkled in concern. "She doesn't seem—"

"I'll be fine. You lot just be careful, that hallway has already collapsed twice, once on Kindle herself. Take Hubert with you, but make sure he doesn't get crushed. Chirp will come and let me know if anything happens." Rubbing her hands down over her face, Rose straightened up, adjusted her glasses, and prepared for another long couple of hours in the presence of someone who clearly didn't like her very much.

"How sweet. Do you actually care if any of us get hurt?" Penny teased, her wings fluttering behind her.

"No, it'd just be more trouble for all of us if you did." Rose scoffed.

"Right." Manu hummed slowly as if he completely understood.

With a huff, Rose turned and walked out into the hall where Kindle was leaning against the wall. She looked annoyed at having been kept waiting, but she didn't say as much, she just turned and led Rose toward the east end of the library.

"Before we get started, I want to lay down some ground rules." Kindle's steps were brisk, in spite of the pain her injuries were probably still causing her, and Rose only just managed to keep up.

They made it past two closed doors before Kindle continued, as if she'd left a pause, expecting Rose to have something to say to that. She didn't. She had expected there to be rules surrounding this whole thing. Kindle was too tightly wound to not have some restrictions. And while Rose had some leverage, she didn't think she had enough to completely disregard any of Kindle's rules.

"No books are to be taken from their respective rooms, unless otherwise authorized by myself," Kindle said. "If you need help finding something you can ask me, but please don't bother Chirp"—Rose secretly delighted in the fact that Kindle had taken to calling the little robot by the name she'd given it—"it has far more important things to deal with than helping you. All books are to be returned to where you found them, no exceptions, we like to keep things tidy."

Their steps brought them to a door that was bolted tight with multiple locks from the outside. None of them required keys, as far as Rose could see, but Kindle had gone through great lengths to keeping something inside, or maybe keep her unexpected guests out. Rose tried to remember if she'd passed the door in the mad dash to get Kindle to a bed so she could be treated, but they'd been running so quickly, and all of the halls of the Great Library looked the same to her, she had no way of knowing for sure.

"You are not, under any circumstances, to enter this room." Kindle gestured to the door, but she didn't look at it. In fact it looked like she was trying to avoid making eye contact with it entirely, her gaze darting anywhere but directly at it. Interesting.

"What sort of books are in there?" Rose asked, her weight

rocking up onto her toes with her curiosity. Was it full of black magic texts? Or maybe Kindle's own history? Or maybe it was her private collection, and thus something really embarrassing, like a host of romance novels. The possibilities were endless. And already Rose felt the twitch in her muscles to get inside.

"No books," Kindle said, bringing Rose's guessing game to an immediate halt. "Just storage that you have no business digging through." Her wings shifted behind her, going rigid. A lie? "If you go into this room, you will all be banned from the library, permanently. Have I made myself clear?"

Rose squinted at Kindle, her gaze shifting from the woman to the door behind her. No books, she'd said. So there was really no reason for Rose to go in there, aside from curiosity. No reason at all. But it didn't look like Kindle was being completely honest, and still the need to know hummed through her veins.

"Focus, Rose. You've got bigger fish to fry." Rose scratched at her neck, wishing Tobias would stop *doing* that. If one more person caught her talking to herself she was worried they'd lock her up.

"Have I made myself clear?" Kindle repeated, her jaw tightening.

"Perfectly." Rose smiled, dragging her eyes from the door. She had always been the child who did things just because she was told not to, who was too curious for her own good, and she wanted to know what was behind that door so badly that her skin itched with the desire of it. But she had the entirety of civilization's words at her fingertips, that would have to be enough to quell the urge for the moment. "Where do we start?"

"History." Kindle spun to go back the way they'd come, seeming to have only brought them there so she could tell Rose not to enter that room specifically which just made

Rose more curious. She lingered for a moment outside of it, her palms sweating where she had them pressed into the fabric of her trousers. It couldn't hurt to take a peek, surely. She wouldn't go in, she just wanted to see. And there was a crack under the door, if she just waited until—

Kindle cleared her throat, and Rose snapped out of it, scurrying after her.

Whatever Kindle had thought it would be like to research with Rose, she hadn't been expecting complete silence. She was used to the quiet tweets from Chirp when the robot found something interesting, of the twittering as it tugged on her pants' leg to share something with her. But Kindle had let Rose loose on the history room, and in the last hour they hadn't even exchanged eye contact. No, instead Rose was hunched over some tome at the desk, her glasses perched on top of her head, a wrinkle in her nose, and her eyes staring intently at the text. As if the entire world outside of the book in front of her did not exist at all. The single-minded focus was unsettling, and made Kindle want to ask the rest of the crew of the *Duchess* if Rose was always like this, or if it was just because she didn't want to interact with Kindle.

"Why did you start at the most recent history?" Kindle asked, when being ignored started to make her spine bunch up in discomfort. The narrow-eyed look of annoyance, and the long sigh from Rose made Kindle almost instantly regret it. Not that Kindle could blame her, she knew how annoying it was to be interrupted while she was reading, and yet, here she was interrupting someone else because a little bit of quiet was making her twitchy.

"I don't know exactly how far back the queen's reign goes." Rose marked her place with a finger, tilting her neck this way and that to loosen out whatever kink she'd acquired from spending the last two hours with her head ducked. "No one does. She stays out of the public for the most part, and doesn't use her name if she can help it. Even Agnes, who's at least a hundred and fifty isn't entirely sure."

"How does that work?" Kindle frowned realizing she'd drawn closer to Rose while she'd been speaking. The cadence of Rose's voice soft in the quiet around them, intimate and personal, more like she was thinking out loud than she was having a conversation. It made Kindle lean in closer, desperate for a peek into the inner workings of that constantly moving mind.

"A spell, I'm sure." Rose's thumb tapped against the edge of the book's cover, her gaze flicking back down to the words. "If I were to hazard a guess, and keep in mind I know very little about magic, I'd say she cast an avoidance spell to keep the people of Daiwynn from thinking about it too long."

"On everyone? That would take a massive amount of power." Kindle's wings rustled on her back. It was a waste of magic, as far as she was concerned. Why would the queen hide how long she'd been in power? Unless it was far longer than anyone realized. Something about that pricked at her memory, making a sharp pain start behind her eye, that she reached up to rub away.

Rose either didn't notice or just thought she'd gotten dust in her eye—she probably didn't notice, she seemed to be so fixated on this theory that little else occupied her mind—because she continued on the topic without pause. "Not if you put the spell on the information itself, instead of the people who would know it."

"Is that even possible?" The pain stopped as soon as Kindle forced herself to focus on Rose's thoughtful expression instead of the queen's age. Strange. "To cast a spell on an idea?"

"In theory." Rose's tapping grew more insistent as her mind worked, her eyes taking on a far-off expression as if she weren't really seeing the library or Kindle anymore. "You can put a spell on any person, place, or thing, you just have to know its true name."

"And what's the true name of such a thing?" It was just a theory, Kindle knew that, there was no proof that the queen had done this, or that it would even work. But it had been so long since Kindle had been able to follow an idea to its logical conclusion with a mind like Rose's. Kindle could almost hear the *click-click-click*ing of gears in the woman's head as she thought over the question, her teeth wearing on her lower lip. Who was this woman? And why had MOTHER locked her in a labor camp instead of using her brain for something more useful? It seemed a colossal waste to Kindle, but then MOTHER was keen on destroying knowledge, and a mind like Rose's could be dangerous. It would probably have been better for them if they had killed her instead of locking her away.

"I'd imagine the year she was born would be the best true name for such information," Rose murmured, her teeth threatening to bite through the skin of her lower lip. Her eyes had gone sharper, the gears in her head *tick-tick-tick*ing faster and faster. MOTHER had probably thought that in locking her away in a camp she'd wither, her mind becoming a dull blade. They'd been wrong. Kindle hadn't known Rose before, but she would wager that she'd only grown keener, more observant, in the gray world of the camps. MOTHER's loss. Kindle's gain. "That combined with her true name would be enough to tie up the spell, I'd think."

"And you plan to combat it by finding the information in the library? Won't you just forget it soon after you find it?"

These questions drew Rose out of her thoughts, and she looked up at Kindle with a smile so slick and cunning that Kindle couldn't be sure Rose wasn't mixed with Kitsune somewhere in her lineage.

"That's the best part about the library," Rose whispered, leaning in closer as if this were a secret just between them. Kindle felt the heat from her words against her cheek, and was glad, for the first time, that her skin was already blotched over with red scales and lizard skin, or Rose might see the warmth that spread through her at such closeness. "It exists in a pocket dimension."

Kindle drew back, hoping Rose wouldn't notice how she put distance between them, and frowned. "So?"

"So, the library isn't technically *part* of Daiwynn." Rose took a step back as well, seeming to have just realized how close they had gotten. There was no redness staining her cheeks, but there was a wide, wildness in her eyes as if she'd just realized a misstep, a mistake, and was working double time to correct it. "Which means any magic cast on Daiwynn won't apply to us here."

"But what about when you go back?" Kindle turned to the shelves, running her fingers across the worn spines of the books, a nervous gesture she'd had since childhood. She'd read them all at least twice over by this point in her life. Not that she could remember every single detail, but she could remember the general idea from every book in her library, that would be enough to help Rose find what she needed, and fulfill her end of their deal. "Will you forget?"

"Maybe." Rose tilted her head back to the book she'd been reading, her feet taking her across the room to the little desk in the corner. She sounded like a scientist, puzzled, but excited to test a theory. There was danger in that, Kindle recognized. In the not knowing what would happen until it happened. Experimenting could get them all killed, but Rose didn't seem bothered by the potential consequences of her actions. A true scientist through and through. "There's only one way to find out, really."

Kindle's shoulders sagged a little. As much as she had thrashed against the idea of Rose finding information on the queen and Uprising leader, she hated the thought of someone finding the information they sought in the library and then immediately losing it, even more. It left a hollowness in her chest, like someone had gone in and plucked out something vital she hadn't even known was there until it was gone, a liver, or a kidney, something one didn't know they needed until they were suddenly lacking it, and forced to function without. Information shouldn't be kept from people like that, no matter what the queen meant by it.

"You could always come with us," Rose said, breaking Kindle from her thoughts.

"What?" Kindle frowned, turning from the shelf to raise her brows at Rose.

"I feel like any magic they've cast on the people of Daiwynn wouldn't apply to you at all." Rose sounded like she was only half paying attention to her words, her head ducked over the book at the desk as she jotted down notes in a journal Kindle had given her, but her mind a million miles away, running her thoughts to their inevitable conclusion. A conclusion that somehow included Kindle leaving the library. "How long have you been here?"

Kindle's heart leapt into her throat, threatening to choke her response. "I'm not leaving the library."

The cold stone of the history room was hard under Kindle's feet where she curled her toes into it to ground herself in her home. To keep anyone from pulling her away from it. Rose was interesting, yes. She wanted to know more about the outside world, yes, even if it was a mess. But the library was her home, and she knew the consequences if she left. She'd seen them spread out before her, in color, a crumpled, dusty mess, that she could never repair or escape if she took a step in that direction. Because once she did, it'd be like falling down a hole. No way out.

Rose's head lifted and she turned to look at Kindle over her shoulder. Her glasses had slid down her nose, so that she was eyeing Kindle over top of the frames. Kindle wondered if that made her harder or easier to see. Was Rose farsighted or nearsighted? And what was the difference? Kindle so often forgot. Maybe she was both. Maybe Rose had bifocals.

"I'm not leaving the library," Kindle repeated, clearing her throat so her voice wouldn't waver, around the thumping of her heart.

"Why not?"

The truth crawled up Kindle's throat like a living thing, wanting to be free, to be shared. Only she and Chirp knew why she couldn't leave the library, not ever. Maybe if Rose knew, she'd understand Kindle better, but what would that achieve? Nothing. Besides, Kindle didn't need to be understood for her to help Rose get what she needed. She also didn't need Rose's pity, her promises, or her creative solutions, because there was little doubt she'd have some. A thinker like Rose, she'd find a way around the collapse of the library should Kindle leave it behind. Or think she had, anyway, but inevitably, the book would be right, and the library would collapse, and all would be lost.

"Because the library is my *home*. Stop wasting both of our time trying to learn about me. Get back to your research." She had hoped the words would come out a little more annoyed, or angry with Rose's questioning, but they mostly just sounded tired, even to Kindle herself. Maybe Rose wouldn't notice. Maybe they could just. . . pretend this conversation had never happened.

Rose opened her mouth like there was something else she

wanted to say, but Kindle grabbed a book from the shelf and buried her face in it, silencing her. It was better that way, Kindle knew. She wouldn't leave, no matter what Chirp thought, or how Rose tried to convince her. And the less they discussed it, the better for everyone involved. Lest Kindle get angry, and lock Rose on the ship again, that would serve none of them.

KINDLE ATE dinner alone that evening, amongst her cushions and her books in the reading room, in spite of the wary look that Chirp had given her. The others hadn't invited her along. They hadn't even seemed interested in much more than a brief wave from a tired looking Persinette as they all loaded back onto the *Duchess* to settle in for the evening.

Not that Kindle had been expecting an invitation, mind. They weren't her friends, and she knew that. Their relationship was begrudging and mutually beneficial. Rose hadn't even looked back at her before climbing the rope ladder. And the image of her walking away, leaving Kindle behind, played on repeat through Kindle's head as she shoveled another fork full of potatoes into her mouth.

Chirp made a grumbled, grinding noise that sounded like a chastisement, and Kindle sighed, leaning back more heavily in the cushions as she ate the meager meal she'd prepared for herself in the cook book room/kitchen of the library. She wasn't even really hungry. Spending an entire day in the presence of another person, especially one like Rose, had left her too tired to be hungry, grogginess clouding all of her senses, making her cranky. But she knew she needed to eat or she'd never feel normal again.

"I wasn't mean to her." Kindle stuffed another bit of bread

into her mouth where it sat stodgy and heavy on her tongue. She just wanted to go to sleep, and not wake for the rest of the week. But tomorrow would be more of the same, another day full of answering Rose's questions, and helping her find information on a topic Kindle didn't like. Not that Chirp would have let that slide anyway, it was too busy regaling her with its general feelings of the crew.

The tail end of another twitter went up in a question, and Kindle sighed, scrubbing at her face with the palm of her hand.

"I don't know why she didn't invite me back to the ship then. Maybe because this is only a means to an end for all of them, Chirp. That's what it seems like, isn't it?" She hated the way Chirp's shoulders drooped a little. It thought it had made some friends, but Kindle knew the truth. As soon they got what they wanted, they'd be gone, and they wouldn't give the keepers of the library a second thought. They didn't care about her or Chirp, even for all Rose tried to pretend she did by asking her to come with them. That was just because Rose was curious, because she saw Kindle as a test subject, another curiosity that had raised questions, nothing more and nothing less. And she'd be quick enough to move onto another such thing were it to catch her attention. Kindle wasn't fooling herself into believing otherwise. It would hurt too much. One of them had to keep their head about them, and Chirp had always been the more emotional of the two. "Look, I'm sorry." Kindle sighed. "But it's the truth. Once they get what they need, they'll be gone, and we'll still be here."

A mournful whistle left the little robot as it deflated further into the cushions beside her. *When did it become so pitiful and in need of company?* Kindle shook her head, finishing off her food.

"Cheer up, Chirp. You still have me!" She nudged it lightly with her foot.

It lifted its head to look at her, then nodded with a soft, sad ticking noise. Rose had really thrown a wrench into everything. She'd upset the natural balance of the library, and Kindle disliked her just a little bit more for that. For making Chirp sad. For making the halls, once they had gone back to their ship, seem just a little bit lonelier. The sooner Rose and the crew left, the better, before they buried themselves so deep into this place that Kindle would spend decades trying to forget what it had felt like to have people who might have almost been friends there.

"How are the repairs going?" Kindle asked, hoping to change the subject, and Chirp let out a long whistle that might have been a sigh.

After that first day, Rose hadn't asked any more questions about why Kindle wouldn't leave with them. She didn't want to see the look of resignation on Kindle's face again. It had left behind an aching rawness in Rose's chest that had her rubbing at her sternum to try to alleviate it. The action didn't help. All it really seemed to do was rub the pain into the very marrow of her bones.

She knew that expression and tone all too well. Knew what it was to resign oneself to a life that there seemed no way out of. She'd lived through that resignation before Agnes and Sully had showed up at the labor camp, spouting their ideas of escape. Even after, she'd felt resistant to the idea of leaving behind what she'd begun to think of as the place she'd surely die one day.

The camp had never been home, it had always been a prison, and Rose had never tricked herself into thinking otherwise, but there had been a time right before they had showed up that she'd decided there was simply no way out. That she'd never know a life outside of the gray walls of the camp. It was a complete, and total loss of hope, and Rose wondered how long Kindle had felt that way, but decided not to ask. That was something she had learned in her days at the camp, sometimes it was better not to ask about people and their past. Better not to dredge up all the horribleness that had come before she knew them. Especially in a world where MOTHER and the queen sought to punish any Enchanted they could find for the mere crime of existing.

Instead, she asked, "how long have you been here?"

She'd asked on that first day, but Kindle had ignored the question to argue about her not wanting to leave the library. Which was fine, Rose supposed, but she really was quite curious. And besides, she couldn't leave Kindle this way. That wouldn't be right. Kindle may have been bitter, and angry when they had first shown up to the library, but she was helping them now, and Rose, well, Tobias would say she had a soft spot for broken things. She was a fixer and a fiddler by nature, and people were not immune to that impulse. Nor were they immune to the impulse to take something apart and put it back together again to see how it ticked. Rose was a complicated woman.

"Since the library was formed," Kindle said, shifting on her bare feet, her talons scraping a little against the stone.

Rose frowned, rubbing a hand over her tired eyes. They had been at this for days, reading in silence, and dancing around each other as if avoiding even glancing at one another would ease the tension between them. It would not, Rose knew that from experience. And she was bored with whatever game Kindle thought they were playing. Cat and mouse. Hide and seek. Ring around the Rosie. Rose was done. She wanted answers.

"Do you just not know?" Rose asked, plainly, lifting her head from the book on the table in front of her. So far, she'd learned nothing new about the queen or the Uprising, but she'd only gone back fifty years or so. The library's cache of history books was almost too thorough, in her opinion.

More shifting was Kindle's only answer, and wasn't that

answer enough? Rose took a deep breath, and pulled on what little empathy she had, before standing and walking over to where Kindle had leaned herself against the shelves. She stopped in front of her, taking the book slowly from Kindle's taloned hands, careful to mark her page with her index finger.

"It's okay if you don't know right now," Rose said when Kindle looked up and met her gaze. It was true, in Rose's mind. To say one didn't know was to invite questions, and curiosity. It was to court research and tests. The first step in any experiment was the initial 'I don't know', and Rose had become addicted to that as much as she had the knowing when she was a child, sitting at her father's knee as he worked on his clockwork machines. He'd taught her the value in 'I don't know', and she'd always be grateful to him for that.

Kindle's dark eyes widened, lending her a stricken look. As if no one had ever told her it was all right for her to not know something. Maybe they hadn't. That kindness wasn't one many people gave themselves, or others, but Rose had learned that sometimes, the joy was in the discovery. Another precious lesson from her father.

The vulnerability didn't last. Kindle quickly regained control over whatever she was feeling, and her expression shuttered. "It's not that I don't know."

"Okay." Rose said, opening the book again, and holding it out to her.

That seemed to confuse Kindle just as much, because she snatched her book back, her lips pressing into a scowl. She lifted the book to hide her face from Rose, and Rose let out a slow breath then returned to the desk. It wouldn't do to push Kindle too hard, too fast. Kindle was more scared animal than person half of the time, and Rose had read enough about scared animals to know what that meant.

"Sometimes you have to give a little, to get a little," Tobias suggested in the back of her mind, and Rose bit down so hard on the inside of her cheek to keep from snapping at him that she tasted metal on her tongue. He really did know just how to pop up when he was least wanted. He did have a point though. Rose had promised to tell Kindle about their escape from the camp. She looked up from her book to see Kindle aggressively turn a page, and decided to try again the next day instead.

"WHAT HAVE you learned about our mysterious captor?" Roy asked later that evening over dinner. They'd all been picking at their food, and Rose could tell they had been waiting for the best time to ask that particular question, or maybe just hoping that she'd supply them with information. None of them were half as subtle as they thought they were. Least of all Roy who had sucked in a breath, making his cheeks look even more chipmunk adjacent, and blew it out before he'd asked.

"Not much." Rose took a mouthful of pasta, ignoring how everyone's shoulders seemed to droop. *Not even a little bit subtle*, she amended. "She doesn't even seem to know how long she's been here."

Persinette frowned, her hand stilling where she'd been twisting her fork through the noodles. "Chirp said something similar. It doesn't remember coming here at all. In fact, from what Hiccup was able to gather, its memory banks only go back a couple of decades."

"It has to be older than that." Agnes shook his head.

"We really have no way of knowing." Owen reached for another helping, piling more pasta onto Benard's plate which seemed to irritate the goblin—his long, pointed ears twitching—although he didn't say as much. "Right Benard? You've heard rumors about it from way back."

"We are not discussing how old I am." Benard grabbed Owen's roll from the side of his plate, and broke it in half before dipping it into his sauce. "But yes, the legends go back further than that. I can't remember when I first heard about it, but I know I was fairly young."

"What's young for you?" Manu snarked obnoxiously, then yelped when someone kicked him under the table. Rose wasn't sure if it'd been Owen, or Benard himself, but Manu ducked down to rub at his shin.

"As I was saying," Benard continued, his gaze narrowed on Manu. "It definitely goes back further than that. Did Hiccup say what came before Chirp and Kindle were here?"

"Nothing." Persinette's lavender brows pinched together in frustration, her freckles becoming a smear as she scrunched up her forehead. "Before the record of the library, there is just emptiness. Have you spoken to Kindle about what came before her memories of this place?"

"No. I don't want to push her too hard." Rose nudged her glasses back up her nose where they'd slid down, and scratched at her cheek. Discomfort with being the center of an enquiry that had nothing at all to do with herself, made her shift in her seat, peeling one leg and then the other up from the hard wood of the chair. "I still don't understand why it matters."

"It might not." Persinette's freckled nose wrinkled too, and she scrubbed at it with her fingers as if it itched. "But I have this feeling that Kindle is important somehow, and I like to trust those feelings."

Rose didn't think that was as good a reason to go prying into someone else's life as Persinette seemed to think it was, and maybe if she didn't have her own reasons, she wouldn't have listened to Persinette, and her gut instincts, at all. But she did have her own reasons, so here they were. "How are the repairs to the west wing going?"

Sully sighed heavily, leaning so his upper body hung off the back of his chair limply, and he was staring up at the ceiling. "Every time it seems like we might have gotten through to the other side, there's more rubble. I'm beginning to wonder if the whole wing has collapsed."

"Let's hope not," Penny mumbled around a full mouth. "I don't exactly want to be the one to tell her that she's lost an entire wing of her library."

"Good thing you probably wouldn't be the one given that job." Rose rolled her eyes, pushing her plate away, she suddenly wasn't very hungry. The thought of an entire wing of the library having collapsed had soured everything she'd eaten already, making bile rise in her throat. And not just because she'd have to be the one to deliver the news to Kindle. But because she had to wonder . . . *What rooms had been lost? What books destroyed? How much history of their world would simply be gone forever? And what would that change?* Maybe nothing. Probably nothing. But as someone who felt knowledge was power, as someone who had known what it felt like to be powerless . . . well. Rose couldn't stomach the idea of so much being lost. Especially when she was fairly certain that the queen had access to such knowledge. It would have been foolish for the queen to have MOTHER burn all those books, and not keep copies for herself. And the queen had proven time and again, that she was no fool.

"Have you found anything we can use yet?" Agnes said, changing topics, and Rose was ever so grateful for it. Grateful for Agnes, not a thing she ever thought she'd be. This whole mission was turning into one big thing she never thought she'd see in her lifetime, and yet, here she was. If there weren't so many hypotheses to test, and mysteries to solve, she might very well be annoyed by it all.

"Not yet. The history section is very thorough, and I started at the most recent and am working my way back." Rose lifted her glasses to rub at where the nose-pads had been pressing a little too hard on the bridge of her nose. She'd needed to adjust them for the last couple of days, but there never seemed to be the time or the energy to do it, even for it being such a mindless task. Her mind was always elsewhere. And she was so tired. Tired from exerting herself to be somewhat amiable. Tired from being "on" all the time. Tired from not getting enough sleep because as soon as her head hit the pillow, and she was allowed the time to think, her mind raced with questions. Just tired. Overall. In general. Exhausted. "It would be better if I weren't the only one searching."

"Maybe you could convince her to let someone else help?" Persinette looked hopeful, but Rose knew better. If there was one thing she'd learned about Kindle over the last few days, it was that when she said something she stuck by it. She didn't change her mind, and she didn't let someone persuade her otherwise. Obstinate, was the word, and Rose was getting rather sick of it already.

"I doubt it," Rose sighed, and the conversation moved on.

GIVE A LITTLE TO GET A LITTLE, Tobias had said, and maybe he was right. Maybe making herself vulnerable would make Kindle feel more comfortable being vulnerable as well. Rose hated being vulnerable, above all things, it was a weakness she'd never wanted to allow herself, but the crew was off working with Chirp, it was just them, and who was Kindle going to tell? No one.

Inhaling deeply through her mouth, Rose straightened her shoulders, and prepared for what was no doubt going to be a grueling trip down memory lane. Gods, she hated those. "I was in labor camp 9c so long, I hardly remember what life was like outside of it."

"What?" Kindle asked. She'd pulled another chair from somewhere in the library and was sitting across from Rose at the desk, reading through one of the history books. They still hadn't come across anything useful, but they were getting close, Rose could feel it. The texts were humming with excitement like bees under her fingertips.

"I told you I escaped from one of MOTHER's labor camps, but I never told you how long, or why, I was there." Rose shrugged, as if that could make the uncomfortable tightness of her skin go away. It didn't. She didn't know if she really wanted to tell Kindle the why, worried she might have to endure more of Kindle's censure. But Tobias's words played on repeat through her head, *give a little to get a little.* She needed more than a little . . . she'd have to give a *lot.* "As for how long, I don't know exactly, more than twenty years at least. I just know that I was there so long that I have a hard time remembering what life was like before that gray place."

Kindle tilted her head this way and that, as if stretching out a knot in her neck, shifting in her seat to give Rose her full attention. "And the why?"

"The why is just as complicated to answer as how long." Rose let out a mirthless laugh, her mouth twisting into a smile that held no warmth. Complicated was an understatement. "There were a lot of reasons. But what it comes down to is that my handler, Gaston, wanted me. He tried to force himself on me, in fact. Which wouldn't have mattered much at all but then he started slinging accusations around, about how there were Uprising spies in MOTHER. And Agnes—"

"The unicorn?" Kindle asked, surprising Rose with the fact that she'd actually bothered to learn the crew's names, and was listening closely enough to apply that knowledge.

"Yes, the unicorn." Rose's fists clenched in her lap. She would never forget what Agnes had done to her, and she didn't think she'd ever entirely forgive it either, but she'd learned to live with it and with him. She understood why he'd felt he had to, and she supposed that was something. "He needed to get the heat off his people, the Uprising he had imbedded in MOTHER, and well. . . Gaston hated me already, you see. He couldn't quite understand why I wouldn't sleep with him the way so many others had. So when I was caught looking perhaps a little too long at another female Enchanted, it was the perfect storm, and Agnes helped it along. Even if he hadn't though . . . it wouldn't have changed the result. Rumors are vicious that way. Especially one as vicious as an Enchanted asset being homosexual."

"Agnes outed you?" Kindle's nostrils flared, smoke drifting from them in her anger, and Rose's whole body relaxed. If Kindle was furious at the idea that Agnes might have outed her, then there would be none of the disgust that Rose had been trying to avoid.

"No. He just repeated what he'd heard and didn't help when I asked for it. Which I did. I begged him to please, make this go away for me. He'd done it before, for others. But he refused. He said someone needed to get the attention off of him and the others. So I was sent to the camps after a group of Gaston's favorite women claimed that I had made advances on them." When she said it like that, it sounded even less like it was Agnes's fault, but Rose had always been taught that doing nothing when someone asked for help was almost worse than hurting them. And Agnes had stood by, and done nothing. He had watched. He had waited. And he had taken advantage of a situation that benefited him more than anyone else. Because he was a selfish bastard like that. He had to be.

"And yet you're flying with him." Kindle frowned, her brows pinched together, the smoke lessening but not quite going away. She didn't understand. That was fine, Rose didn't either sometimes. When Agnes's tone became just a little too condescending, when he got a particularly pinched expression, she didn't understand either. But. . . Well, she also had been the one to walk him down the aisle when he married Sully. So she supposed they were on decent terms now. Not quite friends, but maybe as close as Rose would ever let herself get.

"It's called forgiveness." Rose looked back to her book.

"What was the point of that story?"

Rose turned the page when she didn't see anything they needed in front of her. "The point is, people change, and change is good." Turning the page again, she smiled a little to herself. "Also, I guess I forgive you too. For everything you did when I first came here."

"Oh," Kindle said on a breath, and ducked her head so quickly back to her book that Rose could hear her teeth clack together.

"Oh, indeed," Tobias murmured, a knowing smugness to his tone that Rose didn't like.

Since the day Rose had told her about the labor camp, a truce had formed between them. Kindle understood why Rose was doing what she was, she couldn't fault her for wanting revenge, and maybe wanting to save someone else from going through what she had. That made things both easier and harder for Kindle, because while they were bickering, and she was angry, she could keep Rose and her crew at a distance. Things were better that way, she'd told Chirp. Then she didn't have to worry about them trying to convince her to leave the library to crumble in on itself. She had made her choice, and nothing Rose did or said was going to change that. Nothing. But that decision seemed a little less sharp, a little less pointed, the more Kindle got to know Rose.

"My father was a great inventor," Rose said as if something had just reminded her of him. They had gotten to the history books for a hundred years ago, and were slowly closing in on something, Kindle could feel it. But Rose wasn't letting it make her reckless, she was still taking her time combing through book after book, making sure that no clue was missed, no matter how small. Kindle admired the dedication. Too many who had come through the library over the centuries had been in such a hurry to find what they needed and go. Not Rose. Rose took her time. She was meticulous. Her long brown fingers flipping pages almost reverently. Respect shown to every tome no matter how useful she found it as she carefully returned it to its place.

"Oh?" Kindle asked, when Rose didn't expand upon that statement. She ran her roughened fingertip over the edges of the pages, feeling them catch on the tough skin with a soft *flick.*

Letting out a breath, Rose turned the book she was looking at to Kindle so she could see the photograph of a man with curled black hair, and wire spectacles. "This was him. He was so good that the queen herself commissioned him for things." Her thumb brushed reverently against the paper near the man's photo. Kindle could see the resemblance there, though she supposed Rose took after her mother more so than her father. But they had the same eyes, right down to their shape. A curious, almost mischievous glint behind the lenses of his glasses that Kindle had stopped trying to pretend she didn't find achingly beautiful in Rose's hazel eyes.

"What happened to him?" She regretted the question almost as soon as she'd asked it, but there was no way to take it back, so Kindle merely swallowed around the lump forming in her throat and hoped Rose wasn't about to cry. She was so very bad with crying people. Worse still when it was her fault that they were crying.

Rose smiled tightly, the corners of it cutting at her eyes, and making them water, then turned the book back to herself so she could look down at her father again. "He fell in love with a human. And as you know, mixed marriages like that are not allowed in Daiwynn." She turned the page, and it seemed like she was finished her story for a moment as her eyes scanned over some text in the book. Then she shook her head, and lifted it to meet Kindle's gaze. "They were planning to escape to the Wastes when the queen's men caught them. She couldn't let her best inventor run away, could she? So father struck a deal, his service for his family, and for a while, it worked. But even a genius couldn't keep up with the queen's demands for long, and eventually his work began to slip."

"What did the queen do?" Kindle didn't think she wanted to know the answer, already her stomach was churning imagining what kind of punishment a woman who ran MOTHER could come up with for such a person. Rose looked down at the book, seeming to want to hide whatever expression she was making in its pages. Kindle averted her own gaze, to alleviate some of the pressure, but not before she caught the tell tale shine of tears. "You don't have to answer if it's too painful."

With a little lift of her shoulders, Rose pushed her glasses back up her nose, even though they didn't look like they had slid at all, a nervous gesture very likely. "I don't remember my mother," Rose said, the words sounding like they'd been ripped from her throat.

There was a clench in Kindle's chest, her heart stuttering in understanding. Because she knew that pain all too well, the pain of knowing someone had loved her, but also knowing that she'd never remember them. The ache of vague voices and feelings that lingered, but never became any more detailed, and seemed to fade the more she revisited them. The hollowness of a loss she'd never fully understand, but seemed to experience nonetheless. "I don't remember either of my parents." Kindle had never said that out loud before. Chirp knew it, of course, it had been there through her aching, and her tears, and there was the book of course, but no one who'd ever visited the library had asked Kindle about herself or her history. "I have vague memories of my father, and my siblings, but nothing concrete, nothing I can pin down. Just shapes, and feelings. All I really have is this stupid storybook Chirp and I found a while back in the fables room."

"Storybook?" Rose glanced up from her reading. "Someone wrote a storybook about you?"

"I don't know if it was about me specifically." Kindle wrinkled her nose, shutting the book she'd been sifting through. There wasn't anything. She'd been tempted to grab something from three hundred and fifty years ago to see if that would give them a better understanding of what was going on, but she couldn't explain the impulse to look at that time period specifically, and she hardly thought Rose wanted her research to be led by someone else's gut feeling. "But humans have this way of turning Enchanted history into stories for their children, and this one does feature a dragon, a library, and a clockwork rose."

"A clockwork rose?" Rose sat up a little straighter, interest clearly piqued. Kindle hadn't meant to say that bit, and she frowned a little, biting at the inside of her lip to try to take it back. "Can I see this storybook?"

"Sure... uh... how about you have supper with me this evening? And we can look at it?" She wouldn't be showing Rose the torn-out pages featuring herself, or the crew, but Rose could look at the rest of it. Giving in to the nervous energy under her skin that came with asking Rose to join her for supper, and baring a part of herself she'd never shown anyone, Kindle stood from her seat to return her book to the shelf, and pick up another.

"I'd like that." Rose sounded like she was smiling, but Kindle didn't turn around to see for fear it would only make her leathery skin burn hotter.

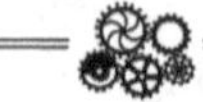

CHIRP WAS DELIGHTED by the idea that Kindle had asked Rose to join her for supper, and even more delighted by the fact that Rose had accepted. It would not shut up about it. The chirping and twittering was getting very annoying, very quickly, but Kindle didn't have it in her to ruin the good mood Chirp was in. It was so rare that they had anything to celebrate in the library—or had visitors at all—that she was more than willing to let the robot go a little overboard with everything.

Of course when she'd imagined a *little overboard*, she hadn't thought Chirp would pull out the nice plates from the dining room, and set up candles. That just seemed like. . . overkill. And she didn't want Rose to think that she was trying too hard. Or that this was like . . . some lame attempt to woo her or something. Because it wasn't. It was a friendly dinner between research partners to share information. Nothing more, nothing less.

Still, there she was, standing in the middle of the room of arts, which was perhaps one of the best rooms in the library. It tended to be the loudest late at night, but in the early evenings the chatter from the artists was drowned out by hundreds of musicians, all playing in harmony. Kindle came there when she needed to calm down, or relax. Rose wouldn't be able to hear it, no one other than the keepers ever seemed to be able to hear the books, but it provided a pleasant background for Kindle at least. And the noise was a good distraction from how the candlelight felt over-warm against her skin.

"This isn't meant to be romantic," Kindle frowned down at Chirp, who looked at her with wide, innocent visual circuits, and blinked as if it didn't understand what she was saying. She wasn't sure where it had learned such a trick, maybe from her younger self, but she wished it would stop doing that. With Chirp's head tilted just so, and that carefully placed blink, Kindle found it increasingly hard to be mad at it. She was going soft, that was the only explanation. "Don't act like you don't know what I mean."

Chirp shrugged, and turned back to setting the table, unbothered by her chastisements.

"You've gotten obstinate. That's something she's taught you." Kindle's fingers twitched around the edges of the storybook. This was her worst idea yet. She wished she could call it off, but she heard Rose's soft footfalls in the hall. It was too late. Far too late.

The robot lifted one shoulder, and let out a soft, disinterested twitter that meant something like, "well somebody had to."

Kindle clicked her tongue.

The music from the musicians swelled, as if they knew what was about to happen, and Kindle spun just in time to see a strange expression sweep over Rose's features. It wasn't a look of confusion, or irritation, like so many of the ones Kindle had seen so far. It was some. . . *other* emotion. Harder to decipher, and the moment Rose realized Kindle was watching her, it was gone.

"This is lovely." Rose smiled, brushing her hands down over her trousers. They weren't covered in grease stains like usual, and it looked like they might be a bit too long for Rose, like she'd borrowed someone else's clothes in order to look presentable. *Maybe I'm not the only one trying too hard . . .* Kindle stamped down on the tiny thrill that thought brought her.

"We have Chirp to thank for that." Kindle pulled out Rose's chair for her, and shot Chirp a narrow-eyed look that said very clearly it should make itself scarce. Not because she wanted to be alone with Rose, but because if she were going to make an absolute imbecile of herself, she'd rather not have an audience.

Chirp chirped out an excuse, and left as quickly as Kindle ever thought she'd seen it move before, apart from when it'd been excited about something. The doors creaked behind it, leaving Kindle and Rose utterly alone to their dinner. Kindle sat down across the table, rubbing her sweaty palms on her pants, and wondered if she hadn't just made a gigantic mistake. At least with Chirp in the room there would have been someone there to alleviate the awkwardness. Now, there was no one. Just Kindle and her inability to talk to people like a normal person.

The silence stretched on, Kindle cleared her throat, Rose shifted in her chair. Yes, she'd definitely made a mistake.

"Is that. . . Do I hear a cello?" Rose asked suddenly, her hazel eyes flicked around the room, searching for the mysterious instrument.

Kindle's stomach lurched. "You hear them?" She raised her brows high, wrinkling her forehead, and her fingers stilled where she'd been fiddling with the worn edges of the storybook in her lap.

"Well of course I do. I'm just trying to figure out where it's coming from. You don't have a record player, and I don't see—"

"It's the books." Heart pounding against her ribs, Kindle leaned in closer, her lips twisting up into an almost manic smile. They shared this. They didn't have much else in common—or at least Kindle liked to think they didn't because that made disliking Rose easier—but Rose could hear the books, just as Kindle had always been able to. She could hear the swelling music, the rising and falling of wind instruments, and strings. And it made Kindle's head spin with a foreign emotion that might have been real, and sincere joy. Gods, how long had it been since she'd been really happy?

"The books?" Rose wrinkled her nose, but it didn't sound

like she didn't believe Kindle, just that she was trying to clarify what Kindle had said, and understand it better. "Is that the whispering I'm always hearing too?"

"Yes. Yes, it is." The chair creaked ominously under Kindle's shifting weight, her wings twitching at her back. This wouldn't be the first dining room chair she'd broken with her increased density thanks to the wings, and usually she was more careful, but she couldn't seem to help it now as excitement crawled over her skin, lifting the hairs on her arms and legs. "No one has ever been able to hear them before."

"Why not?" Bracing herself on the table, Rose leaned forward too, her hazel eyes wide with curiosity, a faint flush of interest staining her cheeks. She was beautiful like this, Kindle realized, and then she also realized how close their faces had gotten in their shared excitement. She could feel Rose's quickened breath against her lips. And if she leaned forward just a little more, she could close the gap between them, and kiss the girl who had been haunting her dreams for these last couple of weeks. Except. No. she couldn't. Because at the end of this, Rose was leaving, and Kindle would be alone again.

"I don't know," Kindle said, leaning back, and clearing her throat. Sweat prickled at the base of her neck, as she fiddled with her silverware. "I just know that no one else was ever able to hear the whispers."

"Do you know why they do that?" Rose lowered herself back into her seat, but she didn't look near as embarrassed as Kindle felt. Maybe Rose hadn't noticed the sudden shift in the air between them as Kindle had, she could hope. "The books, I mean."

"Usually just for attention. Books don't like not being read, and the longer they sit on the shelf, the louder they get." Kindle picked up her napkin and draped it over her lap. "But sometimes it's because the library knows exactly what you're looking for, and they're trying to get you to it faster."

Rose was silent for a moment, her fingers fiddling with the neatly arranged silverware as she thought through what Kindle had said, then she tipped her head to the side and said, "That's useful information to have."

"I would have told you sooner, had I known you could hear them." Reaching over to lift the cloche from their food, Kindle offered Rose a hesitant smile. "Let's eat, and then I'll show you that storybook I was talking about."

Rose nodded, and the conversation lapsed into silence as they both turned their single-minded focus toward eating. Which was better, Rose told herself, even as she suddenly missed the weight of Rose's interested gaze on her skin.

"Are you aware there are pages missing?" Rose asked—the food had been finished, and their plates pushed to the side, so they could flop the book open between them—running her fingers over the torn leftovers of paper as one might a scar, or a child might a missing tooth. She was sure that Kindle knew, there seemed to be very little that went on in the library that Kindle didn't know, but she wondered if Kindle would provide some answer why.

"I am," Kindle said, not offering any further explanation, and Rose supposed she wasn't going to. Interesting.

Rose had learned over the last couple of weeks that there were any number of topics that Kindle did enjoy talking about, but her past was not one of them. She seemed intent to forget all of it if she could, and when she couldn't, she'd just growl about it until Rose moved on. Rose frowned down at the missing pages, her fingers skimming the soft edges where they'd been torn away, not cut. She wondered if any of them had survived, or if Kindle had destroyed them in her bid to forget the past.

The illustrations in the book were beautiful, clearly made by someone who cared about the story, and wanted to bring it to life. There were no names given to the three little dragons, but Rose saw how Kindle knew this book was hers, her nerves over sharing it palpable in the air between them, and she felt the gentle pull it had like gravity, drawing the book and Kindle back together. Rose tightened her fingers around the covers to keep it in front of her. Aside from the illustrations, she could see that the book had been loved. Its spine creaked every time it was opened or closed, the edges of each page were softened with age, and the corners were a little ratty. It was not badly worn, not as if it hadn't been taken care of, but it had clearly been read over and over.

"It's Chirp's favorite." Kindle shifted in her chair, making it creak underneath her.

"I can see that." Rose hummed, flipping to the next page. "Do you know what happened to your siblings afterward?"

"What?" When Rose looked up, she found Kindle watching her with a confused pout, lips pursed, like she hadn't thought of that until Rose had asked the question. Which made sense, if she was trying to distance herself from the past as much as Rose thought she was. It was almost cute. Almost.

"Well, they left you here," Rose said, keeping her tone gentle so as not to make Kindle angry again. It wouldn't solve anything if she got angry, and locked Rose back up on the ship. Not when they were finally making some progress, and Rose was beginning to realize just how fond she was of talking to the dragon. "So what happened to them? Did MOTHER round them up? Or did they die in the war? Where did they go?"

"I don't. . . I don't know." Kindle frowned.

"Did you never look?" That seemed impossible, she would have had to have. If Rose knew she had siblings, she would have looked for them. And if they had done to *her* what Kindle's had done, she would have hunted them down, and demanded answers. Maybe not revenge, she could see how getting revenge on family would be near impossible, but certainly an explanation. She'd want to know why she'd been punished, and taken advantage of, and Kindle seemed the type to not let a question go unanswered either. She didn't seem the type to sit back and take something like that quietly. If she was as much of a child as the book made her sound—Rose didn't understand much of dragons, but it looked like they matured more slowly—then perhaps that was why. Still. Once she was old enough, Rose couldn't see why Kindle hadn't gone to find her siblings, and demand they explain themselves.

Kindle shifted again, her fingers tightening around the edges of the old wooden table, and Rose decided to let the subject drop, at least for the moment. Berating Kindle wasn't going to get either of them anywhere. To head off the frustration that Rose could see beginning to simmer in Kindle's eyes, Rose turned the page in the book to one with the rose, and changed the subject.

"You said this exists?" Rose asked, tapping her finger against the paper.

"It does." Kindle's brows relaxed, her shoulders easing a little as she hunched forward. Deflating from the posturing she'd been about to do to shut Rose up. Good.

"May I see it?" There was something oddly familiar about the design. Like something she'd seen in a dream once, or in a memory from long before she'd known how to write her name. It lingered there, blurry, and indistinct, but maybe if she could see the rose in person, she'd be able to remember better. And maybe ascertain the connection between the rose and the library itself. And besides, it looked like a mechanical marvel, a combination of clockwork and magic the likes of which she'd never so much as dreamed possible. Rose's palms itched with the memory of metal tools in her grip, and the urge to take something apart just to see how it worked sat like lead in her belly.

"No." Kindle growled, reaching over to snatch the book from her, expression sharp.

Rose didn't know what she'd been expecting. Yes, they'd been making progress, and she'd learned more about Kindle in the last day or so than she had in the previous few weeks combined. But Kindle was still volatile, and unpredictable at best. And Rose never knew what would set her off. There was the instinct to fight back, to lash out in turn, but Rose swallowed it down. It wouldn't work with Kindle, it hadn't thus far. Fighting back just made Kindle angrier, and she wanted to still have access to the library come morning.

So, she nodded. "It's getting late, I should head back." Standing, Rose straightened her clothes. "Thank you for sharing your story with me. I think I understand you a bit better now."

She did. She understood Kindle a lot better now. The way Kindle snapped at being challenged. The way she didn't seem to understand social norms. The fact that she was so attached to a place that she was willing to stay even as it crumbled around her. It all made sense to Rose. She didn't know how many years it had been, but if she'd been stolen away and imprisoned before the merging of the realms? It was at least three hundred, maybe more. And all that time, Kindle had been essentially alone, with nothing but the little bot to keep her company. Maybe people had come and gone, like Alys said she had. But there likely hadn't been many, the very nature of the library saw to that.

Kindle didn't rise to follow Rose to the door, or back down the hall to the history room where the ship was waiting, but Rose hadn't expected her to. Besides, it would be better if Kindle did not know that when Rose returned, she didn't board the ship to head to bed, she rolled up her sleeves and turned to the whispering shelves.

"All right library, Kindle said you'd show me what I needed to see if I just listened," Rose said, running her fingers over the spines in reverence, feeling the subtle pull of each book on her. She didn't know where the words came from, but they sprang to her lips like she'd thought them as often as her own name. "Show me what became of Kindle's siblings."

The whispering fell away, the absence of it a buzz in Rose's ears that left her dizzy. Using her finger to rub at them, she yawned, making them pop and crackle loudly. Then there was a voice in a language she didn't understand. The volume wasn't a yell, but it sounded like one in the quiet left behind by the silenced whispers. She followed the sound, her fingers running over the spines as it got louder and louder, until she touched on a book and a shock traveled up her fingers, making the hair on her arms stand on end.

"There you are," Rose murmured appreciatively, pulling the book from the shelf. It hummed softly, vibrating against her skin like it too was pleased that she'd found it. Rose wished she'd known that trick all along, it would have saved her a lot of time, but that was all right, the history books had had some interesting things to say about MOTHER and the Uprising through the years, and she'd gotten to know more about Kindle in the interim. Which she hated to admit, was worth it.

Dropping the book onto the desk, Rose settled herself into the chair she'd been using for the last several days, and set to work. It had been a long day of researching, and the last thing she likely needed was to be reading more with the headache lingering on the edges of her peripheral awareness, but they didn't have time to waste on things like sleep. Not with the Uprising and MOTHER hunting them.

After a quick perusal of the table of contents, she turned

to chapter five. The first two pages were a spread of the draconic family tree, featuring the dragon king, his wife, and their three children. There weren't pictures, just names. The last dragon king had been an only child, but the fact that he had sired three of his own, well... that seemed to be the root of the problem with Kindle and her siblings.

Below him and his wife were the names Eloise, Eddi, and Kindle. Rose stopped, her fingers twitching beside the book with the need to snatch it up, and drag it away to Kindle so she could get some answers. Rose's heart hammered against her rib cage at the revelation. The queen and the Uprising leader were related? Not only that, but they had another sibling. A baby sister, with magic enough to power a library that was constantly moving and updating. If this was true. . . no wonder they had done their best to get rid of her.

Kindle didn't know who her siblings were, didn't remember, that's what she'd said. But this book existed in the library. And Rose knew that Kindle had read everything here, so how did she not know? Or had the library been hiding this book from Kindle? If it had been, why?

Something shuffled behind Rose, and she whipped around to see Chirp skulking in the doorway, looking as if they didn't know if they wanted to be in or out. They froze when they saw her looking, and she sighed, rubbing at her crusted eyes. How long had she been sitting there? It hadn't felt like that long, but then it was always hard to tell how much time passed in a quiet room with a book in front of her. She'd always had the ability to tune everything else out.

"What is it, Chirp?" Rose turned back, hunching over the family tree again. Kindle was going to react badly to this, and Rose wasn't sure she wanted to be the one to tell her. Maybe she could have Agnes do it, then if Kindle decided to set him on fire, there would be no real loss. She shook her head. No, it'd have to be her.

Paper rustled, and Rose looked up to find Chirp setting several sheets of folded paper in front of her. They were colored on both sides, illustrated, and Chirp tapped on them loud enough that Rose could hear the knocking of their metal pincers against the book beneath. When she raised a brow at Chirp, they just tapped again, more insistently.

"All right, all right. You're as bad as she is sometimes." Rose turned her focus to unfolding the pieces of paper, brushing them smooth with her fingers, and frowning at what she saw. They were clearly pages from Kindle's story-book, but the illustrations showed . . . *her*. Holding hands with Kindle. Leading Kindle up onto the *Duchess*. The *Duchess* flying away with them on board. She flipped the page over, and watched the entire library collapse as the *Duchess* drifted higher into the atmosphere.

"This is what she's afraid of?" Rose whispered, fingers brushing over the depiction of Kindle's life work utterly destroyed.

Chirp whistled, nodding their head.

"Well, it *would* be a tragedy," Rose reasoned. It would be. It would be a great loss, not just for Kindle, but for every person of Daiwynn to lose the books the library had spent centuries collecting. All of that history down the drain. All of that knowledge laid to waste. But . . . But . . . "But she can't stay here forever." *And Kindle deserves more than this half-life.*

A soft twittering noise of question left the little robot, and Rose sighed, rubbing a hand over her face.

"Because that's no way to live a life. Books are wonderful, trust me, I know. They can give you adventure, and action, and history, and all the things you could ever want. But you can't bury yourself in them and cut yourself off from the world entirely. Eventually, you need to go back. Books aren't just about escape, they're about learning, and if you aren't using what you learn then what's the point?"

Chirp grumbled, gears grinding against one another.

"What about the rose?" she asked, turning to another page where she could see it in the background. "What does it have to do with everything? And what about Kindle's siblings? Eloise and Eddi? They're..." Rose swallowed, hoping it would make the words come out easier, but they were still thick on her tongue, goopy, and sticky, and hard to push past her lips when they wanted to cling to her teeth. "They're the queen and the leader of the Uprising."

Chirp gave a disinterested whirr as if that meant nothing to them.

"Have you seen this book before?" Rose shoved the storybook pages away, they weren't as important as Kindle's real identity. Rose wasn't sure what it meant yet for Kindle, for the people of Daiwynn, or for their cause, but she knew it was something big. The fact that queen and the leader of the Uprising were related alone, meant the people of Daiwynn had been lied to. It meant that this whole war between the two siblings wasn't really about right or wrong, as they'd always made everyone around them believe, it was about something more sinister, and possibly more frivolous. Maybe Kindle was the only one who could change it, the only one who could finally end it all.

Leaning closer, Chirp's visual sensors swept the book, and they let out a confused, disgruntled little noise, shaking their head. So the library had been hiding it from them both. Rose wondered why it had given the book to her then. Frowning, Rose turned the illustrations from the storybook over again, looking at them from all different angles.

"Did she ever ask the library for information on her family?"

Chirp shrugged. It was being exceedingly unhelpful. Still, it would make sense that perhaps the library had never bothered to provide the book for Kindle because she'd never asked for it. It had taken a specific question from Rose to call it up, and maybe that was part of the trick of the library. Maybe it didn't give the reader certain information unless they asked for it with the correct search terms.

"This isn't all of the pages that were missing from the book. There are still two more, based on what was left in the spine. Where are the others?"

With a motion to the circle that surrounded the *Duchess*, and a long, arduous set of chirps and cheeps, Chirp attempted to explain. Rose was beginning to speak Chirp's particular vernacular, but there wasn't much of what they'd just said that had made sense to her. All it had managed to do was give her a headache.

"She used one of them to summon us," Rose guessed.

Chirp nodded, flapping their arms out in front of them in excitement at being understood.

"And the other?"

Chirp tilted their head to one side, and then the other.

"You're very helpful sometimes," Rose huffed.

A soft twitter that almost sounded like a laugh left the little bot.

"Wonderful. Well, maybe the library will spit it out like it did this book while I'm here. Should we ask it?" Rose stood from the chair, her knees popping where they'd begun to lock up from sitting for too long. The books had begun to whisper again at some point, their voices a faint hum in Rose's ears that she'd grown accustomed to as the days passed. "Has Kindle ever *asked* the library for something before?"

Grinding out a noise that Rose took to be a no, Chirp followed her to the shelf.

"Well, let's give it a go then." With her palm flat against the spines, fingertips tapping lightly against them, she thought about the storybook. "Show me the missing page."

The whispering of the books grew into a cacophony, like they were arguing with each other. Normally Rose couldn't make out the words, but this time she knew what they were saying, "Not here. Not here. Not here."

"If not here, then where? Was it destroyed?" she asked with a heaviness in her stomach that reminded her of that one time Agnes had tried to cook for them on the ship, and given them all food poisoning.

"The rose room," the book just beneath her palm whispered, as if only half wanting her to hear it.

Rose turned to Chirp, and raised a brow. "The rose room?"

Chirp's head jerked from her to the book and back, their visual circuits bright, mouth wide open to show off the little chip in their gears. They seemed almost afraid. They shook their head, but what they were denying, she wasn't sure.

"Chirp," Rose said, kneeling in front of them, her words calm and low so as not to scare the little bot more, "you need to take me there. I know you're worried about Kindle, and what will happen to her. But you need to take me to the rose room. Please. I just want to help."

Twittering, Chirp looked from her to the row of books again as if they might provide them with an answer that was different than the one that had already been given.

Rose took their pincers in her hands, and gave them a firm squeeze, before repeating, "I just want to help."

With a long-whistled exhale, the robot tipped their head forward once, and then turned to lead her from the room. They walked in silence through the halls of the library, followed by the whispering of the books, and Rose could only hope that Kindle had already gone to bed, as she was sure they were doing something Kindle wouldn't approve of. A thought that was only proven correct when they stopped in front of the bolted door, and Chirp pulled a key from somewhere to begin unlocking the multiple locks Kindle had put in place to keep them out.

The hinges screeched as they pushed through into a room devoid of light but for the soft glow of a clockwork rose set on a pedestal. Rose took a moment, tilted her head, and squinted at the strange thing in the middle of the room. It looked like a music box her father had made for her once, she realized. But the thought was pushed aside when a voice in the dark, soft and childlike, said, "here."

Shuffling carefully around the edges of the room, Rose reached a little shelf tucked away in the dark. Her eyes adjusted, and she squatted down to touch the shelf lightly. It was stuffed full of board, and picture books, a child's personal collection. Her fingers brushed the spines, and didn't stop until she found what she was looking for, a little journal that hummed under her fingers, vibrating with the urgency of an answer.

Pulling it from the shelf, Rose settled onto her backside, and turned to face the light. The handwriting on the inside was unsteady, and too large for the pages—like that of a child —in a language she didn't know. But after flipping through a few pages, she found the folded-up bit of storybook paper, and carefully uncreased it.

There on the page was a much smaller Kindle—not yet covered in scales, and leathery lizard skin, wings tucked away—tears glistening off her cheeks. She had fistfuls of paper in her hands, and appeared to be ripping pages from a book.

The storybook. Kindle's storybook.

"She did it," Rose rasped softly. "She destroyed the book, and hid the pages." She looked up at Chirp, her own eyes wide. "But why?"

Chirp shook their head.

It hadn't gone terribly, Kindle reasoned. It could have gone better, but it definitely could have gone worse, and she supposed that might be the best she could ask for given the circumstances. If only she hadn't gotten angry at Rose's continued questions. But there were things Kindle just wasn't ready to share, may *never* be ready to share. And for all Rose pretended like she cared, Kindle knew the truth of it. Rose was there for information, and once she got what she needed, she would be gone again. Leaving Kindle with the whispering books, and the twittering robot. Kindle wouldn't leave the library, and Rose wouldn't stay. That was all there was to it.

It would be nice to say that she had made a friend. To say that she had tried, and succeeded in something her siblings had clearly thought she never would. A victory. A triumph. And the thought of trusting Rose with as much as Kindle already had, it didn't leave behind the heaviness of dread. Instead, there was a lightness to Kindle's bones the likes of which she'd never experienced before.

Yes, this was definitely the beginning of something good. Something that would change everything for her. Maybe Rose would even come back to visit her, Kindle would like that. Humming happily, Kindle made her way down to the kitchens the following morning, fully prepared to make up a wonderful breakfast that would nourish the mind and the body for the day ahead.

Only. . .

Only there was a door open that shouldn't have been open in the hall. One that Kindle had locked up tight. A door that kept mysteriously opening itself. One that made sweat trickle too cold down her spine. Her ears rang with the implications, and she was running toward it before she even fully comprehended which door she was looking at. Skidding across the floor, Kindle turned into the room. She caught herself on the doorframe to keep from crashing inside, her breath coming in hard pants, and she scowled at what she found there.

Rose was sprawled out on the floor, her cheek smushed against the back of her hand which rested on top of a book it looked like she had fallen asleep reading. Chirp had propped itself up in a corner, head bent back against the wall, seemingly in power-save mode.

Growling, Kindle stomped across the floor, every step rattling the glass of the clockwork rose, even as she kept her distance from it. Not wanting to intrude upon its space. "I told you not to come here!"

"Wha-what?" Rose jerked in her sleep, not quite waking, but enough that Kindle knew she heard her. Her brown brow was wrinkled in agitation. Her cheek, where it had been smushed against her hand, was red with the imprint of her own skin.

"Did I or did I not tell you *not* to come here?" Kindle hissed, grabbing Rose by the back of her collar and hauling her to her feet.

Rose scrambled, scooping up the book she'd been looking at, and clutching it to her chest like she was afraid Kindle would take it from her. She might have, if her blood wasn't pounding in her ears, drumming so loudly she could hardly think past it.

"You were forbidden from coming here!" She hauled Rose across the open space toward the door, her head whipping only for her gaze to fall on the rose in the center of the room in fear. It looked the same as it had, but that didn't mean anything. More sweat gathered at the base of her spine, coating her palms, making it hard for Kindle to maintain her grip on the wriggling woman. "What did you do to it? Did you touch it?"

"Touch what?" Rose asked, her eyes jerking around Kindle's face as if looking for a tell, or an answer, or just some clue as to why Kindle was so furious.

"The rose!" Spittle flew as she snarled in Rose's face, her fangs bared in an obvious threat. There was no telling what damage Rose might have done to the library by tampering with the rose. Maybe it would cease to update. Maybe Kindle wouldn't be able to move it the next time she had to. Maybe the north wing would be the next to crumble. Kindle didn't want to find out. She dragged Rose behind her, still by her collar, Rose's boots scrambling on the floor trying to gain purchase and failing.

"I didn't. . ." Rose panted, her breaths loud and heaving in Kindle's ears. She should feel bad that she was making Rose sound that way. That she was likely sending the woman who not but a few minutes ago she'd been thinking of as a friend into some kind of panic attack, but Kindle couldn't find it within herself to care. Rose was no friend of hers. She never had been, and she never would be. That much was clear. All people saw when they looked at Kindle was the library. All they wanted from her was access. The ability to satiate their curiosity. How had she fooled herself into thinking things might be any different with Rose?

"You did!"

"No! I didn't." Rose got her feet under her finally, but Kindle didn't stop to let her catch her breath, and Rose was forced to keep up with Kindle's long, purposeful stride which had her skidding against the floor again. "I didn't touch the rose."

"Then why were you *there?*" Kindle threw Rose back against the wall next to the history room. The entire library seemed to shake under the force, and Rose wheezed to try to regain her breath.

"The library," Rose coughed again, a wet, choking sound that would have made Kindle offer her water, and a break maybe an hour ago, but now Kindle felt gratified hearing it. It was good to inflict pain on someone who had caused her pain. It was good to have that small bit of petty vengeance. "The library led me there. I asked it for the missing page to your storybook, and it took me there."

"You're a liar. The library doesn't lead people places." Leaning in closer, Kindle listened to the way Rose's heart pounded in her chest, to how every breath came out a labored wheeze, no doubt a hold-over from having lived in a labor camp for some time. Rose was terrified, but Kindle didn't care. She couldn't. Because Rose would bring this all down to rubble. Hadn't the book said as much? Hadn't it shown her what would come of her *friendship* with Rose? And she had foolishly thought it was trying to say something else. Thought maybe it was showing her how to make a friend. It had been a warning, not a suggestion. Stupid. She'd been so stupid.

"The whispers, and the music, remember?" Hazel eyes went wide and wild with Rose's need to make Kindle understand. "You said sometimes the whispers were because the library knew what you were looking for, and it was trying to help you find it. So I asked the library a direct question, and it took me there, to the missing page."

Kindle pulled back, her ears ringing a little as her heart fought to try to settle down now that the adrenaline of anger was being replaced with curiosity. Her legs wobbled beneath her, but she managed to stay upright, fixing Rose with a narrow-eyed glare.

"This is the missing page." Rose smoothed her fingers over the illustration, holding it so Kindle could see the little red-haired girl tearing paper from a book.

She stumbled back further. "This is a lie! A trick! You're working with *them*. You came here to drive me mad!" Kindle grabbed Rose by the front of her shirt, and dragged her into the history room.

"With whom? With your siblings? With Eloise and Eddi?" Rose pressed on, seeming unbothered by the rough treatment, her words and tone reckless as if she didn't care what happened to her. Or maybe she thought that if she got the words out fast enough, they'd save her. They wouldn't. Kindle knew better now. Knew not to trust anything that Rose said, no matter how good it sounded.

"Yes. My siblings." Eloise and Eddi, that's what their names were. Not that it mattered, in the end, it didn't change anything. Still, the names rubbed coarse and raw against her skin, sandpaper made to grind her down to nothing. Eloise and Eddi had taken advantage of her trust, and they'd left her here. And now Rose was doing the same thing, *would* do the same thing. Why did everyone who Kindle cared for *do* that?

"I'm here to stop your siblings." Rose rushed, her heels digging into the stone as Kindle dragged her across the circle toward the ship. "The queen. The Uprising. I'm here to stop them."

"My siblings have nothing to do with your queen and your Uprising." Kindle snorted, rolling her eyes, and shoving Rose through the barrier. Rose stumbled, her feet catching on one another, and she tripped to the ground, landing hard on her knees on the stone floor.

With a wince, she turned back to Kindle, her eyes begging, pleading. "You're wrong. Their names are Eddi and Eloise. Eloise is the queen. Eddi is the leader of the Uprising. Please, Kindle, you have to listen to me." Her fingers shook around the book she'd scrambled to bring with her.

Kindle should have ripped it from her hands, and burned it to cinders. But she could never bring herself to destroy any of the books in the library, that was why the illustration was a lie. She'd never do such a thing. This was her life's work. The only thing that made her *useful* and *worthy* of the air she breathed, and the magic she used. Without it, she was nothing. And she knew that. Her siblings had made that very clear to her.

"Please, Kindle. You have to listen." Rose's hand pressed into the barrier between them, the palm flat as if it were resting against glass. "Please."

"You forget, Rose," she said, leaning in closer so Rose could see the rage in her eyes. "I'm the keeper of the library, I don't *have* to do anything."

Then she spun and retreated to her rooms, ignoring the shouts from Rose that followed her down the hall.

"Well, that could have gone better," Sully said, his voice forced into a lightness Rose could tell he didn't really feel.

"You think?" Rose scrubbed at her face. She should have come back to the *Duchess* and slept, but she hadn't. Instead, she'd buried herself in the history of Kindle and her siblings. She'd learned everything she could about them, and what had happened before Kindle had come to be in the library. There were many theories whispered behind hands and in dark alleys in Daiwynn as to what had happened to the dragon king's youngest. Some said that the humans had killed her to keep the Enchanted in check, but there had been no public execution. Some said that she was languishing away somewhere in a MOTHER-run facility, acting as a battery for their portals. And others thought that her siblings had spirited her away to protect her from what was to come. What none of them guessed was that it was jealousy that had ultimately destroyed the dragon heir who likely would have saved them all.

"You didn't really think she was going to take all of that. . . *well*? Did you?" Sully had moved to lean against the side of the ship next to her, his legs stretched out in front of him as he reached over to take the book from her lap. She'd shown him everything she'd found, but history books were a summary of events. And while this one may tell of how the youngest, and heir to the throne, had disappeared, leaving her siblings to fight for the land that was left behind once the realms had merged, it showed no details of Kindle's curse or the library. Nothing Eloise or Eddi might hope to keep the general populace from knowing. If there were a written record of that, it would be in the journals, and Rose hadn't thought to check those before giving Kindle the information. Not that she'd been given much choice in the matter.

"I wasn't thinking anything." Rose tugged on a loose thread on her trousers. Not entirely true, but her thoughts had been so rushed, and scrambled, they'd done very little to help her at all. "There was no plan. I just wanted to get her to stop trying to lock me up again. Besides, I thought she'd be happy to know that her siblings were still alive out there, somewhere."

"And running Daiwynn into the ground." Sully snorted. "How come no one knew they were related?"

"It's been so long, Sully." Sighing, she leaned her head back against the side of the ship to look up at the skylights in the distance. The night was dark, and starless, cold clouds rolled in to blot out the moon. "They probably got rid of anyone who knew, and I know for sure I've never seen that version of history before."

"History is written by the victors," Agnes said, swinging from the rope ladder.

"Right. And I think they've probably bewitched the information, to erase it from the mind of anyone who might still remember. I mean, you were around with the dinosaurs weren't you, Haggy? You should know all about the queen, and the start of MOTHER." Rose turned her head to look up at him, her brows raised in mock curiosity.

Agnes huffed, his shoulders rising, and falling with it, as

he straightened his already immaculately pressed suit. Pursing his lips, he shook his head to keep from saying whatever snappy retort sat on the tip of his tongue. "You need to come see this."

"See what?" Sully had already started to rise, holding his hands out to take Rose's and pull her to her feet.

"A message from Alys." Agnes climbed the rope ladder, not waiting for any further questions.

"That doesn't sound good," Rose mumbled. She straightened her own clothes, tugging them back down into place. They were hopelessly wrinkled from where Kindle had dragged her down the hallway, but that didn't mean she had to look completely unkempt. The rope ladder burned where she'd smacked her hands against the barrier, but that didn't matter. Whatever Alys had to say was likely something that none of them would want to hear. Letting out a long breath, Rose took off her glasses to rub at where the pads had dug into her nose as they made their way down to the helm.

Everyone was there, gathered around the projector. Manu had been given the captain's seat, with Persinette perched on the arm, and Roy behind. The others had found seats or places to lean around him. One thing they all had in common was an expression of unease. Shoulders hitched up around their ears. Lips pursed. Eyes narrowed. If Rose didn't already know they were at war, she would have thought this was the proclamation of it.

"What's happened?" Rose asked, coming to stand beside Persinette, who had the good grace to offer a kind smile. Rose shifted on her feet, she didn't know how she felt about that kind of acceptance. The whole crew had been that way with her since day one. They had welcomed her and brought her on as if she were merely an extension of the crew. They'd never even asked anything of her, aside from when Agnes had roped her into this plan to find the library. But still, Rose hadn't had that, not since Tobias, and it made her insides squirm around, unsettled.

"You'll get used to it," Tobias would have said if he were alive to say it. But it had been months, and Rose still wasn't used to it. She shook herself and gave Persinette a curt nod that she hoped displayed her gratitude. It seemed to work, Persinette turned back to the screen.

"Alys said she didn't want to tell us what she'd found until we were all together," Manu said, his fingers tapping on the arms of his chair. "Alys?"

Alys offered a little wave, before she dove in. "We intercepted a missive between the Uprising and MOTHER."

"They're working together?" Persinette sat up straighter, her fingers clutching at her skirts.

Perhaps this should have surprised Rose. Betrayal should have run through her like an ache, like the sharp stab of heartbreak. But it didn't. She'd always known the Uprising wasn't what it said it was. She'd always known Eddi didn't care about their people. What was one more reminder? What was a little more proof? What was one more stab in the back? Besides, after finding out Eddi and the queen were related, it was hard to be surprised by anything else.

"They always have been." Rose tapped the book she had been reading. It wasn't even a particularly thick volume. A hundred and fifty pages or so. But those hundred and fifty pages had done more to turn Rose's world upside down than any other book she'd ever read. It was amazing the power books held. Although a person never truly appreciated that until their very belief system had been shaken to its core, as Rose's had. As the people around her were about to be. "If this book is correct, which it has no reason not to be, Eddi is the one who originally formed MOTHER."

That revelation hit exactly as hard as Rose thought it might. The room of rebels descended into chaos, everyone shouting over one another to be heard. Rose couldn't make out what anyone was saying, but she did know one thing, they were angry. They all felt they'd been lied to. Rose couldn't blame them for those feelings, they were all perfectly valid, and true. They had been sold a dream that Eddi didn't believe in. Fed a lie that they'd nearly given their lives for. Set up in a game that was rigged. Eddi and Eloise had no doubt stacked the deck against them, and now . . .

Well. Now, Rose wasn't sure that they could win. Even with this new intel. Because Eddi and Eloise had all the resources, and all the knowledge, and what did they have? Two ships, and a small militia weak with fatigue and starvation.

Not enough. Not nearly enough to win the war.

"Why would they do that?" Persinette whispered, her hands shaking where she'd clutched her skirts all the harder. Rose wanted to reach out to her. To unlock her fingers from the fabric, to stop the screaming of the seams as Persinette tugged them near to ripping. But she didn't. Because Rose wasn't the kind of person to do things like that. Not anymore. Not since . . . not anymore.

"Fear," Agnes said, tone detached, but Rose could see where his own fingertips were digging into the fabric of Sully's sleeve. Sully wouldn't be able to keep Agnes from bolting, not if he really wanted to, but Rose could understand the urge to hold onto something or someone like they were a lifeline. She could understand using them as an anchor to keep from drowning in the shifting tides. How many times had she done that with Tobias? How many times would she continue to do it with Tobias now that he was a voice in her head, and not something that could be readily taken away from her?

"Fear?" Penny repeated, her wings rustling behind her. Roy looked like he was holding both himself and Penny up at this point, Rose bit back a sigh. Maybe some of them would have been better off left in the Wastes. Where they would be safe, and would not have to face the consequences of their recent actions.

"People are easier to control when they're afraid." Agnes lifted his chin. The words, *you'd know all about that, wouldn't you*, sat on Rose's tongue heavy like lead, but she swallowed them down. Now wasn't the time to start a bickering match with Agnes, even if she was right about him. Now was the time to think about what Alys said, and what Rose had discovered, and formulate a plan. To get them out of this accursed library, and back to the Wastes where they might actually make a difference *finally*.

"What did the communication say?" Sully asked, thankfully getting them back on topic.

"They're working on a spell to locate the library. They know you're there, somehow." Alys frowned, her eyes shifting to someone behind the camera, as she rubbed at her face. "We don't know how they got that information. Hatter is talking to everyone from the camp, the *Sultana*, and the *Duchess*. My best guess is—"

"We have a spy on board our ship," Benard growled, green eyes cutting between the people around him as if he'd be able to tell who they were by just looking.

"No." Persinette's gaze narrowed, and she jerked her head in a quick motion, dismissing the notion. "It's a possibility, but I don't think so. There must be something else."

"Or maybe there's a spy in the library," Agnes said, his tone arrogant, as if he knew something the others didn't.

"In the library?" Manu leaned forward so he could turn his head in the direction Agnes's voice had come from. "Wouldn't Kindle know if there were someone who didn't belong in her library?"

"Unless Kindle *is* the—"

"She's not a spy," Rose hissed, surprising even herself.

Agnes tilted his head, his lids lowering so he could look down his nose at Rose. "And how would you know? You don't even *know* her."

"I do know her." Rose tilted her chin back when Agnes scoffed. "I trust her."

"What?" Sully blink at her, surprise lining his dark eyes.

"I trust her," Rose repeated, and was absolutely flabbergasted to find that she meant it. She did trust Kindle. She may not *like* her, or even get along with her most of the time. But she did trust her.

"This is an Uprising ship, isn't it?" Roy looked around, seemingly in the hope of alleviating the tension, his fingers moving to peel Penny's away from where she was holding onto him. "Maybe it's been bugged."

"That's our best guess." Alys's shoulders relaxed a little now that the bad news had been given, and they could focus on a way to deal with it.

"No." Manu frowned, his hand taking Persinette's to pull it to his face. Pressing her palm against his cheek, he seemed to draw courage from the touch, his pale eyes lifted. "It's Ivy Werner."

"Ivy Werner? Why does that name sound familiar?" Sully rubbed at his chin, fingernails brushing over the scruff there.

"The Uprising's mole on the ship when we were working with Persinette," Benard supplied helpfully, his face twisted into a scowl. "She was obsessed with the library."

"She was. She's the one who helped me get the hair to find this place." Manu rubbed his face, looking tired suddenly. Guilt seemed to make his posture sag even further. He was a captain, after all, it was his responsibility to look after his crew. And if he had let a mole on board then he'd failed them. Rose couldn't blame him, not really. How was he to have known the Uprising was working with

MOTHER? "I should have known better than to leave her alive after she. . ."

"After she what?" Agnes pressed.

"Cursed him." Persinette gave Manu's hand a firm squeeze. "She meant for it to hit me, but Manu got in the way. I don't know what her end goal was, but. . ."

"So she knows about this place." Rose's hands tightened around the book she was carrying, the cover cutting into her palms. It hurt, but it was a nice hurt, a familiar hurt. "And she knows that you planned to come here eventually."

"In the beginning, it was to find spells for Pers. Ivy was going to train her." Manu tilted his head back, smiling up at Persinette without a trace of bitterness, or blame. "But in the final raid, when all Hell broke loose, she fired the curse. We've yet to find out why."

"The *why* doesn't matter." Agnes growled, his teeth gritting so hard Rose could see his jaw tick. He was right. They didn't need to know *why* Ivy had done what she'd done, just that she had clearly been under other orders by Eddi from the beginning.

"Do you think Eddi knew something we don't?" Penny fidgeted. She was looking between them as if they were suddenly her own worst enemies. Like they'd turn on her at any moment.

"Persinette had too much potential, would be my guess." Agnes's nose had curled up in disgust and Rose wasn't sure if that was aimed at Persinette or Eddi. Possibly both. Not that it really mattered, Agnes seemed perpetually disgusted.

"Potential?" Persinette scoffed.

Agnes shook his head, unwilling to explain himself further, and turned back to Alys. "How long do we have?"

"Hard to say," Alys sighed, tugging the bandana from her white hair so she could ruffle it by the roots in her agitation. "Very hard to say. I don't know enough about the magic of the library, and how it works. Does it move by itself, or is Kindle the one moving it? Does it exist in a pocket dimension? There's just no way to—"

"I'll find out," Rose volunteered, cutting Alys's ramblings short.

"What? But Kindle's mad at you." Sully turned to her, dark eyes wide in his face.

"She is. But this is too important for her to ignore. They can't gain control of the library. And I still need access to the books. We may have gotten some answers on who Eloise and Eddi are, but we don't know how to bring them down yet." Rose pushed her glasses further up the bridge of her nose, ignoring the ensuing headache from lack of sleep. "And now that I have a direction to go in, and a better understanding of how the library works, things will go much faster."

"How are you going to convince her?" Agnes's brows lifted, wrinkling his forehead. "We all saw that fight, Rose. I wouldn't be surprised if she just left us here to rot."

"No." Rose shook her head. "The library is too important to her. She won't leave it as it is, and she needs our help to restore it. Just... you just let me talk to Kindle, and see if I can convince her."

Manu crossed and uncrossed his legs in his seat, then leaned forward to brace himself on his knees. "Are you sure Pers shouldn't? I mean she got Stella on our side when I thought—"

"Let me do this." Rose lifted her chin, planted her feet, and said something she never thought she'd say again. There was far too much of that going on these days, and she was really going to have to sit down and rethink her world view once all of this was over. But there would be time for that later. Hopefully. "*Trust* me to do this."

Manu opened his mouth, to make some other argument, but Persinette gave his hand a squeeze and stood.

"We trust you, Rose," she said, stepping in front of Rose and offering her a wide, toothy smile. "What can we do to help?"

"I uh..." Rose drew a blank. How long had it been since she'd let someone help her instead of the other way around? How long since she'd been anything but a dutiful little minion doing as she was told? Even with Tobias, she'd just done what he asked of her. Fix a med droid. Send out a message. Keep Agnes alive. "I'll think about it."

"Perfect." Persinette hummed, then turned to the others, and clapped to get everyone's attention. "In the meantime, the rest of us should look to see if we do in fact have any bugs on the ship."

With minimal grumbling, and fussing, the crew of the *Duchess* turned their attention to finding out if the Uprising had bugged their ship, and left Rose to think.

Chirp had grown brazen in the time it spent with the crew of the *Duchess*. Before, while it might have lectured Kindle, it had seemed to know when to quit. It had known how to tread the fine line between being annoying and being full-out infuriating. It didn't seem to care now. They had spent the last two days avoiding the history room—even though Kindle could hear the books and people calling to her every time she passed, wanting to tell her things, to turn her world upside down again—and focusing all their efforts on finishing the clear-out of the west wing. It went deeper down the hall than she'd hoped, at least to the first door which was, thankfully, a room full of outdated catalogs—not everything people printed was useful years later—which had also collapsed. The snow from the previous days had settled into the thin pages, making them soggy, and turning some of the thinner ones into not more than pulp.

Kindle had taken one look at the mess and decided to leave it. The catalogs had been fun to look at when she was bored and didn't have the energy to read, and she was sure there was someone, somewhere, who would appreciate the historical significance, but they weren't her top priority. The seed library was three doors down, and they still hadn't dug it out, even with all the help.

The disgruntled noise that came from Chirp as it kicked at some of the rubble was enough to have Kindle groaning. She didn't want to have this discussion *again*, but she wasn't being given a choice. Much of her life was about her not being given a choice in things. Her home, her companionship, what she did with her life. None of it was her choice. All of it had been pre-ordained for her. And as much as she loved the library, knowing that it hadn't been *her* choice rankled. And now she had names to go along with the people who had done that to her. Eloise. Eddi. She wasn't sure if that made it better or worse.

"No." Kindle rubbed the sweat from her brow with a kerchief, throwing another shovel full of rubble into the wheelbarrow. She was running out of places to displace the mess. If she wanted to be able to plant seeds in the spring, she couldn't cover up the ground in the garden, the etiquette room was already full, and the space around the edge of the garden was quickly beginning to encroach on useable land. She supposed she could start putting the rubble in with the catalogs. They were trash anyway. "I *couldn't* have been nicer to her."

Chirp muttered something, its pincers latched onto its little shovel to help, of that Kindle could be grateful. At least it was finally starting to understand the true danger of the situation they were in. Winter had settled in, and if she didn't get to the seed library by the time spring turned—or if the seed library was destroyed—she'd starve, because she wasn't leaving.

"Rose wasn't trying to help me." Kindle had been telling that to herself over and over the last couple of days, and she was so tired of saying it. She knew it was true, but every time she thought about the time she had spent with Rose, how close they had gotten, how Kindle had trusted her, she had to remind herself again. And the reminder opened the wound anew, leaving it stinging and gaping for the cold air of the library to cut into. "She was trying to help herself."

Rose may have found an answer for her. She might have found the names of Kindle's siblings, and where they were, but she'd only done it because in finding them she could sway Kindle to her cause. That was all Rose and the others wanted, to draw the dragon heir into their war. She was the rightful queen of Daiwynn, but she didn't want it. She doubted she ever would. Her siblings could keep the world, Kindle had the library.

"So what if my siblings are tearing the world apart?" Kindle asked when Chirp didn't continue on its tirade. The words made her stomach turn a little. The world was where books came from. People were the ones who told and wrote stories. If Eddi and Eloise were left to their own devices, there might never *be* any more books.

Already, people were writing down their stories less and less. She was sure they were still telling them, that was the nature of being alive, but they were probably spreading them by word of mouth now. It was safer that way. Then MOTHER couldn't find evidence of them. Still, Kindle missed finding an early draft for a novel tucked away in the drafting room. She missed the thrill of fresh words from a fresh voice, that left her feeling like she knew the person because no matter how original a writer tried to make a piece, they always put something of themselves in it. Their experiences, everything they'd ever read, all of that added up to create a writer, and it was fascinating to see that play out across the page.

"What does that have to do with me?" Kindle turned to

face the little robot who had been working in silence while she thought about all the things she'd miss if her siblings tore the world apart. The library would survive, it always had before, and it would now, if Kindle had anything to say about it. But there was so much of the library that wouldn't be the same. And the books. . . the books would mourn.

She remembered the first time the books had mourned. It took days to get her ears to stop ringing from all the screaming the books had done. And another month before she found out why they had been screaming. It had been the first mass burning of books by MOTHER. Kindle felt like screaming right along with them after she'd read that. The sound clawing at her throat, razor-sharp and raw, but she hadn't, not that time.

By the time the third mass burning happened, she'd been so heartbroken she'd let herself grieve with them. What was worse, looking back, was that her siblings had never had to worry about if they'd have access to those books. They never had to concern themselves with destroying the last known copy. Because they could always come to the Great Library should they need it. But anyone else, any other reader, could not. The very memory of her own screams made Kindle's ears ring, and she had to hold on more tightly to the shovel to keep her balance as her weight tipped.

Chirp made a soft noise of concern, its cold pincer reaching out to help steady her, and Kindle inhaled a deep breath in through her mouth, out through her nose. Once she was firmly on her feet again, Chirp twittered a soft question. It didn't translate exactly, but it was something like *you don't really believe that, do you?*

And no. No, she didn't. She knew that whatever her siblings did was because they had gone about unchecked. Their father had meant for her to rule, he'd left their world in Kindle's hands, and instead of fighting for it, she'd let her siblings lock her away. What. . . what *good* was she to anyone?

Cut from her strings, Kindle collapsed to the floor as her stomach gave a sick lurch. She could have stopped the burning of the books. She could have stopped Enchanted being rounded up and systematically worked to their deaths. She could have saved Rose the pain she'd gone through. But Kindle had been too scared to leave the library. Yes, her siblings had put checks in place to keep her there, but in the beginning, they weren't powerful enough to stop her, not if she'd really wanted to leave. Only . . . only she'd *let* them stop her. Even knowing what her siblings were like, she had hidden away. Let them have the power, and the world, since they were so keen to have it.

Chirp settled onto the floor beside her, cold pincers scraping her skin where it brushed her hair from her face, and tapped softly at her shoulders. A good friend, that's what Chirp had been to Kindle since it had come there, and how had she repaid it? By trapping it there with her, and never letting it go. It wasn't fair. None of this was far. Twittering quietly, Chirp pulled Kindle into a hug.

With a deep inhale, Kindle nodded to herself. It was time to stop being afraid, and help Rose in any way she could. Even if she couldn't leave the library for fear of its collapse, she could help Rose find the answers she was looking for. She could help the crew of the *Duchess* stop her siblings.

"Well. I'm going to need a peace offering, aren't I?" Kindle asked, pushing to her feet, and brushing the dust from her pants legs.

A happy little cheep left Chirp, and it rose beside her, to follow her through the halls of the library. *First things first, I had to make amends.* A simple apology wouldn't do for what Kindle had done, she knew that, so it was off to the greenhouse to see if she could dig up some fresh fruit for the crew.

Fresh fruit was always a good way to get people to forgive, or at least Kindle assumed it was, people gave fruit as gifts a lot in some of the novels she'd read.

She rounded the corner to head out into the greenhouse, eyes not yet adjusted to the dim light of the hallway. Her feet crunched on something. Frowning, Kindle bent to pick up whatever it was, and the sharp bite of glass sliced into her finger, making her hiss, and rear back. Once her eyes had adjusted, she saw it shimmering all over the hall connected to the greenhouse. Little shards of glass everywhere.

Her heart pounded so hard it seemed to be crawling up her throat, threatening to lurch free from her esophagus and out onto the ground. She swallowed hard to keep it in place and took another step into the hall to get a better look at the damage. Her heart gave another sickening lurch, followed by her stomach, and whatever meager contents she'd put into it in the last few hours—it hadn't been much, but that hardly seemed to matter at the moment. Stumbling forward, she grabbed at the wall to steady herself, and better assess the damage.

The greenhouse was destroyed. Her only source of food during the winters had collapsed in on itself just as all those rooms had, just as the entire west wing had, but worse. So much worse. Because where books could be salvaged, most of the time, the food could not be. Glass glittered through all of it like newly fallen rain, making it inedible.

Chirp's distressed whirr brought Kindle back to herself.

Her shoulder drooped at the question, hopelessness weighing them down. "It's all gone, Chirp. All of it."

With a questioning grinding of gears, Chirp crunched across the glass to get a better look. It wouldn't be able to do anything about this, neither of them could.

"I have enough food to last a month, maybe two if I stretch it. But without fresh produce. . ." Kindle shrugged. It didn't matter. None of it mattered. "Maybe the *Duchess* can leave me some of their provisions to get me through till spring. But. . . Chirp—" She swallowed, the hot saliva burning her raw throat. Had she been screaming? She felt like she'd been screaming. "It's only been a week, maybe two, since the west wing collapsed—"

Chirp interrupted with a muted series of tweets, placating, trying to minimize the damage they both knew the decay was doing to the library. Kindle didn't know what was causing it, not yet, but if they didn't stop it, if they didn't reinforce the place with magic, there would be nothing left, whether she went with the crew of the *Duchess* or not.

"No, Chirp, it wasn't just the hall." Kindle scrubbed at her face. Everything was raw, the air burning against her skin like a brand, leaving her aching and stinging all over. "I don't know how far the damage goes, but it was much more than just the hall. And it's happening so fast now. We used to go years between collapses, and we've had three this month. Chirp. . . I don't know how much longer the library will survive like this."

Hanging its head, Chirp let out a mournful little whistle, and Kindle sighed, patting its shoulder.

"It's all right. We're going to figure it out."

A questioning cheep was Chirp's response.

"No. Rose and the others need to focus on the war." Sad but true, the crew of the *Duchess* had other things to worry about. "We'll figure this out *on our own*. In the meantime, let's get the library searching for what she needs." Kindle pushed off from the wall, lifting her chin. She could make this work. She could help Rose and the others save Daiwynn, *and* find a way to save her library. It would all work out. She had this under control.

Heading to the first open room, Kindle brushed her

fingers over the spines of the books. "Help us find any information you have on Eloise and Eddi."

The library fell silent for a moment, and then it started muttering, the books shuffling around.

"When you've collected them," She tapped gratefully on the spines and turned to Chirp again, "bring them all to my private reading room. You need to make room on the shelves there. Stack our private collection along the walls, in the chairs, if you have to. Just make sure there is room for these."

With a reprimanding hiss of steam, Chirp braced its pincers on its hips.

"You let me worry about the library, Chirp." She bent to pat her hands on its shoulders, giving them an affectionate squeeze. "We'll make it through this without any help. Just as we have before. Right now, we need to end this infernal war between my siblings. Okay?"

Chirp huffed, but nodded.

"Good. Now, get to work. I have to go and apologize to Rose." Kindle brushed her fingers through her hair trying to put it back into place, but it just made it look more unkempt, she was sure. She should probably brush it, change, and clean the dust from her face. But there wasn't time for that. If the library was failing, there wasn't time for *any* of that. The *Duchess* needed the information and they needed to go before the library completely caved in on itself, and took them with it.

Walking back toward the history room, Kindle passed the open rose room. She stopped, looking in at the little device. It was beautiful, when separated from what her siblings had done to her. Something anyone would treasure, but for Kindle, it had always been sinister. She didn't know what it meant, or how it was connected to her imprisonment, but she knew it had always been there, and that was enough to terrify her.

The rose ticked, the little minute hand moving one notch closer to twelve, and Kindle flinched.

There wasn't time enough to worry about what it meant. She could deal with that after Rose had what she needed to take down Kindle's siblings.

If the library was still standing to even bother.

TWENTY-FIVE
ROSE

"You're allowed to like her," Sully said, his tone gentle.

"She has a terrible temper." Rose's fingers tapped on the pages of the history book she'd read cover to cover. She'd gotten no more from it than that Eddi and Eloise had risen from the ashes of the draconic ruling family, and built a place for themselves, burning anything and everyone that stood in their way. The historians didn't guess at their motives for why MOTHER had been created, or how it had turned into what it was today, but Rose was willing to bet that Agnes was right, it was all about fear for Eloise and Eddi. If they could keep the people of Daiwynn afraid, hateful, and turned on one another, then the people would never realize who their real enemies were, and Eloise and Eddi would stay in power. It was as simple, and as complicated, as that. It was enough to turn Rose's stomach, and she could see that those around her were feeling the exact same way.

They had given their lives to the Uprising, to helping overthrow MOTHER in the hopes of freedom.

Sacrificed. Bled. Lost.

"So does Agnes," Sully said, leaning in to knock his shoulder against her own in camaraderie the likes of which Rose was once sure she'd never experience. People didn't form attachments like the ones the crew of the *Duchess* had, in the labor camps. It was too easy for those attachments to be used against a person. Too easy for a friend one day to use their knowledge to garner favor with the guards the next. Rose had had Tobias, and that was it. Now she had. . . a whole slew of other people. She hesitated to use the word family, but somewhere in the back of her mind Tobias scoffed at her reluctance.

"She locked us all up here, and gave us no means of escape." Even Rose could hear her arguments weakening. The fact of the matter was, she *did* like Kindle. She found her engaging when Kindle actually bothered to have a conversation beyond growls, and grunts. She found her interesting. And there was a beauty in the way her draconic self lingered around the edges. It had been terrifying at first, but Rose saw more and more that it was a brand of Kindle's strength, her resolve. Kindle had been left to die, and instead she had thrived. Not many could say that. *Rose* couldn't say that. When she'd been left in the camp to die, she'd let herself wither, let herself get as close to dying as possible without actually being put in the ground. Kindle was so much stronger than she knew.

"People make mistakes." Sully felt like the only person Rose could really talk about this with. She knew the others wouldn't mind talking to her, and they may even have some good advice, but Sully's relationship with Agnes was the only one that seemed as tumultuous and care-worn as this fragile thing Rose saw growing between herself and Kindle. Sully's relationship was built on grit, and blood, and trust. He knew what it was to be afraid of the person you gave your heart to, and afraid for them as well. It wasn't a hearty and tested thing like Owen and Benard's, or a romantic, soft thing, like Persinette and Manu's, developed through long nights of sharing their *feelings*. Gross.

"Gave your heart, aye?" Tobias asked, a delighted quality to his voice that Rose didn't care for.

"So I'm just supposed to forgive her?" Rose asked, shrugging off Tobias's question. She hadn't meant it that way, and certainly not about herself and Kindle, that would be crazy talk. They'd hardly known each other more than a hand full of days. Still, there was something about Kindle that drew her in. A fire of intelligence in those dark eyes. The cut of wit on her tongue. Rose wanted to know more, see more, understand more about Kindle and all that had turned her into who she was. If Rose had thought the itch to dissect her crewmates had been strong, it was nothing compared to the frenzy going on beneath her skin when she was near Kindle.

"If she apologizes." Sully leaned forward more, stretching out his back and shoulders.

"If she doesn't?" She wasn't fool enough to think Kindle would apologize. Why should she? She'd instructed Rose not to go into that room, and Rose had ignored her. If anyone was supposed to apologize, it'd be Rose. Sure, it had been an overreaction, but this was Kindle's home, and she had opened it up to Rose, taught her its secrets, and Rose had repaid her by breaking one of only a few rules.

"Maybe *I* should apologize," Rose said, when the silence stretched on too long. Sully's smile twitched a little, as if that's where he'd been going with this all along. Sneaky.

"Maybe you should," he agreed, and stood back up, patting her on the shoulder as he turned. How had Rose wound up surrounded by all these old men who seemed intent on giving her sage, and very useful advice? *Annoying.* "And it looks like you're about to get your chance."

"What?" Rose frowned. She looked in the direction Sully had jerked his chin toward, and her lungs squeezed, making it hard to breathe. It was anxiety about the confrontation that was about to happen, she was sure of that. She'd never been particularly good at apologies, and the one she was about to make might change everything, for all of them. Or it might change nothing. Even if she did make up with Kindle, could she convince her to leave the library behind? Probably not. Either way they went, there was heartbreak. Rose would just have to choose which heartbreak she was willing to accept.

"I'm sorry," Kindle called across the space. The books had gone oddly silent a little while ago—but Rose was only just noticing, so Kindle's voice echoed in the big open room—sound waves bouncing off the side of the ship like water might have once upon a time. "I. . ." She stopped, stuffing her hands into the pockets of her overalls so deep that her arms almost disappeared up to her elbows. "There's no excuse for how I lost my temper like that, or how I treated you."

There wasn't any excuse for the physical reaction, but the emotional one, Rose could understand. And what she'd said to Sully was true, Kindle wasn't the only one who'd been in the wrong. "I'm sorry too. You asked me not to go there, and I did anyway. I could have asked first, but I didn't. That was disrespectful to you, and this place."

Kindle rocked back on her heels, her wings fluttering a little in surprise, and Rose wondered if Kindle had ever been apologized to. Likely not, considering her siblings had decided to lock her in the library instead of including her in their plans.

"You don't have to. . . You don't have to apologize." Kindle laughed a little, rubbing at her face, making a particular patch of scales look a little irritated.

"I do, and I did." Rose nodded to herself, grateful she'd taken Sully's advice, not that she'd ever tell him as much, he could be just as smug, if not more, than Agnes. "Now can you come let me out of here? I have some important stuff to tell you."

"Let you out of— Right!" Kindle shuffled forward, her head ducked far enough that Rose could see heat lingering on the back of her neck where her draconic skin hadn't settled quite yet. Blushing. Kindle was *blushing*. The barrier fell completely for the first time in days, and Rose's ears popped at the difference in pressure. "Your people can move about the library as they wish."

"What?" Rose frowned. She felt someone standing behind her, likely Sully, but he had the good grace to not add his two cents to the conversation, not yet at least. He'd likely stayed in case she needed moral support, and she tried not to think about how grateful she was for that. How much he and Agnes had become like brothers to her. "But your rules."

Kindle shook her head, but gave no further explanation as she climbed the rope ladder to meet Rose on the deck. Dark eyes flicked to Sully over Rose's shoulder, and though wrinkles appeared around her eyes—no doubt from embarrassment—Kindle just gave Sully a little wave. "Kindle."

"Sully." Sully stepped forward to hold his hand out for her to shake, but when Kindle just stared at it for an awkwardly long moment, he dropped it.

"So," Kindle turned to Rose, her hands moving to brush flyaways back from her face. She was a mess, Rose realized, likely worse for wear than Rose herself who had done little outside of studying, and tinkering with a device to track any approaching ships for the last couple of days. "What is it you have to tell me?"

Rose tried to stand up taller, to give off the commanding presence that Persinette and Agnes both seemed to have without trying, but she knew she fell short. They were born leaders, she was just an inventor. "Eddi has sent MOTHER after us."

Kindle blinked, unfazed by this news.

"One of their prisoners, Ivy Werner," Sully continued for

her, seeing how Rose faltered—maybe it was good to have backup sometimes after all— "was an Uprising agent on this ship with Manu for a time. She bragged about having a means to find the library when she was with the *Duchess*, and we think—"

"No one can find the library, no matter what they have to hunt me." Kindle laughed, shaking her head. "People have tried before, but the library is only found when it wants to be."

"She had some of your hair." Rose hedged, not wanting to contradict Kindle and make her upset again.

"This is not the first time." Kindle rolled her eyes. "The only way they'd be able to find this place is if it wanted to be found, and even—"

"Or if Eddi did something to it to make it visible." Rose sighed. Gods, she was so tired, so unbelievably tired. She really needed a nice long nap, or to sit without her glasses on for a little while. But neither of those was an option right this second.

This, at least, seemed to make Kindle take a moment and think. She still didn't seem as worried as Rose thought appropriate for the situation, but that was fine, Rose could be more than worried enough for the both of them.

"I've created something that will let us know anytime a ship gets close enough to the library that it might be able to see it," Rose continued. "That should give the library enough time to move itself."

"Move itself?" Kindle scoffed, her brows raised so high they almost disappeared into her hairline. "The library doesn't move *itself*. I move it."

"You what?"

"I use my magic to move it. I always have." Kindle lifted her shoulders up towards her ears, as if it were nothing. "But if Eddi is closing in on you, we don't have time to worry about that. We need to get your crew everything you need, and send you all off before they show up here."

Rose turned to look at Sully. She didn't know what her face was doing, but she was reasonably sure it was mirroring the confusion and horror she saw plastered across his.

"Kindle. . . what else is your magic tied to in the library?" Rose moved toward her, taking Kindle's hands in her own, and giving them a squeeze. It was the first time she'd actively reached out to another person, she realized belatedly. Not since Tobias. The crew of the *Duchess* were always touching her, not the other way around. But it didn't feel strange like she'd thought it might.

"Everything." Kindle huffed a laugh, like this wasn't the most earth-shattering thing Rose had ever heard.

"*Everything*?" Rose squeaked, her knees nearly buckling under her. No wonder! No wonder the magic was wearing thin! No wonder Kindle couldn't shift all the way between one form and the other! As the library grew, so did the strain on her magic. It didn't matter how powerful she was, no being could sustain such a large piece of magic, something would have to give. And something had. First it had been Kindle's ability to shift. Now it was the very library itself. How much longer before there was nothing left?

"Come. Come. I've had the library gather everything you need." Kindle tugged on Rose's hands. Her smile wide, beautiful, and sharp-toothed, her eyes dancing with the thought of helping someone find what they needed. Someone else. Never herself. As cruel as Kindle had seemed at first, she was never selfish, Rose realized.

"I need. . . I need a moment." Rose whispered, pulling her hands from Kindle's and ducking back below deck to hunt down Persinette with Sully hot on her tail. She was near frantic by the time she found Persinette in the helm, watching the radar, her face pinched in worry. "Persi."

"What? What's happened? Is everyone all right?" Persinette whipped around, her short legs eating up the space between them so she could meet Rose near the door. She didn't reach for Rose, but Rose could see that she wanted to. Her hands lifted halfway between them, and then stopped, only to fall at her sides where they clutched her dress like a lifeline.

"We have to take Kindle with us. She needs. . . *Can* we take Kindle with us? She can't stay here. She'll *die*."

Persinette's eyes jerked from Rose's to Sully's over her shoulder. "I don't know, Rose."

"We *have* to."

"All right. All right. You just. . . you focus on research. See what you can find about the magic that's tying her here. And if you can convince her to leave, we'll bring her along. She and Chirp. We have plenty of space. She can come with us." Persinette smiled that smile that she gave everyone, the kind, and caring one. The one Rose had thought fake for the longest time. It wasn't fake, Rose saw it now. It was. . . Persinette *cared*. What a strange thing for someone to actually care. Especially about a person that they didn't know, and who had trapped them on a ship, and forced them to do manual labor for information. Rose didn't think she'd ever understand Persinette.

"No one will mind?" Surely someone would take issue with it. "We won't. . . she's not a *weapon*."

"No. She's not," Persinette agreed readily. "And we won't treat her as such. She won't be coming with us to take down her siblings, or to fight in the war. We can take her to the Wastes, and she can live there with the other refugees if she wants until everything is settled. I promise, we won't make her do anything she doesn't want to."

"Okay." Rose swallowed around what felt like tears clogging her throat, and words that might have been 'thank you's, before she grabbed Persinette and pulled her into a tight hug. It was good, she realized, to have people who cared about her enough to care about the things she cared about. It was good to have family.

Kindle had thought Rose would be delighted to know that her access was no longer restricted, but she didn't seem to be. Rose hadn't smiled when Kindle had told her as much. She hadn't bounced on her toes the way Kindle had come to associate with a happy Rose. No. She'd looked at Kindle with all the awe and horror of someone who was perhaps truly seeing the beast for the first time. Which wasn't possible, because Kindle had shown Rose the worst of herself when they'd first met. She'd been cruel, and unyielding. She'd been. . . she'd been exactly like her siblings, she blanched.

Instead of the *thank you*, and the squeal of excitement over getting to read whatever she wanted that Kindle had been expecting, Rose had ripped herself away and fled down into the ship. The ghost of her warmth lingered on Kindle's fingertips, tingling. She'd almost reached for Rose, to pull her back, but managed to stop herself just in time. No one was looking, but Kindle didn't want anyone to see that weakness, because the truth of it was, she didn't know how she'd let Rose go. Not now. Things had been so different since she'd spent time with Rose. The halls seemed emptier, the whispers of the books louder, like everything was closing in around her. Still, she would let Rose go. Rose had a war to win, a people to free, and wrongs to right. How could Kindle ever get in the way of that? She couldn't.

"I see you two made up," a deep voice said from off to her right. Kindle turned to Agnes with a narrowed gaze. Someone *had* seen that foolish display of softness after all. Damn.

"So we did." It was strange to think that maybe Rose had talked about her with the others. Maybe she'd told them about Kindle and all that had passed between them. Or maybe they'd just made assumptions, as people seemed wont to do. Either way, the knowledge that the others knew about her sent a tremble down her spine, and under her skin. She couldn't decide if it was anxiety or pleasure, and thus decided to ignore it.

"Are you really giving us the run of the place?" Agnes tilted his head, his boots padded gently against the deck as he made his way over to her, eyes narrowed. If Kindle didn't know better, which she did, she'd say he could hear her thoughts. Unicorns were powerful creatures, but from what she'd read, they didn't have *that* ability. Unless they'd kept that bit to themselves and never allowed it to be written down.

Some Enchanted were like that. Secretive, tricky creatures. That's why the humans had been afraid of them from the first. That was also probably why MOTHER had taken to locking them up. Not that it was the Enchanteds fault. It was no one's business what kind of power they could wield but their own.

"I am." Kindle's eyes flicked back to where Rose had disappeared, wondering what she'd run off to do. Maybe she'd never come back. Maybe Kindle had well and truly scared her away. Maybe this was all finally over. A leaden weight settled into her stomach. She might have already lost Rose. Before she was ready to give her up. What would she do if that were the case? How would she fix this? How would she—

"Without us helping you repair the library?" Agnes asked, bringing her spiraling thoughts to an abrupt halt.

The question landed like a blow, the implications so heavy her knees went weak under them. Agnes *knew*. No one else seemed to, or at least Kindle hoped they didn't, but the unicorn knew. He understood the sacrifice she was making, and everything it would cost her to make it. Kindle swallowed hard around something threatening to crawl up her throat, maybe her stomach, or her heart, and forced her posture into something more relaxed. "You're running out of time, and my siblings need to be stopped."

"How do we know you're not working with them?" Agnes's eyes narrowed further, their color brightening to something luminescent as he called on his magic. A clear threat that Kindle wasn't sure if it was in defense of himself, his crew, or Rose. Maybe all of the above. "How do we know you didn't summon us here to trap us so that we couldn't stop them?"

"Would I be giving you the books if I had?" Kindle raised a brow, lifting her chin.

"Maybe the books are just a way to keep us busy while MOTHER and the Uprising close in. A lure as the noose draws tight around our necks."

He made a valid point. But she didn't like the scrutiny or the accusation that she was using Rose's curiosity to keep them trapped there for some reason. That she was working with her siblings in any way shape or form. "I wouldn't do that."

"You wouldn't do that, or you wouldn't do that to *Rose*?" Agnes lifted one dark brow, his lips twitching into something like a smirk. He thought he'd caught her, doing what, Kindle wasn't sure, but she could tell that this had all been some elaborate way to examine her and find her wanting. Manipulative bastard. Maybe Kindle should have taken the time to learn more about Rose's companions. But it was a little late now.

Kindle's shoulders stiffened. "Both things can be true."

"I suppose they can." His gaze flicked over her, taking in Kindle as a whole. "I'm Agnes."

"I see." She wondered if that meant she'd passed his test or not, but didn't ask. It'd probably be better not to know, honestly. "Is there something you want to research specifically in the library?" Those eyes were too clever, too perceptive, and Kindle would do anything to get them pointed elsewhere. Preferably somewhere that Agnes wouldn't be able to notice the softness under her armored skin. He seemed the type to take a blade to those soft spots just to see how much they'd bleed.

"Do you have any blueprints?"

"We do. I can have Chirp show you the room once Rose gets back." Kindle wished Rose would hurry up about it if only so she could escape the heaviness of Agnes's gaze. How was it that he and Rose were even friends? They seemed nothing alike.

"Much appreciated." Agnes bowed his head, then turned to saunter through a door on the other side of the ship that seemed to lead into a long narrow hallway made of other doors. Kindle tilted her head, watching him go, she wondered what Chirp would think of that interaction. If the little robot would have anything to say about everything that had happened in the last half an hour. But she'd left it behind in the hopes it would be able to finish with the reading room before Rose needed it. It would have been nice, still, to have a friend at her side for support, even if Chirp wasn't very good at that whole . . . supportive thing.

"Are you ready?" Rose asked, her voice jerking Kindle

from her reverie. Kindle whipped around to find Rose wild-eyed, a little flushed, and achingly lovely.

"What was that about?" Kindle's palms itched to reach out to Rose again, to thread their fingers together, and show that the physical affection, however limited it had been, had been welcome. But she didn't. Because Rose was carefully keeping space between them, her shoulders rigid, just out of reach. Something had happened. Something had changed. Kindle didn't like it, but what was done was done. That might make things easier, she thought, to say goodbye and send Rose on her way knowing that there was nothing between them now that Rose had seen how truly monstrous Kindle was.

"Nothing. I just wanted to check some things with the captain." Rose smiled, but the expression didn't reach her eyes.

"Come," Kindle said with a nod toward the rope ladder. "I've had the library pull everything you'll need, and deposit it in my reading room. Chirp is there organizing everything."

"Your reading room?"

"Yes." She hadn't thought about the implications of Rose in her private space. Of how telling that reading room was. But it was too late now, they were already on their way there, and all Kindle could hope was that Chirp had at least made it look presentable. Although, Rose had seen her bedroom, and not even blinked, and that was far messier, but less personal to some degree. For the bedroom was simply where she slept. Things ended up there, but they weren't often things she put much thought into, hence the mess. Rose would likely be too distracted by her research to look at the books that Kindle and Chirp had gathered for themselves anyway, Kindle reasoned.

Chirp was waiting for them outside of the reading room, its pincers wringing in front of its chest, making a grinding sound that left Kindle's ears ringing. It looked up at them when they stepped into the light of the lamp near the door, visual sensors brightening for a moment. Its head jerked from Rose to Kindle, and then behind them, like it couldn't decide where to look, and was afraid of meeting anyone's gaze for too long.

Kindle ushered Rose inside, shutting the door behind her, and whirled on Chirp for an explanation.

"What did you do? Why do you look so guilty?" She hissed, grabbing the little robot by the shoulders and tugging it down the hall where it would be difficult for Rose to over-hear them without actively pressing her ear to the door.

The twittering started immediately, Chirp's sounds layering over each other in a dizzying way that made it hard for even Kindle who had known the robot for years to know what it was trying to say to her. Its arms swung wildly in either panic or exasperation, and then it produced a book from somewhere. It was a familiar looking, ratty journal.

"Where did you get this?" She snatched it away, opening the cover to find *Eloise* scrawled across the first page in a flourished handwriting. *My sister, the queen*, she had to remind herself. The book left her fingers tingling with latent magic, a soft buzz against the roughened tips, and Kindle realized where she'd seen it before.

Chirp whistled, rocking back on its heels dangerously as if it would tip over backward with just a breeze. It wasn't going to answer, but it didn't need to, because Kindle knew where the library had found this book. It was the same place where the library might find an entire collection of books that Kindle had hoarded away at one time or another. In piles upon piles that a younger Kindle had clearly hoped would hide whatever lay within, tucked under her bed, or in the cluttered corner of her room. Somewhere that she would know they were safe, but she'd never have to look at them. Over the years, she'd forgotten why she'd collected them to begin with, but she hadn't forgotten that she was protecting them, hiding them.

"Answer me, Chirp. Where did you get this?" The book hummed louder under her tightened grip, threatening. How many more like it had been tucked away in her room? Hidden there for centuries where no guest of the library, and not even she would find it unless the library itself pulled them out. How many more had the library seen fit to gather and give to Rose? Kindle's stomach gave a sick lurch. It was too late now, much too late, for her to put that particular clown back in the box.

Looking down as its metal feet scuffed against the stone floor, Chirp's shoulders heaved.

"I'm not. . . I'm not angry with you," Kindle said, scrubbing at her face. She didn't know who she was angry with, not really. She didn't really even know why she *was* angry. That had been the deal, she'd given Rose access to anything and everything she needed. Even if that meant she needed the things Kindle herself had hoped to never see again. "Just. . ." she let out a breath, her shoulders hunching forward, "just take it in to Rose. She'll probably need it."

Chirp whirred a question, pincers firmly held in front of it.

"No. I am not going to look in it." Kindle wiggled the book in front of it, the cover closed over the pages so she didn't have to see them. Eloise's journal. She could find out so many things about her oldest sibling. Maybe even learn why Eloise and Eddi had done what they'd done to her all those years ago. Maybe even how to escape. But it wouldn't change the past, would it? Nothing would. Ultimately her siblings had loved the idea of power more than they loved her, and in the end, that's all she needed to know about them.

Chirp cheeped, its head tilted in question.

"Because I don't want to know any more about them than

I already do. I just want to go back to taking care of the library and not thinking about it." Which, Kindle was sure, was exactly what she'd been thinking all those years ago when she'd ripped the pages from the storybook, and hidden away this journal. It would be better not to know. She'd been right then, knowing hurt too much. It settled like an ache in her bones, making every joint stiff. It hurt too much and it didn't change *anything*. "Go on Chirp, see to it that Rose has everything she needs. I'm going to. . . I don't know. Maybe try to dig out the greenhouse."

Chirp took the journal, still watching her with a tilted head and visual sensors turned up to full brightness. When she didn't pull the journal back to herself, it took it, and turned to shuffle back down the hallway.

Good. Better that Chirp help Rose and the others get what they needed and leave as quickly as possible. Before it was too late and they succumbed to the destruction of the place just as she planned to.

A captain always went down with their ship. Why shouldn't a keeper go down with their library?

TWENTY-SEVEN
ROSE

Rose had never been the type of person to convince people of things. She wasn't positive, and sunny, like Persinette was, seeing the good in the world around her. Nor was she as pragmatic as Agnes, seeing potential in every person—maybe not always good potential, but potential nonetheless—and how best he could use that potential for his own gain. She didn't have a bright smile like Sully, nor the charm Manu seemed to ooze. Rose was just. . . *Rose*. Just someone who didn't know much about people.

She preferred machines, for that very reason.

If a machine didn't act the way she wanted it to, there was a fix, sometimes that fix was to give it a good swift kick, but it was a fix ultimately that was diagnosable, and easy enough to put into place provided you had the right parts. People didn't have quick and easy fixes like that. They had too many moving parts and things like feelings that made no logical sense whatsoever. People were messy.

Rose was in over her head with Persinette's current plan, and she knew it, but she was the only one close enough to Kindle to really enact it.

Convince Kindle to come with them.

How Rose was supposed to do that, she didn't know. If the library crumbling around them and nearly crushing

Kindle wasn't enough to send her running onto the *Duchess* without looking back, Rose didn't know what would.

So, over the next week, she focused on what she *did* understand, research. She gathered as much as she could on Eloise and Eddi, as did the others. Agnes had pulled blueprints from every building Eddi might be using as a hideout, and the palace. Sully had focused his attention on the numbers they might face, and how best to circumvent them. Penny and Roy had set up a constant watch on Rose's radar to ensure no ships got close to the library without them knowing. Owen and Benard were in constant communication with Stella and Alys, telling them everything they found. And Persinette and Manu had settled into the books of magic to try to find a way to counteract the curse Ivy had cast on Manu.

While they'd been doing all that, Rose had been avoiding doing the one thing she knew she absolutely needed to, convincing Kindle to leave with them. She'd learned a fair bit about Eloise and Eddi, all their ticks, how they'd risen to power, how they built their empire on fear and hatred. But she hadn't been able to say one word to Kindle regarding her departure from the library. It was a failing, Rose recognized it as such, but she didn't know what to do, or say. She just . . . *didn't*. And that was her own fault. She should have practiced more. She should have learned from Tobias's excellent example. She should have not kept herself at such a distance from the others.

Regrets wouldn't change anything, but they weighed on her, making her movements and thoughts sluggish. How much time had she wasted?

"Jabberwocks are magnificent creatures," Rose said apropos of nothing, because she still hadn't thought of anything to say, and she couldn't take another evening where she came back to Persinette and reported that she had failed without at least giving it a try. Clearing her throat, Rose looked up from the book she'd been skimming to find Kindle looking back at her with wide eyes. "Terrifying, but magnificent."

"What?" Kindle asked, her brow creasing in confusion.

It wasn't exactly what Rose needed, and it didn't make this conversation any easier to have, but it was an opening, and that was more than Rose had found in the last week. She was going to take it. *Here goes nothing.* "I'm just saying, some things are like that, they're terrifying, but they're worth it to see. I was scared, and it was the ugliest thing I think I've ever laid eyes on, but I was glad I'd seen it." Rose tapped her fingers on the cover of her book, shifting her weight a little where she sat. "I spent. . . I spent a *while* in the labor camp, and I remember waking up one day, and thinking that that was it. That I'd spend the rest of my life there. And there was a strange *safety* in that certainty.

"I wasn't safe, obviously, but I *felt* safe." That didn't need saying but the words dribbled out of Rose in a torrent. Now that she'd started, she was finding it hard to stop. "It was a comfort to know that every day would be the same from then on. To know that I'd wake up, and go to sleep in the same place."

"Why are you telling me this?" Kindle frowned, her nose wrinkling enough to make one of the scales on the bridge of it stick up oddly. *Cute.*

"Because I want you to know that I understand why you're so resistant to leaving." Rose swallowed around a dry tongue that stuck to the roof of her mouth. She wished she had some water for this conversation, or maybe that Kindle would stop looking at her like she had all the answers when really she didn't have *any.* "Because when Agnes and Sully came to the camp, I wasn't sure I wanted to go with them either. A way out seemed too good to be true. I didn't trust it. But I'm glad I left that place."

"Because you got to see a jabberwock?" Brows raising, Kindle gave Rose a doubtful look. Rose could understand that, she'd be doubtful too. But it was true. It was all so true.

"Because I got see a jabberwock." Rose huffed a disbelieving laugh. It was hard to fathom, even for the person who had lived it. But it was also so, *so*, achingly simple. "And I got to see a train that had been converted into a caravan for people to live in. And a library that keeps itself updated through magic. And any number of other things I haven't actually gotten to see yet, but I'll have the chance to now because I let Agnes and Sully drag me out of a place I had considered safe."

"Hmm. . ." Kindle hummed, her head bending down over the book she'd been reading. Rose wasn't sure what that meant. Was she thinking over what Rose had said to her? Had she merely brushed it off? There was no way to really tell.

Rose opened her mouth to ask. She hated to press, but she needed to know if she'd at least made progress in this fight. Things would come to a head soon, so *very* soon, and she needed to be ready. If nothing else, she just needed to make sure they had an escape plan for when—

The doors to Kindle's private reading room opened with a clatter, slamming against the walls to either side. In the tall block of light from the hall stood a small lavender-haired woman, Pesinette's shoulders heaving with hard pants.

"They're here, Rose." Persinette rushed across the space to start gathering up the materials Rose had spread around her.

"Who's here?" Kindle didn't move from her spot, but Rose was already helping to stack her books into something resembling orderly.

"MOTHER," Persinette let the word out on a hard pant,

then she turned to meet Rose's gaze, her wide green eyes wild with fear. She shook over the word, "Gaston."

Rose froze, her fingers trembling where they'd been reaching for one of the journals she'd found useful. "No." Her heart pounded against her chest, making her ribs ache. "No. No. No. *No.*"

Kindle's gaze had jerked to her, her eyes narrowing as if assessing the fear on Rose's face. Rose wasn't sure what her face was doing, but she felt the blood drain away from her extremities, making the tips of her fingers go numb and tingly.

She wasn't afraid of Gaston. She *wasn't.* But she knew the cruelty he was capable of better than anyone else except maybe Agnes. And the thought of being faced with the man who had sent her to the camps out of jealousy, and wounded pride, it made her stomach roll with nausea. When Alys had announced that he'd be the head of the MOTHER contingent sent to capture the crew of the *Duchess*, she'd wanted to fight back. She'd seen it as her chance to finally—*finally*—get revenge for what Gaston had done to her. For locking her up in that place, and throwing away the key. She hadn't thought of what that vengeance would look like, but she knew that she was going to get it.

But now, when faced with it, Rose faltered. Letting out a breath, she stiffened her shoulders, and closed her eyes for a moment before opening them again, and looking at Kindle. "You need to move the library."

Kindle pursed her lips, and Rose wondered what she might be thinking. There was something going on behind her gaze that she wasn't going to put into words, which worried Rose. What could she be planning?

With a hard exhale that seemed to make Kindle look so much older than she ever had, she lifted her chin. "Go to the ship, I'll deal with everything else."

"To the ship?" Rose's brows knitted together, the stack of books in her arm wobbling a little. Persinette's head whipped between them, following the expressions on their faces like some kind of sporting event.

Kindle didn't say anything else, she just finished helping them gather the books Rose had been looking over, and pushed them toward the door. They were halfway down the hall before Rose finally got her feet under her enough to slow them down.

"What are you doing Kindle?" Rose turned, the books in her arms wobbling a little, but Kindle wouldn't let her slow down. She kept pushing, even when Rose's feet stopped moving, making her boots skid across the stone floor until they were right in front of the history room. "Kindle," Rose rebalanced the books on her hip so she could take Kindle's wrist, giving it a squeeze to get her attention, "what are you doing?"

"I'm going to move the library." Kindle wasn't looking at Rose, her gaze was somewhere over Rose's shoulder, maybe watching the ship. It sounded like the truth, Kindle's tone harried but sincere. "How long do we have?"

"An hour, at the most." Persinette moved to the side of the ship and began climbing the rope ladder one-handed, the books she'd taken from Rose precariously balanced against her stomach. "I've already got Manu and Roy figuring out our best mode of defense, and Penny went to get Agnes and Sully."

Kindle jerked her chin toward the deck, giving Rose another hard shove toward the rope ladder. "You go up, and get settled. I'll handle everything else."

"Why can't I stay with you?" Rose wasn't sure why it mattered, why she even wanted to, but something felt *off* about this. Kindle's words settled over her like an ill-fitting sweater—itchy, wrong. They rang like a lie through the air.

Rose wanted to call her on them, to tell her that she knew what Kindle was doing. But she didn't, not really. She just knew that Kindle wasn't telling the truth. Was it that Kindle was planning to turn them over to MOTHER and wanted them all in one place for when the Collection team came? Then why allow them to bring the books? That didn't seem to fit. There was something else, something Rose was missing. Something it seemed like Kindle had communicated to Persinette without Rose ever having noticed.

How long had they been planning this? How long had they left Rose out of the loop? She was hovering over a precipice, just waiting for the bottom to drop out from under her, and she didn't care for it, not one bit.

"Because it'll be easier for me to deal with the ship as an object, instead of worrying about a bunch of moving people. Trust me, this is better." Kindle handed the books Rose had in her arms up to Persinette when she climbed back down to take them, and then took Rose's hands tightly in her own. Rose had been with Kindle all day, she'd watched her movements, and looked into her face, but as they stood under the bright sunshine filtering in from the skylights above, Rose noticed for the first time the dark circles under Kindle's eyes. Her cheeks looked hollowed out, and haggard. And there were bigger patches of red, leathery skin than ever before. One of Kindle's sharpened eyeteeth had grown so long it was hanging out over her bottom lip. More dragon than woman at this point. If she didn't leave now, cut herself off from the library, there might be nothing left of the woman to save. "Trust me."

"Okay." Rose's hands shook where Kindle's talons dug a little into her fingers. She trusted her. She didn't know why, or how. But she did. She had since before the moment Agnes had posited the idea that Kindle might be a spy. Strange how those things could sneak up on a person. "Okay. I'll come down when this is all over."

Kindle smiled, baring sharp teeth, but it didn't crinkle her eyes. *A false flag of surrender.* Was Kindle giving up? "Of course you will. I'm sure you'll be bothering me again in no time."

"I will. I definitely will." Why did this feel like a goodbye? Why was Kindle looking at her with a softness that Rose didn't think she'd ever seen before? What did it all mean? Rose wished she had more time to examine the situation, to step outside of herself and see what was happening from someone else's perspective. She might be able to make more sense of it then. But Kindle wasn't giving her that chance, because she'd dropped Rose's hands with one last squeeze and shoved her toward the rope ladder again.

"Go on, we don't have much time."

Rose looked over Kindle's shoulder to see Sully and Agnes running up with Roy, rolled-up blueprints tucked under their arms. They were acting like they weren't—

Like they weren't coming back! They were acting like they weren't coming back! Rose struggled, but Sully had already grabbed her and hauled her over his shoulder as he ascended the rope ladder, not much more than a sack of potatoes.

"Are you sure you won't come with us?" Sully asked, his brow scrunched up in concern.

"My place is here, in the library," Kindle said, a soft, sad smile on her face. Rose jerked her chin, trying to meet Kindle's eyes even as Sully climbed the ladder, but Kindle wouldn't look at her now, and Rose couldn't find her voice. It had been lodged somewhere in her chest, and she couldn't get it out past whatever was blocking it. She had words, so many words, but they wouldn't *come out.* "I'll send you back to the Wastes. Hopefully you'll be safe there for the time being."

Sully nodded quickly, and finished climbing the ladder. He didn't put Rose down though, instead he waited at the rail of the boat, keeping his back away from Kindle, making it so Rose couldn't watch her as she did whatever magic she was doing.

"Put me down, you brute!" Rose kicked him, struggled against him, found her words finally as she banged her fists on his back. But Sully was tall, and broad, and the months since the labor camp had been kind to him. He'd bounced back to the weight and strength he'd had before, whereas Rose had spent years there, and was recovering more slowly from the near starved state she'd spent so many of her days in. "Sully! Put me down!"

There was a sucking sound, like a vacuum tube getting caught on a sock, and then the world went dark, blinking out of existence, before it was bright again, sound cascading into Rose's ears so quickly that it hurt. She blinked hard against the brightness as Sully set her on her feet, and she got a good view of Alys's caravan in the Wastes. Exactly where they'd started.

"NO!" Rose spun on Sully, shoving him hard in his chest. "NO! We could have helped her! We could have brought her with us! We should have! Why didn't we?! Why did we leave her *behind*?!" And then she was sobbing, wailing, her vision blurred with hot tears, and her knees weak from the feeling of anguish that had washed over her.

Why hadn't they brought Kindle with them?

Why hadn't she worked harder to convince Kindle to come?

Why? Why? *Why?*

TWENTY-EIGHT
KINDLE

The betrayal that widened Rose's eyes just made Kindle more determined. She'd made the *right* choice. She'd known it had been the right choice days ago when Rose had first told her about MOTHER and the Uprising coming for them.

The memory of that choice came back to her now as the consequences of it played out right before her eyes.

It had been three days ago when she'd taken her fate into her own hands for the first time in centuries.

Failure had made sweat gather at the base of her spine. There had been fear in Rose's eyes when she said that MOTHER was coming for them, and although Kindle didn't know everything that had happened to Rose in that camp, or even before when she had worked for MOTHER, she knew that she couldn't see Rose go back there, not if she could help it. She needed to get ahead of this. Cut them off before they could reach the library.

If she moved the library now, it would take MOTHER and the Uprising time to pin down its location again.

She left Rose in her private reading room, her feet moved almost soundlessly through the halls of the library, her home hummed with the magic it knew she'd need to do what was necessary. The rose room was closed off, still, although Rose hadn't tried to enter it since that last time, and the clockwork sculpture at the center seemed to glow brighter as Kindle approached. The glass was cold under her fingers, the books around her taking a deep inhale and holding their breath, waiting to see what would happen.

Lifting the dome off of the pedestal, she sat it on the floor at her feet with a soft, hollow sound. Silence fell, not even the hint of a whisper from the books of the library, and then Kindle's fingers brushed the thorned stem, and the air was sucked out of her lungs. She fought to hold on, to take a deep breath, but it didn't help. Still, she tightened her hold on the rose, the metal thorns cutting into her palms to leave behind deep gouges in her skin.

The metal grew hot under her hands, burning into the already aching nerve endings. Closing her eyes against the pain, Kindle thought of a dot on the map, someplace no one would never find the library again. Out off the coast, an island left empty by the wars, and the collapsing realms. Uninhabitable if not for the pocket dimension where the library was housed. It would serve as a good enough tether for the time being until the crew could go back to the Wastes.

Her focus narrowed to a point, *that* point. It would be safe. Kindle was sure of it. If she could just *get* them there. Only the longer she focused, the darker the edges of her awareness became, and not in the way she was used to when she moved the library. No. This darkness wasn't just around the corners, sitting idle, it was closing in. And it pulsed painfully. Scattering Kindle's thoughts, making it harder and harder to focus. Things went fuzzy for a moment, and she lost the point she'd been hoping to get to. It slipped from her mind like water through her fingers.

With a grunt, she tried to refocus the magic, drawing up the image of the map again, but no sooner had she managed to pin it down than it slipped away again. She struggled, over and over, pulling out the mental image only for it to be lost.

The thorns seemed to be growing, digging deeper into her skin. Blood ran hot, and slick down her wrists, taking with it what little strength she had clinging to her bones. She swayed on her feet, her grip slackening on the rose, hearing the glass dome beside her clatter against the stones and roll away, the sound a death knell for what Kindle was trying to do. The rose slipped from her fingers, and Kindle stumbled back, falling onto her backside. The fall jarred her back, and she hissed, rubbing at her spine, before lowering herself to the stone to stare up at the skylights overhead until the spots cleared from her vision.

Smacking her hands against the stone, Kindle reached out with what little magic lingered under her skin, trying to feel where the library was. A vision of a wide-open field over-looking Maximus flashed through her mind, and she growled.

The library hadn't moved an inch. *Blast.*

Persinette. She needed to speak to Persinette.

Kindle's arms screamed as she pushed herself up, the muscles aching from exhaustion and strain. When she looked down at her hands in her lap, she found them free of the wounds that the rose had inflicted, though blood clung to her forearms and wrists, leaving traces of her failure. She'd have to scrub them away before she went to see Persinette.

PERSINETTE HAD BEEN in the history room, humming to herself, her long, pale fingers dancing over the spines of the books. Kindle didn't know what she was looking for, but she didn't suppose it mattered, she'd given them freedom and the crew was more than happy to take advantage of it. *It's good they do,* she reminded herself. They'd find everything they needed to bring down Eloise and Eddi, and Kindle could finally rest knowing that someone had gotten vengeance on them for her.

"Is there something you needed, Kindle?" Persinette asked, her head tilted to one side to brush short lavender hair away from her eyes. She was a pretty, little thing, petite, and unassuming. But Kindle had learned that being small didn't mean anything. Persinette, for all she didn't look like much on the outside, was their leader, from what Kindle had ascertained. And that meant that she was the only one who could help Kindle with this. Possibly, she'd be the only one to really understand it. At least, Kindle hoped she would.

"When MOTHER comes, I need you to take Rose, and run." Kindle's fingers were tight in her pockets, her gaze focused on a single freckle to the right of Persinette's nose. It wasn't making eye contact, that would be too painful for what she was asking Persinette to do, but it was close enough. If Persinette noticed, she didn't say anything, she just let Kindle look where she wanted.

"You're not coming with us," a statement of fact, but not a surprised one. Kindle wondered what other things Persinette had realized before the rest of the crew did. She seemed the type of person who simply knew people. The type that could look at someone and take their measure in a few seconds. Not in a bad way. Kindle didn't feel judged by her, she felt *seen.* In some ways, that was worse. Kindle didn't want to be seen. She wanted to hide away from the world, and let the library take her wherever it was going when it disappeared entirely. That's what all this was about.

"No. I'm not coming with you." There were a lot of reasons why she wouldn't, *couldn't.* None of them would make any sense to anyone else. Nor would Rose agree with them, Kindle knew that. But she couldn't leave the library to crumble in on itself without trying to fight it. What would happen to the books? The world would be darker for all of that lost knowledge. No, if Kindle could keep the library going by sheer stubbornness, she would. Leaving with the *Duchess*, however, would ensure that didn't happen, and she wasn't willing to take that chance—may *never* be willing to take that chance.

"She's going to be upset," Persinette said, turning back to the books and pulling down one seemingly at random. She flipped through the pages, her thumb pressed hard into the edges. "She'll fight us."

"That's why I'm speaking to *you*." There didn't seem to be any other option, not that Kindle had given herself much room for debate. She'd seen the storybook, she knew what would become of the library should she leave. That wasn't something she could allow to happen. And she liked to think that if Rose really thought about, if she weren't emotionally invested—not that she was—she'd see that this was the only way this could ever have turned out. Chirp was going to blow a gasket.

Persinette hummed thoughtfully, replacing the book where she'd found it, and turned back to Kindle. She didn't look happy about what Kindle was proposing, but she didn't look like she was going to stop Kindle either. *Good.* "I've spoken to Rose. She has a theory that your magic is the only thing sustaining this place, and if we leave you here, you'll die. I think you know that's true. Maybe you always have. And I think you've decided that's what's best for everyone." Persinette's green eyes had gone sharp, disappointed. The muscle in her pale jaw was working like she had more to say, an argument sitting heavy on her tongue that she was biting back.

"I don't know, not for certain," Kindle said, with a little

shrug. She wasn't sure, there was no way to be sure. But she did know that if she couldn't get to the seed library, that her death was a very real possibility. Maybe not right away, but eventually. She wasn't going to tell anyone that, least of all Persinette who saw too much.

Persinette's gaze narrowed further on Kindle, making her want to squirm, but Kindle refused to shift under it. Whatever Persinette saw, she'd see it no matter what Kindle did, no point in trying to hide it. After a moment of careful scrutiny she said, "We'll leave you with some rations."

"You'll need them in the Wastes." Kindle shook her head, frowning. Extra rations would help, yes, but the crew needed them more. The people of the Wastes needed them more. And they may not do her much good, not if the library simply collapsed. Kindle had lived this long without help, she'd find a way to continue doing so. "Let me worry about how I'll handle things here. You focus on your crew."

"We'll leave you with some rations," Persinette repeated, and then she turned back to the shelf, effectively dismissing Kindle from the conversation.

There was little point in arguing after that, so Kindle hadn't bothered, she'd left Persinette to whatever it was she was doing.

Now, days later, Kindle couldn't help but wonder what would have happened if she'd made a different choice. Not that it mattered. There was no taking something like this back once it was done. She'd learned that a long time ago.

She panted, biting hard into cheek to ignore the pain in her hands as the world swam around her. Moving a ship was easier than moving the library, it took less magic, to be sure, and as it was not something built upon what should have been unmovable ground, it didn't take as much finagling. But the days had not been kind to Kindle's magic, and the library didn't seem to care for her displacing something that was inside of it. Like it had lain claim to the *Duchess* and didn't want to give her and her crew up.

The thorns on the rose bit into her hands. They had grown larger, more jagged, as they sapped from her the magic the rose required to move something the library considered its own. Kindle didn't dare look down at the damage they had done, worried she'd find the thorns poking out of the backs of her hands. Her ears rang, and the world around her shook, shivering like the earthquakes she'd read about a few years ago.

Then everything stopped.

The shaking. The shivering. The ringing in her ears, and strange pulling sensation of the rose sucking her dry, and she knew they were gone. With trembling knees, Kindle pulled back from the rose, took a deep breath to keep down the bile that had begun to burn at the back of her throat, and turned to go to the history room. Every step sent a tendril of pain up her legs into her spine. The weakness in her muscles made all movement a struggle.

"I wish Chirp were here." But it wasn't. Kindle had sent the little robot along with the others, because there was nothing left for it to do at the library other than watch Kindle fade into nothingness as her magic was drained away by her home. She couldn't bear the thought of her only friend having to witness that. Plus, the *Duchess* could always use the extra help.

Maybe that should have been sign enough to give it up, to let it collapse in on itself, and disappear, to succumb to the natural progression of time and history, but she couldn't. She wanted to, on some level, but every time she thought to do just that, her stomach would twist, and her palms would sweat, and Kindle would realize that there was nowhere else in this world that she belonged. In spite of Rose's magnificent and terrifying jabberwock.

That had almost been enough. Rose's speech about seeing things that were scary but wonderful, it had *almost* convinced Kindle to go with them. To leave the library behind, and let herself see things instead of experiencing them only through books. But then Persinette had said the name Gaston, and Kindle had seen all the color drain from Rose's face, and the decision had been made.

She wouldn't let Gaston catch Rose. Not so long as she could stop it.

Kindle's knees finally gave way when she reached the history room. In the open doorway, looking across the vast emptiness and seeing only shelves, and books, and a big empty space where the room hadn't returned to normal, Kindle crumpled to the ground. They were gone. Everyone was gone. It was just her, and the books now.

Something hitched in Kindle's chest, and she only recognized it as a sob because of the hot trail of tears slipping down her cheeks as she leaned forward to press her forehead to the ground.

Gone.

They were all. . . gone.

And she was *alone*.

Confusion. Fury. Disbelief. They all rushed through Rose in such quick succession that she was left disoriented. She had convinced Kindle, or *almost* convinced her, she was sure of it. Maybe Kindle hadn't said as much. Maybe her face hadn't shown that something Rose had said had changed her mind. But the air had shifted between them, and something in Kindle's eyes had told Rose that she was thinking about it. About all of the things that were out in the world that she could experience if she just left the library behind. A thrill had run through Rose at the realization that maybe she could be the one to show Kindle those things.

But she'd run out of time, that's what it ultimately came down to. Gaston had closed in on them far more quickly than she'd thought he would, and she had wasted precious days not saying anything. That was her fault, entirely. She shouldn't have lingered as she did, floundering over what to say. If she hadn't, maybe Kindle would be with them now, standing beside Rose on the deck of the *Duchess*.

"We have to go back," Rose said, the sound strangled. Night had fallen at some point while she'd been in the reading room with Kindle, and her words were almost lost to the shrill sounds of over-sized crickets in the Wastes. "We have to go back and get her out before they attack."

"They were less than an hour away Rose, there isn't time." Sully was trying to be reasonable, but Rose wasn't having it. Not when her heart pounded hard against her chest. Not when she knew that if they didn't get Kindle out of there Gaston would kill her, because he was a vile, repulsive person who liked to pluck the petals off roses, liked to hurt beautiful things. And Kindle was beautiful, with all her righteous fury, and smoking breath, she was so achingly beautiful. Rose hadn't noticed it before, but now, with distance between them, she noticed.

"There *is* time!" Rose snarled, baring her teeth at Sully in an action she recognized as something Kindle would have done. Funny the things she had learned from Kindle in such a short amount of time. "I'll go alone. If you don't come with me, I'll go alone."

"Calm down, Rose. Just breathe a minute." Sully held onto her shoulders, keeping her from flying off across the deck to start gathering whatever she'd need to go back to the library.

She didn't even know where it was—maybe Kindle had moved it already—not to mention how she'd get there if Manu and Persinette wouldn't take the ship. And how could she reach a place she'd never seen from the outside? She didn't know. She didn't care. She'd figure it out. She just had to hurry lest she was too late. She was probably *already* too late.

An image of Gaston banging on the door to the library flashed through her mind. His too-white teeth bared in what he considered to be a winning smile, but really came off as more of a sneer. He'd worn that expression all those years ago when he'd dragged her away to be hauled off to the labor camps. When he'd looked at her and said, "if you don't want me, fine. Then you won't have anyone." And that had been the end of that. Terror made her ears ring and her fingertips tingle as she remembered that day, the day she'd officially lost what last shred of freedom she'd had.

The clattering of dishes, the chattering of people, the Enchanted cafeteria loud around her, all of it had made her head throb. She'd known it was coming, that was perhaps the worst part. She didn't know *what* was coming, but she knew it was something. Something that two days prior she'd begged Agnes to save her from, and he'd said he'd do something about.

Only as Gaston stepped through the doors, did the entire room fall silent, and Rose knew—she *knew*—that Agnes had broken his promise. It was hard to keep track of what happened after that. Sounds and voices swam in her ears, distant, behind glass. Then there was the sound of her asset number filtering in. The only thing every MOTHER agent had ever called her, the number Gaston had always used in place of her name. She knew it was a tactic, she always had. To demean her, to make her feel small.

She was not *small*.

Rose had stood from her seat, her chin held high. She didn't look at the others gathered around her, or turn her head to face the rainbow-haired man she could just see out of the corner of her eye. It was too late for Agnes to do anything now, and he'd betrayed her anyway. Thrown her to the wolves to keep the eyes of MOTHER off of him and his Uprising.

She didn't remember what she'd said during the exchange, all of it went so fast, and her heart was pounding so hard in her ears that she could barely hear herself think. But she remembered that sneer on Gaston's face as he took her chin in his hand, a mirror image of the time he'd tried to kiss her weeks before, the scene that had started it all. And then she was on the ground, clinging to consciousness like one did when they were on a cliff's edge, sure they would die.

The ache of betrayal had come later. After they'd thrown her in the camp. A bone deep ache that she'd been sure she'd never get rid of, the chill of a long cold night that left her feeling that she'd never be warm again.

But now—*now*—Rose recognized all of that for what it was. Agnes had done what he had to. He'd taken the only route available to him, she forgave him for that. And he'd done what was best for her, even if she couldn't see it at the time. If Agnes hadn't let Gaston arrest her, he never would have stopped trying. Eventually, Rose knew now, Gaston would have stopped asking for what he wanted, and merely taken it. Agnes had saved her that agony in the same way she'd only just managed to save him back in the camps.

"I can't. . ." She paused, trying to catch her breath where it had begun to rasp from her in hard pants as if she'd just run miles and miles instead of standing still on the deck of the Duchess. "I can't leave her to *him*."

Agnes was beside her now, Rose didn't know when he had joined them. He reached for her shoulders, turning her to him, and crouched so he could meet her eyes. There was a serious set to his jaw that she recognized all too well from those days in the camp, after he had come back to himself and decided there was something left worth fighting for. "Who said we were going to?"

"But. . . But. . ." Rose looked around confused, her eyes finally focusing on the crew that had gathered on the deck. They weren't standing still. Maybe they hadn't been since Kindle had sent them away. Purpose lined their steps and movements as they set about tying off ropes, and preparing munitions. "What are we doing?"

"We're going back to save Kindle, of course." Agnes raised

a brow as if to ask Rose what else they would be doing. "We're not leaving her there to MOTHER's mercy."

"But the library?"

"Well, that'll be up to you, Rose," Persinette said, holding out a spare pistol when Agnes stepped back to begin arming himself. "We can't hold the line against MOTHER, and Kindle can't move the library. We have to get her to leave it behind."

"Then why did we leave in the first place?" Rose asked. None of this made sense. Her hands shook, the pistol rattling lightly in its holster as she strapped it around her waist. She didn't even know what she'd do with a pistol, but she supposed it was better than going in unarmed.

"There were certain books we had to get to safety first." A second pistol was strapped to Persinette's opposite hip, her fingers already sparking with the magic they would need once they got back to the library. "Things we didn't want to lose when MOTHER came through with their torches. We had to get all that back to Alys and Hatter so they could start planning our final assault on MOTHER and the Uprising."

"Then why not just bring Kindle with us when we left with the books?" Everything was moving so quickly, like someone had hit the fast-forward button on one of those recordings she'd once seen in MOTHER's library.

"We just ran out of time to convince her," Agnes said, scrubbing his face with his hand. "And when she came to Persinette and told her to make sure you left with us—"

"She did what?!" Fury flared in Rose's veins. How *dare* Kindle make that choice for her. How dare Kindle try to order her around that way. Who did she think she was!

"We also figured it might be best if they not know we'd been there," Sully added, tone reasonable. "Stella and Persinette are going to bring the ships up behind MOTHER's forces, while we send you in to get Kindle out. That way it looks like the library was destroyed before we ever had a chance to get information from it."

"Allowing us to keep the element of surprise!" Stella called from across the gangplank where she was pulling it over onto her ship.

"Right." Persinette motioned for someone to start their ascent. "While you were keeping Kindle distracted, Roy and Penny were able to discern where the library is located."

"So we're going to fly there?" Rose's stomach lurched. "That'll take too long Persinette! We won't make it in time!"

Persinette scoffed—Rose thought that might be the first time she'd heard Persinette make such an undignified sound. Oddly, it worked for her. She thought Persinette should be snarky more often. "No. Alys and Hatter have the traveling arrays all setup. While we were away, they managed to adjust them to create a portal, we just have to fly through and we'll be right outside of the library's doors."

"But the wards. . ."

"Are down. If they weren't we wouldn't be going anywhere right now. Kindle can't keep them up in her current state." Agnes shook his head. "So, are you ready to go save Kindle and possibly get revenge on Gaston in the process?" He held out a little dagger. It gleamed in the lights from the ship. "Or are you just going to hang out on the deck and wait for us to do all the real work?"

Rose took the dagger, the hilt of it cold in her hand, and held on tight enough that she felt the edges dig into her palm. It was closer to a tool than a pistol would ever be, but in the end, it still felt unwieldy and strange in her mechanic hands. "Gaston is mine."

"Thought you'd say that." Agnes tipped his head back, his lips spreading into a ferocious baring of teeth that some might confuse with a smile, but just looked like a snarl of victory to her. "All right Persi, take us up!"

THIRTY

KINDLE

The front entrance to the library had been lost some decades ago in the constant shuffle of expansion to make room for new information. But Kindle knew which rooms needed to be most protected. Which halls needed to be barricaded and which would be fine being left alone. She knew what rooms were the most important.

The west wing, she decided, was a lost cause, but the east one, where the rose and the journals, history and spell books resided. . . that wing she'd protect with her life.

Stories were so infused into their world that she was sure they could be rewritten from memory, maybe not word for word, but close enough. And much of what MOTHER had burned hadn't been fiction, it hadn't been stories, it was history, magic, and culture. It was the books that went against their narrative. Pages that held the true age of the queen and information on the worlds that had existed before the realms had merged. Stories of the land that had existed before Daiwynn, and how so much of what humanity had done to itself had then been turned around on the Enchanted of Daiwynn. It showed how history repeated itself, over, and over, and over, and it showed how the downtrodden, and unwanted had always found ways to fight back, to thrive.

History was a narrative of how people could only be

pushed so far before they ultimately would not give any more. And MOTHER would do anything in their power to keep that narrative from being told. Because, unlike the novels, and storybooks, history couldn't be brushed off as nonsense, there was always some truth in it. MOTHER had sought to erase that truth, and it was up to Kindle to preserve it. It always had been.

When this was all over, when MOTHER and the Uprising were gone, when the people of Daiwynn were free, they would need those books to rebuild. They would need a past to look to, so they could shape a better future. And they would need the hope that knowing their people had been there before and survived, and maybe they could prevent the same things from happening again this time, would bring them. It was Kindle's responsibility to make sure the library was there when that happened. What else was she good for if not this?

Kindle heard them coming long before she saw them. Tearing through the halls of the library, their shouts echoing off the walls. The smell of burning paper drifted through the air, stinging her nostrils, as they set flame to anything and everything in their path, uncaring of if it might be useful or not to future generations.

The library cried out at the injustice of it, books screaming loud, and shrill as they were reduced to cinders. A place of knowledge lost. A sanctuary forgotten. A home collapsing around its singular inhabitant.

The walls shook violently with a concentrated blast, making Kindle's stomach lurch. Canon fire.

Flexing her feet against the stones, Kindle readied herself as best she could without any actual weapons, to keep MOTHER from accessing the east wing. The first shot of a pistol sounded like a pop, echoing off the walls. They were closer now, one more turn and they'd be upon her. But that was all right, she was ready for them.

"There you are!" a familiar voice called, and a warm hand wrapped around Kindle's wrist from behind and dragged her into the darkness of the history room. The door shut behind them quietly, and Rose raised a finger to her lips to silence Kindle when she opened her mouth to ask what in the name of the gods Rose was doing back at the library.

A group ran by outside, their tread heavy. Kindle felt Rose relax beside her.

"I was meant to be keeping them from entering the east wing," Kindle hissed, spinning on her unwanted rescuer. "Now they'll get into the—"

"No they won't." Rose lifted her chin, proud, a little smile on her face. "The crew is here, they're mounting offensive maneuvers."

"How? How did you get back here? I sent you away! To the Wastes!" *For a reason*, she didn't add. *To keep you safe*, she swallowed down. None of that seemed to matter to Rose who was standing in front of her with a smear of soot across her cheek, and a smirk on her lips. She looked even more startlingly stunning than Kindle remembered, and she'd sent Rose away less than an hour ago.

"You gave a crew of highly motivated, reasonably intelligent, people free rein of the library, and you're surprised by this?" Rose tilted her head, a short curl falling against her cheek where Kindle itched to brush it away. She was supposed to be gone. She was supposed to be gone, and safe. But instead she was here, putting herself in more danger, and for what? *For what?!*

"Why did you come back?" Kindle rubbed at the bridge of her nose, wondering how long it would take her to convince Rose and the others to leave again so that she could get back to fading away with the only place she remembered calling home.

"Because, we couldn't let MOTHER destroy this place." Rose blinked up at her, as if this were the most obvious thing in the world. "Whether you want to come with us or not, we couldn't let MOTHER destroy it." It didn't sound like that was the whole story. Kindle could see Rose chewing on her words, even in the dark, teeth gnashing over vowels and syllables she refused to give voice to. "Come on."

"Where are we going?" Kindle frowned, but she let Rose grab her wrist again, and lead her out into the darkened corridor. Whoever had run past them had knocked out all of the lights, leaving only shadows in their place. Kindle squinted through the gloom, hoping that no one lingered there, hidden away, and waiting to attack. Tension crept up Kindle's spine, making her shoulders lift to her ears.

"I wish you'd come with us," Rose continued, without answering Kindle's question. "I know you think that you can't be anything outside of these walls, but that just isn't true."

"Isn't it?" Kindle muttered under her breath, only half-hoping that Rose would hear. Based on the grumble, she had.

"No. It isn't." Rose stopped in front of a door Kindle knew all too well. One that she'd been nervous to share with Rose, but ultimately had. One that she'd come to call her own. A room that was her sanctuary in a world that felt every day like it didn't want her. The reading room was a place where Kindle and Chirp had built a home inside the library. And it was the room that held all of her favorite books. Stories that had gotten her through the darkest of nights. Journals that had made her feel less alone.

This place was where Kindle had come for solace. It, too, would be gone when the library fell. And based on the fact that Rose and the others had entered without her being alerted, she'd guess that that might be very soon, as the library no longer existed in the pocket dimension at all. It was probably a crumbling building on the hillside outside of Maximus now. Something that had appeared overnight that the people of the city far below would avoid for years to come, an odd curiosity, as it crumbled away into nothing.

"Then what am I, if not the keeper of the library?" She refused to be dragged into that room. She didn't know what Rose had planned, but she knew that whatever it was, Kindle didn't want to be a part of it. Maybe Rose thought that Kindle could use her magic to push MOTHER out of the library. Maybe she thought that Kindle could use it to move them again, leaving behind whatever rooms MOTHER resided in. Or maybe she planned to have Kindle gather up the books that meant the most to her, and take them with her. Whatever it was, it wouldn't work. The only way to get rid of MOTHER was to fight them, and Kindle had been ready and willing to do just that until Rose had dragged her away.

"You're Kindle," Rose said simply, as if that was a thing Kindle could just *be*. As if just being a person was a thing people did. Not a keeper of the library. Not a dragon. Not a queen. As if she was none of these titles that she had defined herself by throughout her life before she was simply Kindle.

"If I leave, the library falls." She hadn't said those words, not out loud, not in front of another person. She had some suspicions that Rose had known. That Chirp had shown her the storybook pages that showed what would happen. But Kindle had never actually admitted out loud to another person, what would happen to the library if she were to leave. It made the inevitability of it feel even more real.

"So?" Rose asked, her head tilted to one side, and then she pushed into Kindle's private reading room, and dragged

Kindle behind her while Kindle gaped, trying to come up with a good answer to that.

"What do you mean *so?*" Kindle jerked back, her neck craning to try to get a better look at Rose. It didn't help, she still looked undeniably like herself. Tightly curled hair, a brown forehead permanently wrinkled from thought, and shining spectacles. She was still Rose. Even for how alien the words were coming out of her mouth.

"I mean, so what?" Rose repeated with a shrug, making her way over to the shelves to run her fingers over the spines as if they had all the time in the world. They didn't. The crew of the *Duchess* was holding MOTHER off, but for how long? "What happens if the library falls?"

"All the knowledge will be lost." The words sounded robotic, forced, scripted, even to herself. It was the truth, all of the knowledge *would* be lost, but that wasn't what scared her the most about losing the library. She knew that. She had always known that. That's why she'd ripped those pages from the book, hidden away her siblings' histories and journals, distanced herself from any reminders of who and what she'd been before the library. It was easier that way, than to think about the fact that they hadn't wanted her. And no one had missed her.

"Knowledge is lost all the time." Rose spun to face Kindle her hazel eyes open and earnest. "Data, memories, bits of paper, that's all knowledge, and it's lost every single day. But we keep going, don't we? The world doesn't fall apart just because we overwrote a file, or lost a shopping list, or forgot that one person's name we met years ago."

"This is different." But was it really? Rose was right, existence was loss. People went about their daily lives losing bits and pieces of their history, of themselves, and somehow they still managed. But this was. . . it was so much *bigger* than all that. "I'm the keeper of hundreds of years—"

"*You*," Rose said, holding up a hand to silence her, "are a person who has spent hundreds of years thinking that your only worth was this *building*."

The way she said building made Kindle jerk back, blinking hard. "Building?"

"That's all it is, isn't it? A building. It's just a big, stone, building. The books are what makes a library a library. And the books, don't have to stay here."

"We can't take them all with us." But she was grasping at straws now, Kindle could feel it. Because Rose was right. The books were the important part, not the place they inhabited. The library was magical, yes, but the books were what stored the knowledge.

"Then you won't have a library, you'll have a private collection." Rose grinned, grabbing a book from the shelf seemingly at random and holding it out to Kindle to add toa bag she'd pulled from somewhere while Kindle was distracted. But Kindle saw the spine and knew why Rose had chosen it, out of all the ones on that shelf, it was the most worn, the most often read. A favorite. "This is a good start, I think."

"A private collection won't update itself like the library does."

"No? Well, I guess you and I will just be spending a large chunk of our time hunting down new books, won't we?" Rose turned from the shelf her eyes squinting to accommodate a smile so large, Kindle was sure it made her cheeks ache. And heat bloomed in Kindle's chest, spreading up and out to her extremities the way the fire in her belly sometimes did.

"But. . ."

"No buts." Rose moved, the book still in her hand, and held it out to Kindle, a peace offering, a promise, and a question all in one. "You are more important than this drafty old building, Kindle."

"I. . . I. . ." Kindle swallowed, her fingers fluttering over the book's spine before she took it, pulling it away from Rose and into her chest. She held it close, as if to shield herself in a moment of vulnerability. Her heart was hammering so hard in her chest that she could hear the *badump-badump-badump* in her ears. And Rose was suddenly too close and too far away all at the same time. Tightening her hold on the book, Kindle swallowed around a sharp, clogged, throat, sucked in a deep inhale that didn't help her suddenly panting breaths, and said, "Okay."

"Okay." Rose moved up onto her toes and pressed a kiss to Kindle's cheek that made the fire in Kindle's veins burn hotter. Then she pulled back, and held out a hand, turning her body back to the shelves. "Come help me get the rest of your favorites, and let's get out of here before MOTHER notices us hiding in here."

She spun, and started loading the bag up with the books with the most broken spines. Kindle breathed a moment through the thrill that traveled up her back before she moved to help.

hey had gotten lucky so far, Rose knew that. The crew were providing enough of a distraction that MOTHER wasn't too bothered with finding anyone who might have been residing in the library. It likely helped that the library looked abandoned, but either way, lucky. And in her experience, luck usually ran out.

She and Kindle had packed their bag full to bursting with books for Kindle's private collection, and it was heavy enough that Kindle had to carry it because Rose couldn't. Maybe they shouldn't have packed it so full. Maybe Rose should have cut Kindle off. But once Kindle got going, it was easy to see how she lingered over certain books, and how difficult it would be for her to let them go. So Rose hadn't made her. Every book that was a maybe went in the bag, no questions asked. She only regretted that decision a little, as it did slow them down while they slunk through the halls of the library.

"Agnes and Sully managed to get us in through the skylight of the courtyard. It was a tight fit for both ships and could mean we'll be blocked in if MOTHER figures it out, but we hope to be gone by then." Rose leaned forward to peer around another corner. So far, they hadn't come upon any conscious MOTHER agents. But she wasn't willing to try their luck by not being careful.

"How did they get past the wards?" Kindle sounded like she was out of breath, but when Rose looked back to check on her, she was keeping up fairly well. Her wings were wrapped tightly around herself to make for a smaller target, and to act as protection should she need it. Likely for the best, Rose didn't have any weapons to spare now that she was out of bullets.

"The wards are meant to keep you in, not keep people out. Plus, they're malfunctioning." Their footsteps were soft over the stone floors. One of the rooms off the hall was thrown open, pages scattered about the corridor like fallen leaves, but at least they hadn't decided to set fire to that room yet. It probably wouldn't be long before they did. MOTHER would leave nothing behind.

"Well, well, well, look who it is," a deep, rasping voice said from somewhere behind them. Rose spun, tucking Kindle's much taller form behind herself, dagger at the ready. Gaston stepped from the shadows, his eyes narrowed, lips pulled back to show off a neat row of teeth. "As I live and breathe. If it isn't that little halfling. Rosevelt, wasn't it?"

Fear spiked through Rose, making her hot and cold all at the same time. Sweat pooled in her palms, the dagger nearly slipping from her grip. She tightened her fingers until they ached, but refused to lower the weapon. "Let us go, Gaston. You can finish off the library, but just let us go."

He barked a laugh, short and sharp, and then lunged, knocking Rose off her feet. She went down hard, the breath leaving her, her head knocking against the stones with a sickening crack, but managed to keep ahold of the dagger. With a grunt Gaston landed a blow to her side, something in her torso snapping, a rib very likely. Rose cried out, but didn't let it stop her from wedging her knee between them to try to keep his weight from bearing down on her. She just needed to get enough space between them to jam the dagger between his ribs. But every time she thought she had, he knocked her hand away, or blocked her.

Another blow to her side made breathing a struggle. If she hadn't been suffering from a lack of oxygen—and possibly a punctured lung—all of a sudden, she might have taken a minute to calculate how long it would take her to heal from her injuries.

She sliced at his arm with the blade, making him snarl, and then he grabbed the hair on the top of her head, and slammed it down against the stone. Stars fluttered around her. Her ears rang. He was gaining ground. His hands moved for her throat, thick fingers closing around her windpipe. Rose floundered, choking on the need for air, and the dagger flopped around in her hand, useless but for a nick here and a scratch there. She couldn't get the pressure she needed on it. Maybe he'd broken something in her arm too, and she just hadn't felt it for the pain in her ribs. Or maybe it was the lack of oxygen. Or maybe it was the dizziness from the concussion. There was no way to know. Hubert would have known, with all his vast medical knowledge. But medicine had never been Rose's field of expertise. She might regret that if she lived through this.

Rose gasped, her fingernails digging into the backs of Gaston's hands to try to pry him off her, or at least loosen his grip so she could breathe again, to no avail. And she'd lost the dagger, she realized, probably dropped it in her need to grapple his hands away from her throat.

"I should have killed you when I had the chance," Gaston spat, spittle spraying her face, and he tightened his hold, "twenty years ago!"

There was blackness around her vision now. Closing in. Narrowing it to a point. She'd lose consciousness in a matter of seconds. But maybe Kindle had gotten away. Maybe Kindle had—

A roar sounded, or maybe that was the rush of blood in Rose's ears from a heart threatening to give up, it was hard to tell, and then someone or something tackled Gaston off of her, taking him, and whoever it was to the ground.

Rose wheezed, the air rushing back into her lungs, and making them rub against her broken rib. Pain registered a second later, and she was wincing, then coughing, then choking again. The retching followed shortly after, and she only had just enough time to roll over before she choked on her thick saliva. It was then that she saw Kindle's red wings beating against the stone. Her talons tore into Gaston wherever she could find purchase.

Gaston was losing. Bleeding from a split lip, and a deep gouge down the side of his face. But as Rose lay there trying to regain her breath, and clear the spots from her vision, she saw him scramble for the dagger.

He grabbed it, and Rose had just enough time to choke out a warning before he'd plunged it into Kindle's side.

Kindle roared again, her arm swinging wildly, talons looking for any soft bits of Gaston she could slice into to get him away from her.

The dagger lifted and plunged again.

Kindle's next growl was wet with blood. But she managed to draw back enough to focus her rage. Her talons sank into Gaston's throat a second later.

Dark eyes widened in surprise, and Gaston gasped, scrambling back on one hand while the other uselessly held his throat, trying to staunch the bleeding. Rose forgot about him after that, moving onto her knees, and crawling over to Kindle.

"Kindle. Kindle. Look at me. Come on, look up here." She turned Kindle gently, her hands flying to peel the torn sweater from herself. Wadding it up into a ball, Rose pressed it into the wounds on Kindle's side. She pressed hard, ignoring the way the brown fabric darkened with blood. Sweat gathered on Rose's skin, making her camisole cling to her. "Hey. Hey. Can you look at me?"

Kindle's lids fluttered open, dark eyes made impossibly darker by pupils gone too wide, and face gone too pale with shock.

"There she is. That's my girl." Rose forced a smile, but she felt her lip wobbling as her bloody fingers lifted to brush red hair away from Kindle's sweaty face. "You hang on, okay? I'm going to get us help."

Kindle tilted her chin forward once, but it looked like the motion took what little energy she had. Rose couldn't leave her like this, in the middle of the hall in a pool of her own blood, as a battle waged on around her. But they needed help. They needed to get Kindle stable, and then back to the ship where Hubert and the medic could look after her.

With trembling fingers, Rose reached for one of the books scattered on the floor—Kindle must have dropped the sack in her rush to protect Rose—and pulled it close. She didn't know exactly how the magic of the library worked, and Kindle didn't seem to either, but she knew that the books were alive as much as this place was. And this place had been a part of Kindle for so long, it would want to keep her alive, surely.

Pressing a little of her own magic into the cover, she silently begged the pages to get them help, to bring someone to them, to light the way. There was a fluttering, a whispering, like when the books had been speaking to her before, and then there were voices, a cacophony of so many people all trying to talk over one another. But they were all saying the same thing, over and over again, "This way. This way. This way. Help us. This way."

The loose pages on the floor sparkled with latent magic, fluttering up from the stones like butterflies, and then flapped away down the hall to carry the message, the words followed behind. "This way. This way. Help us. This way."

Rose didn't know how long she sat there, brushing her fingers through Kindle's hair, and trying to soothe her with one hand while she tried to keep the blood inside of her with the other, but eventually, she heard running footsteps. She didn't have to look up to know that they were her people, her crew, coming to help her when she needed it most.

Sully was lumbering down the hall, Agnes right behind him.

"What happened?" Agnes asked, falling to his knees beside Kindle to get a better look at her injuries.

"Gaston stabbed her, twice." Kindle had grown clammy and quiet while they waited. Her breathing shallower and shallower. Rose hadn't noted the signs before—no, *not* not noted. She just hadn't wanted to see them. Had purposefully disregarded the information even as she subconsciously collected it. Because she knew what it meant. Kindle was fading. Fast. Too fast. "I don't think. . . It doesn't seem like her magic is doing anything to try to combat the injury."

Agnes shook his head, bending down to get a better look at the wounds on Kindle's side. They looked bigger, and deeper than Rose had thought before she'd shoved her shirt into them hoping to staunch the bleeding. Gods. Kindle was going to die, wasn't she?

"It's the library," Sully said from Kindle's other side, where he'd taken her limp wrist, and pressed his fingers to her pulse. "She's still maintaining it."

"How?! She's not even conscious!" Rose was trembling all over. And the shout made her wince when it pushed on her own injuries.

"She's not conscious when she sleeps either." Agnes shook

his head, pulling his shirt from his back and motioned for Sully to do the same so he could begin to rip them into strips. "They must have used something to tether her here. Something that would absorb magic from her to fuel this place."

"Something to absorb— the rose!" Rose jerked back when the realization hit her like a blow, pulling at her own injuries again. "We have to destroy the rose."

"That might do it." Sully agreed, and she was grateful anew for the friendship she'd formed with Sully and how well he listened. His fingers still worked quickly to help Agnes wrap the bandages around Kindle's torso. They were already soaking through, but it was better than nothing for their journey to the ship.

"Can you two get her back to the ship on your own? I'll take care of the rose." Rose brushed off her pants, and stood as the two men lifted Kindle carefully between them.

"How will you get out?" Agnes shifted his grip on Kindle, drawing a soft moan of pain from her.

"You let me worry about that. You two just get her to the medic as quickly as you can." Rose bent to gather as many of the books as she could into the bag, threw it over her shoulder, and started for the rose room.

It wasn't far, thankfully, by the time Rose got there, her ears were ringing again, and her breathing had gone shallow enough to make her lightheaded.

The rose glowed brightly at the center of the room, and Rose stared at it for the length of one painfully deep inhale, and exhale before she swung the bag of books—the top gathered tightly closed—and knocked the blasted thing, along with the glass that had been covering it, from the pedestal.

For all that the clockwork rose seemed to be made of metal and gears, it hit the stone floor with a sound like glass shattering, and splintered into a million tiny pieces. Crystalline shards flew about the room. Rose held up an arm to shield her face, and took another breath, before looking down at the pieces of glittering red clockwork.

Then the ground rumbled beneath her feet.

"Gods, it's falling apart," she hissed, hitched the bag up on her shoulder again, and took off at a run praying that the stitch in her side was just that and not one of her broken ribs threatening to puncture a lung.

EPILOGUE

"You were right," Kindle said, not turning to look when Rose joined her in her new library days later. It wasn't really a library, per se, and Kindle had been quick to point that out to anyone who called it such. But Alys had found some old shelves somewhere among her camp, and Rose had found a corner of the room she now shared with Kindle to put it, and it was perhaps better than the whole of the Great Library put together because it was mobile, and because she wasn't alone anymore.

"I usually am," Rose shrugged, and then winced when the motion jarred her injured ribs. "What about?"

"There are some things worth seeing in person." Kindle hunched further over the stack of books she had spent the last couple of days organizing and reorganizing. In spite of the fact that breaking the curse had left her exhausted, she refused to be bedridden. These books didn't move to be where she needed them to be, and it was making her crazy. Agnes had suggested that she could train Hiccup to do that. Chirp would have been the better choice, but when she'd gone looking for it on the ship, it was missing. That above everything else had left her aching. She could deal with the injuries, and the bone deep exhaustion as her magic replenished itself, but Chirp? That robot had been her best and only friend for as long as she could remember.

Rose nodded, a slow, sad smile splitting her face that made Kindle want to pull her in close, and tuck her in behind her wings, protect her from anything and everything that could hurt her.

"But you were wrong too." Fingers tapping against the worn paperback cover, Kindle sat it back on the shelf, puzzling over the feeling of a missing limb not having full access to the library induced. She'd been looking for something amongst her collection when the realization had come to her, the understanding jolting through her like electricity.

"Oh?" Rose moved to sit on the floor beside her, eying the stack of books Kindle had pulled to show the others.

"Yes." Kindle took a deep breath, and turned to meet Rose's searching gaze. "I *do* have to help your people bring down my siblings. I *do* need to help end this war."

"Kindle, Persinette said you don't need to. You aren't a weapon, and we don't plan to use you as one. If you want to stay in the Wastes, then that's fine, we'll all understand. Even Agnes and he's—"

Kindle shook her head, her hands tightening to fists in her lap. Without the library to sap her dry, she'd begun to regain more and more of her humanoid form. Her talons returned to bitten down nails. Her patchy skin had remained the same, but her teeth were no longer cutting into her lip. She hadn't tried to shift into a dragon yet, but she would be willing to wager that maybe soon she'd be able to without fear of being stuck that way.

"Just like there are some things worth seeing, there are some things worth saving," Kindle said, quiet and sure. "And I want to help stop Eloise and Eddi."

"All right." Rose leaned over to take one of Kindle's hands, working her fingers slowly open until she could thread them together with her own. "All right. Then I guess we're both going to war."

Chirp

THE RUBBLE SAT heavy on one of their metal legs, and they couldn't feel it anymore. They wondered if the circuit had merely been shaken loose, or if the connection had been severed entirely. Would they ever be able to fix the damage the collapse had done? Maybe. If they could get out from under the stones of the collapsed history room.

"Well. Well. Well. What do we have here?" a voice said from over Chirp's shoulder where they couldn't turn to look. But they didn't need to see the man to know the voice. They'd heard it so many times in their dreams. The ringmaster. "So this is where you've been hiding. You know, I didn't believe Eddi when they told me, but here you are." The ringmaster clicked his tongue, and Chirp could imagine him shaking his head, long goatee getting caught in the buttons of his marching band style jacket.

Chirp stayed still, hardly even blinking their visual circuits, hoping and praying that if they were quiet enough, motionless enough, the ringmaster would assume they'd been irreparably damaged in the collapse.

No luck. A moment later, Chirp heard the grunt of one of the ringmaster's trolls. "You want us to move all this?"

"Yes, and hurry up about it. The sooner I can repair them, the better," the ringmaster snapped. "You're coming home with us, darling. Don't you worry," he soothed as he took a step closer to bend over and look down into a crack between the debris. "Don't you worry at all."

Acknowledgments

First off, thank you—the reader—for joining me on another adventure in Daiwynn. This cast of characters has been with me for a few years now, and I've grown quite attached to them, so I hope you love them as much as I do.

Although this book is over, Daiwynn has at least one more adventure in it. So keep an eye on my social media accounts for information about The Marionette and the Clockwork Circus.

Next, I'd like the thank my small hoard of beta-readers. You guys gave some excellent insight, and I really appreciate all of your hard work!

And last but certainly not least, are my writing support group. From the friends I've had for decades who have helped me to grow into the writer I am today (Elle, Tiss, and Jasmine) to the new ones I've acquired through MTP like Nancy, Brindi, Hannah, Adina, Nicole, and Steph. And of course my beautiful, supportive editor, Meg. Writing a book takes a village, and you guys are my village.

About the Author

Born and raised in a small town near the Chesapeake Bay, Lou Wilham grew up on a steady diet of fiction, arts and crafts, and Old Bay. After years of absorbing everything, there was to absorb of fiction, fantasy, and sci-fi she's left with a serious writing/drawing habit that just won't quit. These days, she spends much of her time writing, drawing, and chasing a very short Basset Hound named Sherlock.

When not, daydreaming up new characters to write and draw she can be found crocheting, making cute bookmarks, and binge-watching whatever happens to catch her eye.

Learn more about Lou and her future projects on her website: http://louinprogress.com/ or join her mailing list at: http://subscribepage.com/mailermailer

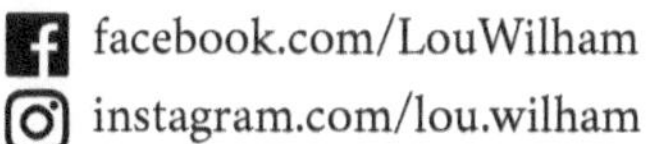

facebook.com/LouWilham

instagram.com/lou.wilham

ALSO BY LOU WILHAM

The Curse Collection
    The Curse of The Black Cat
    The Curse of Ash and Blood
    The Curse of Flour and Feeling

The Clockwork Chronicles
    The Girl in the Clockwork Tower
    The Unicorn and the Clockwork Quest
    The Rose in the Clockwork Library

The Heir To Moondust
    The Prince of Starlight
    The Prince of Daybreak

The Witches of Moondale
    The Hex Next Door

Sanctuary of the Lost
    Of Loyalties and Wreckage

Completed Series
    The Tales of the Sea Trilogy
    Villainous Heroics

Sneak Peek!

continue reading for a sneak peek of Lou's

Chapter 1

"What the fuck," Rus muttered, her gaze fixed on the Moondale town sign. She'd said she'd never come back to this place. But that was the thing about where you grew up: it had the power to drag you back like the fucking Bermuda Triangle. And Rus would know—she'd been to the Bermuda Triangle four or five times in the years since she'd left Moondale behind. The particulars weren't important. What was important was that Rus was sure she'd wind up there four or five more times before she died.

"Rus?" Nesta tilted their head, a piece of floppy black hair falling into their eyes. They looked just how Rus remembered them, and she still wasn't sure how to feel about that. But she'd likely beg for Nesta's skin care regime before the day was done.

"Nothing. Let's just get this over with." Rus shook herself and jerked her gaze back to the view through the windshield.

Moondale looked different and yet the same. It had sprawled out past the little dot on the coast where its founders had originally settled, up into the mountain beyond to include a ski lodge and even a few big name-hotels. Of that Rus was grateful; she didn't think she could stay in one of the inns in town with the kids. Not if she wanted to keep the Board of Magic off her ass for more than a week.

Nesta was still glancing at her from the driver's seat. Rus could feel those cunning eyes looking for . . . something. Maybe some sign of what Rus was thinking. They wouldn't find anything. More than a decade spanned between them, and Rus had learned long ago to keep her thoughts tucked away where they couldn't be used against her.

"I just can't believe you became a realtor." Rus tilted her head, letting a teasing smile tug up the corners of her mouth. It would hopefully be enough to keep Nesta from asking inconvenient questions.

Nesta shrugged, turning down one of the side streets off Main Street. They were headed toward the older part of town, the buildings around them changing from relatively modern retail to small suburban homes to Gothic-style houses that would make the Addams family jealous.

"How did your parents take it?" Rus pressed. Anything to ignore the way her stomach was writhing with nerves. She hoped she wouldn't see anyone else she knew, not before she was settled. But in a town that hardly had more than a few thousand residents to boast, that was likely impossible. At least *she'd* be at work, so Rus could avoid that particular awkward encounter. "I mean . . . a cupid not becoming a matchmaker for the board? That's—"

"I told them I didn't think the board would be using matchmakers much longer," Nesta said, and they sounded smug about it. Like they'd realized a new hairstyle would be trending long before anyone else could.

"And?" Rus had to know, because she could just imagine old man Holyore absolutely losing his shit at his child chucking tradition out the proverbial window. He might quiver right out of his beard.

"And they didn't agree . . ." Nesta's mouth twisted up into a knowing smirk, their eyes still firmly on the road. "At first."

Well. That sounded like a story and a half. One they probably didn't have time for, and it would likely require wine. Lots of wine. Rus snorted, rolling her eyes. "Okay, but a realtor though?"

"Why not? The same principles apply. It's all about listening to harmonizing energies. And this house?" Nesta put the car in park outside of yet another Gothic-style house perched on the far end of one of Moondale's more ancient-looking cemeteries. "It wants you, Rus."

"Ew. Don't make it sound creepy." Rus huffed, her hand twitching to give Nesta a fond shove, but she resisted the urge. They weren't friends like that, not anymore. So instead, she turned her attention to the house.

Rus blinked up at it. It looked like something out of Hansel and Gretel, with a small porch, three walk-out balconies off the rooms upstairs, and a legit tower. Or . . . maybe *tower* wasn't the word for whatever that was, but Rus imagined the room inside would be the perfect place to put a reading and playroom for the girls. The only thing was—

"Nesta, you are aware that this house is . . . *pink*, right?" Rus cocked her head. It wasn't unbearably pink. It didn't reek of Barbie Dreamhouse. But it was most definitely a shade of pastel that Rus was sure she'd never worn in her entire life.

"Lilac, actually. And what's that saying about not judging a house by its siding color?"

"I'm pretty sure that's not a thing."

"You ready to see inside, or what?" Nesta asked, already reaching for the door to climb out.

Rus nodded dumbly, scrambling from the car to follow them through the little wrought iron gate and up the walk. The door opened onto a small foyer bedecked in black walls, and a little gray bench off to the side with hooks hanging above it for coats.

Nesta was saying something about the history of the house, and the remodeling, and something about all the furnishings coming with the place if that's what she wanted, but Rus had largely stopped listening. Because the house—157 Mourning Moore—was exactly what Rus had always imagined when she'd thought of a home for herself. The walls were all black, but there was enough natural lighting about the place that it didn't feel dark and gloomy. And there were pops of color here and there: A throw pillow on the bench in the foyer. Silver birch tree wallpaper in the study. A collection of velvet pillows in the strange round room of the tower that Rus had decided would make a great study and playroom. It was—

"Who's watching the kids?"

"Huh?" Rus shook herself, tearing her eyes away from the frankly spectacular nursery. Aihuan was a little old for a crib, but that was an easy enough fix. She'd love the brightly painted forest critters on the black wallpaper. "Oh. Their Uncle Fernando. But I can't leave them with him long, or by the time I get back they'll have given him a makeover. Buzzcut included. Meiling is a menace."

"Fernando?"

"Yeah. He's one of the witches I met online. Good kid. Little awkward, but who isn't these days? He'll be moving in with us for a bit until we're settled in and we can find him his own place." Rus moved to the window. The view from the nursery was of Moondale, and not the cemetery. She'd have to check to make sure Meiling's window didn't overlook it either. Neither of her girls needed to see the spirits that were standing on the edge of the property looking up at the house. Even now, Rus could feel their gaze on her, making the hair on the back of her neck stand on end. Really, she'd thought the board had Rules about letting spirits languish without rest like that. But then . . . maybe they hadn't had another medium in town since she'd left. And if those spirits weren't doing anything other than just floating around, no one would notice them outside of a medium.

"Is he your . . . ?" Nesta drifted off, their perfectly plucked brows turning down to wrinkle in the middle.

Rus laughed. "Goddess no. We're just friends. He's good with the girls, though."

"I see. Well. There's still the attic." Nesta gestured to the narrow stairs that led up to the last room in the house.

"Lead the way." Rus gestured for Nesta to go first and followed them when they turned on their heel to head upstairs. She'd have to set wards to make sure the girls didn't leave the house without her knowing if she wasn't on the same floor as them. But what was magic for if not to keep her girls safe?

The little door at the top of the steps opened to a large bedroom with stripe charcoal on black wallpapered walls, an awkwardly cut ceiling, and a heavy-looking fourposter bed. In the one little nook in front of a window that overlooked the cemetery was a small desk, which would be perfect for Rus's more . . . unsavory experiments. And opposite that was a small bathroom with a clawfoot tub, two tiny stand sinks, a toilet, and a plant in front of a window that would definitely not live to see the end of the week if Rus had anything to say about it.

"Okay. You're right." Rus laughed a little to herself as she turned to tip an imaginary hat to Nesta. "Me and this house are soulmates."

"I hate to say I told you so—"

"No, you don't."

"I'll go grab the paperwork out of the car. Meet me on the back porch. And feel free to look around the yard."

"Is it screened in?"

"Would I show you a house with a porch that wasn't?" Nesta winked, and then disappeared down the steps.

Rus went back into the bedroom and turned on her heel, looking around. It would need some personalization, but she could see herself being quite happy there. "Well," she said to the house because places, like people, liked to be acknowledged. "I hope you'll take good care of me and my girls."

The house didn't respond. They never did. But when Rus made her way past the nursery again, the crib had been swapped out for a little gray loft bed with a slide and a toy chest underneath. And, she supposed, that was enough of an answer.

The yard abutted two sides of the old cemetery, which seemed to have been built around the house instead of vice versa. Rus exhaled loudly, her breath pushing strands of chin-length bright pink hair out of her face.

"I'm going to have to do something about you, aren't I?" she said more to herself than to the spirits toeing the line between the yard and the cemetery. There was no fence to distinguish one from the other, but it was clear where her yard ended and the graveyard began because the spirits wouldn't cross the property line. "The worst part is, the board probably won't even give me credit for it. They'll attribute the lowered negative energy to like . . . their attempts to promote unity through more frequent clan and coven meetings or some shit." Rus snorted, rolling her eyes.

"It's warded." Nesta slapped a manila folder down onto the back porch table.

"Hm?"

"The whole property is warded against malignant energies. That's one of the selling points."

"Who did the wards?" Rus sat in one of the wrought iron chairs and started flipping through the contract, pretending to read it. They both knew that was bullshit; Rus had never read paperwork a day in her life. But she liked to pretend she was an adult who considered big commitments like a house carefully.

"Crimson Tide Coven."

"Of fucking course it was them." Rus huffed. "You think Greer will be super pissed if I take them all down and put up my own?"

"Probably. But when was the last time you cared what Evander Greer thought? Plus, if you sign here"—Nesta tapped the paper with one neatly rounded fingernail—"it'll be your property and there's nothing anyone can say about it, not even the sheriff."

"Doesn't mean the board won't try," Rus grumbled, grabbing the pen to start signing her life away. "Wait." She stopped halfway through the fourth page. "Did you just say *sheriff?*"

"Yeah. Sheriff Evander Greer." Nesta tilted their head, but their mouth was twitching up at the corners.

Rus groaned, dropping forward to smack her head on the table. It hurt. But likely not as much as a run-in with Sheriff Greer would. "Remind me to stay out of his way for the next like . . . hundred years or so."

"Oh, don't be silly. I'm sure he's not still holding a grudge because of the time you—"

Rus lifted her head just enough to raise one brow at Nesta.

"Well, maybe he is. But either way, you'll be fine. I mean, you've got your girls, and the house, and the business. There won't be time for you to stir up trouble."

Rus continued to stare at them with the same brow lifted.

"I won't tell him you're back in town, and maybe he'll never find out?" Nesta sagged.

"That's all you had to say." Rus sat up and went back to

signing the papers. "Maybe I shouldn't have come back, though. We could have gone . . . somewhere else."

"Why *did* you come back?" Nesta pulled out a chair to sit across from her, their face suddenly open with curiosity.

"Moondale's got a good school system for witches." The lie slipped easily off her tongue. It wasn't even really a lie— Moondale did have an excellent magical school system. But she was sure she could have found someplace equally as good in Europe if she'd wanted to. Or even taught the girls herself. But there was safety in a place as steeped in magic as Moondale was. The very earth the place was built on would give off enough ambient energy to hide Rus and her children. Or so she hoped.

"Fine. Keep your secrets." Nesta leaned over to watch Rus scrawl her untidy signature across page after page of legalese.

Rus lifted the pen to shake out her hand where it had started to cramp when she finally got to the last page.

"So, are you going to see Azure?"

Rus's hand jerked, the pen skittering and leaving a nasty mark across the page that she was sure Nesta would need to reprint. "What?"

"Azure Elwood. Are you going to go see her? Does she even know you're moving back?"

"I'm pretty sure Az hates me," Rus said, instead of telling Nesta that no, Az did not know she was moving back to Moondale. She finished the final signature with a flourish then pushed the folder over to Nesta for them to sign.

"*Hate* isn't the word I'd use." Nesta closed the folder with a snap.

"What?" Rus frowned.

"What?" Nesta tilted their head, their nose crinkling up in an expression of innocence that no one who knew anything about Nesta Holyore would ever believe. "You can start moving in tomorrow. You're keeping the furniture, right?"

"Yeah. I mean, I don't have any of my own, so." Rus stood, stretching out her neck from side to side where it had grown stiff from being hunched over the papers.

"All right then. I'll have my crew come by and help out if you need it?"

"That'd be great. I have to finish opening up the shop tomorrow, and Fernando needs to be there to help wrangle the kids while we work."

"You know, I never asked." Nesta headed back through the house toward their car. "How old are your kids?"

"Aihuan will be four in October. And Meiling just turned thirteen. I've already got her signed up over at Moondale High."

"Ah, so they're . . ." Nesta drifted off, looking like they expected Rus to fill in the blank of what they were trying to say. But Rus had spent the last six months filling in the blank for people, and she wasn't about to do that. Not here. Not anymore.

"They're amazing," Rus said. It didn't matter if they weren't hers biologically—they were hers in every way that mattered.

"Right. Well, you can stay the night here if you want." Nesta pulled a key from their pocket to hold out to Rus. "I'm sure the bedding is clean. The house generally takes care of all that."

"Before you go, can you tell me what happened to the previous owners? I mean . . . it's so well-behaved, I can't imagine a magical family just up and leaving it."

"Well," Nesta said, a little smile crinkling their eyes as they looked back to the house. "It's got a bit of a sassy streak. I guess the previous owners didn't find that amusing. But I'm sure you'll get along with it just fine."

"A sassy streak?"

"You'll see." Nesta winked, and then they climbed into their car and pulled away from the curb without another word.

Rus crossed her arms over her chest and turned back to the house. The little cherry blossom out front was swaying gently, its orange and red leaves falling to the ground in a hush.

"You're not going to give me any trouble, are you?" she asked the house.

The house didn't respond.

"Didn't think so." She pulled her phone from her pocket and dialed Fernando. "Hey. You can bring the kids to the house. I'll send over the address."

"Do we need to bring the truck?" Fernando's voice was soft on the other side of the line, but Rus could hear Aihuan squealing at something and Meiling talking probably too loud for the small hotel room.

"No. Nesta said they'll send by movers to help us. We'll deal with all that tomorrow. For tonight I'll just order us a pizza, and we can rest. Do you need me to come help get them in the car?" A crow cawed, its black body swooping low over the cemetery to better assess the threat levels before Darcy came to rest on Rus's shoulder, his talons digging into her thick hoodie. "Cause if not, I've got some cleaning up I need to do around here."

"I don't think so." Fernando was smiling into the phone; Rus could hear it. "I think I've finally figured out Aihuan's car seat."

"If you need help, just ask Meiling. She knows what to do. I'll have dinner waiting for you guys when you get here."

"Is that Aunt Rus?" Meiling asked in the background.

"Yes." Fernando pulled his face away from the phone, and

Rus could imagine him turning the full softness of his smile onto Meiling.

"Did she get us a house?"

"Yes! I got you a house!" Rus shouted into the phone, her excitement unseating Darcy, who cast her an annoyed glance that she shrugged off. "The perfect house! You're going to love it, A-Ling!"

"YEEEEEEEES!" Meiling cheered. "Huaner! We have a house!"

"We have a house! We have a house! We have a house! " Aihuan shouted, feeding off her big sister's excitement. It sounded like Fernando had put Rus on speaker.

"But that means you two need to help Uncle Nando get packed up and get over here so you can see your rooms." Rus felt her cheeks aching from the smile that split her own face.

"Okay!" Meiling called, and then Rus could hear some commotion on the other end as she presumably got to work picking up all of Aihuan's toys or maybe just shoving stuff into the oversized duffle Rus had left on the floor by the door.

"You sure you don't need me to come help herd the cats?" Rus asked with a little laugh.

"No. I've got it covered." Fernando's shirt rustled against the phone as he too began to help packing. "I think you managed to get all the really important stuff into the car before you left."

"Toys are important!" Aihuan shouted.

"Right, sorry, of course, Huaner. Anyway, we'll see you there." Then he hung up, and Rus was left standing on the porch of her new house, listening to the silence of it. Darcy settled on her shoulder again, giving his witch an affectionate nip to her ear. A gentle reminder.

Movement out of the corner of her eye made her turn her head, and she saw the restless spirits on the edge of the graveyard again, turned milky in the fading light of early evening. "Right. Got to deal with them real quick before the girls get here."

She tucked her phone into her back pocket and strode across the yard.

If you loved the first chapter of *The Hex Next Door,* you can grab your copy at https://books2read.com/u/3Ln7z7

More Books You'll Love

If you enjoyed this story, please consider leaving a review.

Then check out more books from Midnight Tide Publishing!

Alter by H.R. Truelove

WHO DO YOU TRUST WHEN YOU CAN'T TRUST YOURSELF?

Lennox, Erris, Wisdom...
There are many voices in Laura's mind but no one,
not even her family will believe her.

Laura's life is far from normal. After spending years in a medical center for seeing visions no one else can, Laura is transferred to the Tomlinson Institute of Research. There, she's promised, lies the truth she's been after her entire life.

But as her eighteenth birthday looms closer, Laura's already complicated life takes a sudden turn. When she discovers what hides behind her unusual abilities, Laura's reality is blown to pieces, and she must learn to make sense of her supernatural gifts. With a little help from the voices in her head, Laura needs to fight to save herself, the world she lives in-and every other world in the multiverse.

Alter is a gripping and intricate tale of conspiracy, mad scientists, and broken lives. A multiverse of blurry lines, lies, and deceit where we come face to face with the best of humankind... and its very worst.

Available Now

The Last Daughter by Alexis L. Menard

She's cursed with a dead witch's power over fate, he's a heart-less demigod born for revenge and redemption. Once her enemy, now a conflict of interest. The fate of the Nine Realms dangles on a dangerously thin thread.

Fate was cruel enough by dealing Ailsa with a fatal illness. But when her father and sisters are killed at war, she becomes the Last Daughter in a long line of shieldmages. This power comes with a price, however, coincidentally getting her kidnapped by an elfin she's only heard of through legends.

Vali's realm is dying, inflicted by the black magic, sedir, and the only way to heal his land is by delivering the Tether to Odin, king of the gods. When he finds this power bound inside a mortal woman, he is forced to bring her and her shapeshifting wolven back to his home in Alfheim.

But their journey across the Tree of Life is perilous, and betrayal is imminent. Vali and Ailsa must depend on each other for survival, a mutual dependency that turns into a passionate love affair. With Odin waiting on this promised power, a kindred spirit found in her enemy, and a dark threat neither Ailsa nor Vali intended to find in the bright lands of Alfheim, what started as a simple quest has turned into a fight to save all gods, mortals, and fae alike. Vikings meets magic in this fresh retelling of Norse Mythology.

Available Now